CAVE OF IMMORTALITY

Books by Philip S Davies:

The *Destiny's Rebel* Trilogy:

Destiny's Rebel (2015)

Destiny's Revenge (2017)

Destiny's Ruin (2018)

The *Immortality* Series:

Cave of Immortality (2023)

War for Immortality (2025)

Cave of Immortality

Book One in the Immortality Series

Philip S. Davies

First published by Brittain Fisher, 2023.
This revised paperback edition, 2025.

www.philipsdavies.com

ISBN-10: 1-916767-00-1.
ISBN-13: 978-1-916767-00-3.

Map of Albany Valley
N
E
S
W
TO GORGE CITY & PLAINS
HIGH WAY
ALBANY
RUBBISH DITCH
TOWN HALL
SCHOOL ROOM
MILL
INN
FARM
WARLOCK'S PLATEAU
CAVE
WATERFALL
HEISMITH RANGE
MEADOW WOOD

Dedicated to the wonderfully talented young people
in the Creative Writing Clubs at:
North Oxfordshire Academy in Banbury,
The Warriner School in Bloxham,
Wykham Park Academy in Banbury.

CHAPTER ONE

Roza couldn't believe her luck. Or couldn't decide whether it was good or bad luck.

The forest was warm that day with early autumn sunshine, so she chose a shady clearing to saw and chop the wood. She hung her cloak on a branch and worked in her tunic and trousers. The logs were dry and splitting well, and the crash of her axe echoed across the valley.

Her barrow was half-loaded with kindling when the corner of her eye caught a flicker of movement between the trees.

She straightened, watching. Was that a deer … or a bear? Or someone else coming through the forest? Wild beasts and bandits were rare in the valley, but not impossible, so she gripped her axe to defend herself. She'd always been tall and strong for her age but was conscious of being alone.

And then he appeared in the form of a young man. He stepped out from behind a tree, and she could only stare. His wavy, shoulder-length hair was the auburn of copper beech leaves and his tunic the green of grass in the sun. His muscular arms, legs and feet were bare, and his face … well, she'd defy anyone to resist being entranced.

Her limbs locked in shock, her heart and breathing stopped, and for one stunned moment she gazed at him, his eyes sparkling with the greens and yellows of a summer meadow. He smiled and must have known the bewitching effect he had on her.

A curious fascination with him made her lurch forward.

He laughed and disappeared.

It wasn't that he ducked behind the tree or ran off into the forest. No, he vanished before her eyes, reverting to invisibility.

Her heart hammered back into life. She stared and waited, trembling inside, hoping he'd reappear. For a while she heard his laughter in the rustle of the leaves.

But he didn't return.

She searched beyond the clearing in the direction she'd seen him vanish, but there were no footprints. Why couldn't he have stayed longer? It wasn't fair that he'd appeared to her for such a short time.

When at last she gave up on looking for him and resumed chopping the wood, too often she missed the log because one eye scanned the trees for him. As daylight faded, she trundled the barrow of kindling back to her parents' cottage.

It was the most exciting thing to happen to her since forever, but Roza didn't mention him to her parents. They wouldn't understand. Or would say she was seeing things. They – along with everyone else – seemed to fear anything magical, giving her childhood warnings not even to say the words 'dragon' or 'warlock' for fear of summoning the evil against them. So, she decided to keep the mysterious young man in the forest as her secret.

Early the next morning, she returned to the clearing, giving her parents the excuse of stocking up on firewood for the winter. They remarked that she seemed distracted, and Roza's stomach clenched whenever she thought of him. It wasn't that he was annoyingly gorgeous, she told herself, but because she was desperate to meet an invisible magical being again. Yes, that was why she returned.

But he didn't reappear that day.

The vision of him so consumed her thoughts, she came back there every day, drawn to wait and search for him. She went over in her mind what manner of being he might be. Which creatures had the power to appear and disappear at will? She'd lived in this forest all her life, and although there were legends about spirits in the wood, she'd never seen anything so powerful or magical before.

She wondered why he'd revealed himself to her at all. Was it just her good luck – or bad luck – that he'd appeared to her? Or could he possibly be weary of his lonely existence too?

In the following days, she gathered plenty of firewood for the coming months, but her only companions were the rabbits, squirrels, and birds. She began to compose other excuses to give to her parents for coming here.

But then, in the cloudy afternoon of the fifth day, he returned. He walked from between the trees to within only a few paces of her. She froze, but wasn't so surprised this time, except that her axe thudded to the ground.

His tunic was darker, matching the gloom beneath the trees, and she wondered if each day he wore the colours of the forest. Perhaps his eyes also changed with his mood, for today they were the green of holly leaves, with a silver speckle of starlight. Now he was closer, she saw behind his shoulders the rainbow shimmer of wings, like sunlight on a soap bubble.

"Is that the best you can do?" He indicated towards her fallen axe and the wood. His voice had a teasing lilt, and his mouth a twitch of playfulness.

She bristled at the jibe, knowing she was skilful and strong, but her mind blanked and her voice failed her.

His eyes surveyed her, from her light brown hair to her bare arms, to her scuffed leather boots. She endured the scrutiny, trying not to feel self-conscious.

"What's your name, girl?"

She cleared her throat to recover her power of speech. "Rozabella," she managed, "with a 'z'. Most people call me 'Roza' for short."

"But you're not, are you?" he chuckled. "Short, I mean."

Oh, ha ha. Her irritation rose because she always had to endure men making fun of her height.

He controlled his grin. "Well then, Rozabella with a 'z', why is a girl like you out here chopping up wood? Not very ladylike, is it?"

She swallowed, distracted to be talking at last with this magical being. But what did he mean? Everyone needed firewood, and she had to do this because of her parents, but she wasn't going to tell him that. And how dare he comment on being ladylike? Her mother's example had taught her to correct any man who presumed to tell women what they could do.

"We all need to stock up on firewood for the winter," she said. "And I can do anything men can."

His eyebrows rose, as though he disagreed with her, so she prepared to continue the argument. But he smiled and stepped closer instead. "I'm pleased to meet you then, Roza," he said, and held out a hand.

Was he letting her touch him? She hesitated, wondering whether she should fear him, that his touch was some charm or trap. But she wasn't afraid, only curious and intrigued. Or was she trusting strangers too easily again?

She cringed at being sweaty from the chopping and wiped her palm on her trousers. His arm was the tanned brown of a sapling, and when she took the offered hand, it was warm and strong. She'd have held it for longer if he'd let her.

"I'm called by many names," he said. "In your language, you can call me Kerenzi."

"Kerenzi," she repeated. She ought to stop staring at him but couldn't tear her gaze away. She drew a deep breath for her heart and brain to function properly and whispered, "What sort of being are you?"

His grin broadened and he swept his arm around the surrounding trees. "There are various spirits who dwell in this forest – wood nymphs and dryads in the trees, sylphs in the air and naiads in the streams – and I am their master. When your legends speak of a spirit lord, they mean me."

"A spirit lord," Roza repeated. She looked around the trees and blurted out, "Is this forest full of spirits then?"

Kerenzi frowned. "Not full of them, no. But some of us live here. We rarely appear to mortals, though."

"Why have you appeared to me, then?" Her curiosity had won out over feeling awestruck.

The spirit lord tilted his head and started pacing around her. "When I visited the other day, I was bored, and it was a bit of fun. But then I noticed something." He stopped and pointed a friendly finger at her. "I'm pretty good at sensing another person's spirit, and there's something different about you. Something I've never seen before. I can't put my finger on it, but there's definitely something there."

"What do you mean?" Roza demanded. "There's nothing different about me. My family has always lived in this valley, so I can't see what makes me anything special."

The spirit lord shook his head. "No, it's not about your family, it's about you. But I can't pin down what it is."

Roza shrugged, folding her arms. But inside she was basking in the idea he thought her special, unique. Her good luck then, rather than bad.

Kerenzi stepped further around to get a different view of her, so she straightened her back. "How old are you, girl?"

She cleared her throat again. "Seventeen."

Kerenzi nodded and smiled.

Roza needed to correct something. A few times now he'd called her 'girl', and she was determined he should consider her as more than that. "Yes, I'm seventeen," she declared, "so a young woman rather than a girl."

To her dismay, Kerenzi burst out laughing. He shook with mirth, resting his hands on his knees.

Roza's cheeks burned as he laughed at her, and she planted her hands on her hips. "What's so funny?"

When at last Kerenzi wiped his eyes, he shook his head. "A young woman at only seventeen years. We shall see."

She glowered at him, wanting to get her own back. "How old are you then, young man ... or should I say, boy?" As soon as she said it, she knew she shouldn't address a spirit lord so. This was not some boy from the town.

His eyes widened at her impudence, but he seemed content to continue the game. He gazed up at the sky, thinking, or counting. When he looked back at her, his eyes had changed. A deep grey of sadness had come into them as he said, "How old am I? As you count the years, it would be ... tens of thousands."

Her mouth fell open. *"Tens of thousands?"*

He looked down at the grass. "So, what does that make me: a boy, a young gentleman ... or a very old man?"

Before she could think of a reply, a net flew through the air and caught the spirit lord from behind, enmeshing him in its ropes. Kerenzi's screams reverberated around the valley as he struggled against the tightening cords, until he collapsed to the grass.

Roza tore her terrified gaze away from the stricken spirit lord, jerking her head to where someone crashed into the clearing. She caught a glimpse of black robes before fog covered her eyes. Then a crushing weight threw her to the ground, into the realm of forgetfulness.

CHAPTER TWO

She awoke to pain all over her body. She lay on a rough, hard surface, her face squashed against a cold slab of stone. Ropes bound her ankles and wrists, making her arms and legs ache, and her mouth was firmly gagged. Opening her eyes made no difference, for wherever she was, it was pitch black.

It hurt to struggle, so she lay there in pain. Powerless to do anything else, she tried to think, her eyes wide in the dark. Where was she? How had she got here?

She couldn't remember anything. Nothing at all. Her memories seemed to be there, somewhere in her head, but she couldn't reach them. Her mind could fix on nothing before waking here moments ago.

The lack of memory started a rising panic that felt worse than her pain and bonds. Her name was…? Nothing. Why couldn't she remember? Maybe she'd hit her head. Or had gone mad. Was she tied up because she was dangerous?

As her eyes accustomed to the blackness, a faint light was filtering in from behind her, but she could make out only vague shadows and shapes. Was it daylight through a heavily curtained window? No, it wasn't bright enough for that. Gritting her teeth against the pain, she rolled onto her back. Before she passed out, she saw the dim outline of an arched cave entrance, with a glimmer of starlight beyond. Then the agony robbed her of consciousness.

When she came to again, the light hurt her eyes. It had to be hours later. She lay on her back, facing the rocky roof of a cave. She turned her head and squinted through the entrance, to where bright sunlight streamed down from a blue sky onto grass and trees. Where was this?

Everything hurt: her head, back, and limbs. But the pain was less sharp than during the night. Now in daylight, she looked for injuries and saw the blood all over her arms. Her wrists were lacerated, with cuts up her forearms, the blood smeared and congealed across the open slashes. How had she got these?

She was also parched and starving. Had she been in an accident, injured or attacked? She still couldn't remember a thing. The gag and ropes meant she was captive, but with no idea about when, where or who. And what was that horrible smell?

In her confusion and pain, she was determined about two things: she would work this out, and get herself out of here. She had to.

A rustling behind her made her jump. She froze and listened hard. She'd thought she was alone. Her captor was here in this cave. A beast, or a person? The gag and bonds suggested more than animal instinct.

The sound was a rustle of clothing rather than the padding of pawed feet. This was a good sign, a reassurance of not being eaten. Whatever her fears, she needed to turn over and know what she was facing.

She rolled onto her side, away from the bright cave entrance. She almost swooned but remained conscious and focused her eyes.

The cave was inhabited. The daylight showed a large rocky chamber, adapted for human habitation. There were cupboards and shelves on the walls, and ancient furniture: large tables, chairs, stools and workbenches, and everything looked dirty and decrepit. A polished wooden coat stand stood in front of bookcases filled up to the roof. Every surface was cluttered with paraphernalia: pots and pans, bowls and plates, cups, jugs, cutlery, and other utensils and implements. There were pieces of parchment everywhere, old books, lamps, candlesticks, jars, buckets, and boxes. The place gave the impression of nothing being thrown away, even when broken or useless, but simply piled up somewhere or added to a stack in a corner. As though someone had lived here for a hundred years and never tidied up.

Beside her lay a bound young man with long auburn hair, but she only glanced at him, because of what else she'd seen. One area of the cave looked like a kitchen, where a large black cauldron stood. The source of the rustle of clothing – the occupant of the cave – was turned away from her, tending to a small fire beneath it.

No, no, the cauldron and the fire couldn't be … to cook her?

All she could see were long, black robes, tattered and dusty. Strands of greasy, grey hair slimed down onto the shoulders of the hunched and stooping figure.

The fire had ignited, and the person straightened up. Her captor shuffled to a large basin, scooped up a jug of liquid, poured it into the cauldron, and then looked up and saw her watching.

The face made her gasp. The eyes were of piercing blue, staring out of sunken eye-sockets where the skin had sagged, leaving them bloodshot. The nose was long and hooked in a face so lined and wrinkled it seemed beyond what old age could do to it.

Her captor was so ancient, she couldn't tell whether this creature was male or female, until he gave a cackle, and the croaked voice was a man's, deep and chilling. Putting down the jug, he stepped towards her, and she shrank in trepidation, an icy grip clenching her insides. When he opened his mouth, one or two teeth were missing.

"She decided to wake up, did she?"

His voice rasped like sandpaper, and he coughed and wheezed. His approach revealed him as the source of the foul stench, of someone not washing their body or clothes all year. It turned her stomach, making her gasp breaths through her gagged mouth, not her nose. Her tongue was dry and in desperate need of a drink.

"A pleasant surprise to find herself here, isn't it, yes, enjoying the hospitality of the warlock," he chuckled to himself, and set off a choking fit.

The warlock? This answered a question about her captor then: a warlock, someone who used magic. But if legends said warlocks were old, then the stories did no justice to the reality. Did warlocks devour human flesh, then? Or did this one? A morbid fascination in the disgusting kept her gaze fixed on him.

"She must be in pain, yes, we guess, from our BodyCrusher Spell, but that couldn't be helped, could it? It'll soon wear off."

He'd cast a spell to hurt her? These pains throughout her body? The vicious brute.

How could she keep him away from her? She struggled to squirm away, but he knelt beside her prostrate body and leaned in closer. His sharp blue eyes bored into her, examining, appraising, as though assessing an item at a market stall, or the flesh on a joint of meat. His pale tongue licked his thin lips and saliva dribbled into his wispy beard.

"Trussed up like a turkey, isn't she?" he croaked, and spittle flew onto her clothes as he spoke. Long bony fingers, with nails like claws, began to paw at her.

Get off me, she wanted to grunt through her gag, furious but powerless at his touch.

He mistook the sound as her desire to speak. "Wanting a little chat, is she? Let's see what we can do, yes."

He hummed to himself as he fumbled behind her head and neck. This brought his body and robes so close to her nose, that she held her breath. His stench of sweat and urine and unmentionable others was overpowering.

At last, the gag loosened and came off, and he leaned back. She breathed easier through her mouth, worked her jaw muscles, licked her lips and tried to swallow. Her first need was a drink. "Water," she whispered.

The ancient face brightened, and he levered himself to his feet. "Water?" he cackled. "Water!" He shuffled towards the kitchen area, inspecting the progress of the cauldron and fire as he passed, and filled a large cup with water from a jug.

He came back, stood in front of her, and drank the whole cup of water himself.

"We needed that, didn't we," he sniggered. "Drinking helps with our coughs and wheezes, doesn't it?" He gagged and spluttered with laughter. "A good idea and a kind suggestion, wasn't it, yes, it was."

A wild rage exploded inside her. In a haze of fury, she swore and raged, kicked and cursed, shouted at him, thrashed about, but to no avail, for she was too tightly bound. But it seemed to frighten him. He backed away from her.

She stopped her violence and tried to control herself. Raging and thrashing might not achieve anything. She was shaking inside, but needed to think, be smart, work this out. Her thirst was painful, but after some deep breaths, her anger subsided into a cold determination, and she gasped, "Not for you. Water for me. Why won't you help me? Why are you being so cruel?"

He stared at her. "She doesn't like our jokes, does she? Doesn't find them funny, no. No more joking or teasing then. She should have said she wanted the water, shouldn't she?" He shuffled back to refill the cup from the jug, muttering to himself as he went.

"And why are you holding me prisoner?" she shouted at him, but it hurt her throat, and he ignored it.

Drinking from the same cup as him revolted her, but as he returned, she raised her head and opened her mouth to receive it.

He seemed uncertain how to do this, as he knelt beside her, holding the cup in both hands. Perhaps her violent thrashing had scared him more than she thought, because his hands were shaking. As he tipped the cup, the water sloshed into her face.

She swallowed a mouthful, licked as many drops as her tongue could reach, and opened her mouth again. His beady blue eyes watched her as he tipped again, but his trembling hands dropped the cup, and the water spilled all over her.

She choked and spluttered, while he stood up and backed away, retreating to behind the cauldron.

The cold wetness doused her with a new focus, as she slumped back onto the stone-hard cave floor.

If she was his prisoner, he must think he could get away with whatever he did to her. Even though she hadn't done anything to him. Had she? She didn't know. Because she couldn't remember.

Whatever else happened, she promised herself this: she would find out what was going on, escape her captivity, and get him back for this. Somehow, she would make him pay for what he was doing to her.

But first, she needed to think. Why had this warlock imprisoned her?

Maybe it was a battle. Perhaps the warlock was trying to break her, but if so, she needed to be strong and to resist. She couldn't let him see how much he revolted and infuriated her, as that would only spur him on. She wouldn't give him that satisfaction.

If she steeled herself to take his abuses, she might find out what he was after, why she was here. If she knew what he wanted from her, that could help in devising a plan to get out of here.

She noticed again the polished wooden coat stand in front of the bookcases and had the strangest sensation that it was looking at her. Two knots in the wood at the top looked like eyes, and she could have sworn the coat stand turned away slightly, as though having been caught watching her getting the water.

She shook away the stupid notion and looked over to where the warlock pottered around the cauldron, stirring in pinches of ingredients, dipping in a spoon to taste it. He seemed in an excellent mood and highly pleased with himself.

"What are you going to do with me?" she demanded, but her parched throat managed only a whisper. He didn't appear to have heard, or else he was ignoring her. "What are you going to do with me?" she called up from the floor, in a louder croak.

This time he heard her, or else chose to respond. He continued working at the cauldron and talked to her across it. Or he could have been talking to himself.

"What are we going to do with her? Yes, what are we?" he murmured. "Getting the cauldron ready, aren't we?" He must have noticed her horrified reaction, for he went on, "Should we explain to her? Nice and hot, we need it, don't we? It'll soon be simmering away, and there's plenty of room in here, isn't there, as we mix it all together."

"You're going to eat me?" She cut across his stream of gabble.

"Eat her? Eat her?" He shook his head. "No, no, not eat her. She's too big and tall to fold up into here, isn't she? Wouldn't fit her in, would we?" He chuckled and coughed again. "Not all at once, no, just a tiny little bit at a time. Drink her, yes, drink her, that's more like it, isn't it?"

"You're going to put me in your cauldron, and boil me up into one of your potions?" She glared at him, in disbelief as much as rage and despair.

He stopped stirring and fixed her with his piercing blue eyes. "Boil her up? No, we'd have to chop her up very small to get her into here, wouldn't we? No, just some bits and pieces."

Most of her didn't want to know, so she shuddered as she asked, "What sort of ... bits and pieces?"

"Oh, a little bit of this, and a little bit of that," he sang to himself, almost like a young boy. All she could do was stare at the stooped, capering figure by the cauldron.

"I thought you weren't going to joke or tease me any more."

This made him stop his humming and bobbing about and look back at her. "Worried about herself, isn't she? Shouldn't do that, should she, think only of herself. That's not very nice. It's selfish, yes, it is. What about her friend? Yes, her friend, the spirit lord, what about him?"

She didn't understand. What friend? She didn't know of any friends.

With a jolt, she remembered she wasn't the only prisoner in this warlock's cave. There was the bound young man with the long auburn hair. The warlock jerked his head towards the corner behind her, so she twisted around to look at him properly.

In the darker corner beyond her feet lay the slumped figure against the wall. He was deathly pale, his muscular frame bound around with ropes from neck to ankle. His tunic was ripped and bloodied, his wavy auburn hair dishevelled, and between the ropes she saw gashes and bruising on his head, arms and legs. He was gagged and unconscious.

What had the warlock called him? The spirit lord? Looking closer, beneath the battered body lay a pair of crushed and crumpled wings.

CHAPTER THREE

Seeing the wounded spirit lord tied up against the cave wall made her long to remember. She'd no idea who he was, or how they'd got here, but their current predicament meant they were on the same side. She found herself hoping they'd met before, or were friends, and so were together when the warlock attacked, injured, and captured them. Could she and this young man with wings possibly have known each other before?

The warlock had called him the spirit lord. What that meant she didn't know, except that it sounded powerful and magical. But her fellow prisoner looked wretched, and her curiosity was piqued.

She found comfort in not being alone. She didn't need to face this warlock by herself, for she had an ally, a comrade in the fight, even if he was worse off than she was. They were in this captivity together, and they would get out of it together.

But the spirit lord's condition was worrying. Why was he so trussed up like that, with more ropes binding him than she had? He looked more injured too, paler, more bloodied. She hadn't inspected her own wounds very well but couldn't help him while still bound herself.

From over by the cauldron, the warlock chuckled again. "Worry about him, yes, she should, shouldn't she?"

The horror of their situation returned. "Why should I worry about him?" she demanded. "What will you do with us?"

"Bits and pieces, bits and pieces," the warlock reminded her. "A little bit of this, and a little bit of that."

He went on humming while she tried to control her anger. She mustn't let him get to her. He had them both at his mercy, and it was up to her to get them out of this. She drew deep breaths and closed her eyes while she lay still, bound and helpless.

In time the warlock's humming stopped. The only sounds were the gentle crackle of the fire, the bubble of the cauldron, and his shuffling footsteps.

Maybe she should try a different approach. He expected her to be disgusted, appalled and furious, and so far, that was how she'd reacted. It would throw him off guard if she managed to be calm, polite, determined. Any way of extracting information from him could be useful.

But she refused to have another conversation with him from lying on the floor, her face squashed against the rough stone. She would look him in the face. Her side was numb where she lay on it, and although it would be painful, she might lever herself into a sitting position. The cave wall was close behind her, and she could lean against that.

Gritting her teeth, she wriggled backwards to the rock wall. She almost cried out in pain but was determined not to do so. He was watching what she did but not lifting a finger to help. Not that she wanted his fingers anywhere near her body.

When her back bumped the stone wall, she gathered her energy and resilience for the effort to sit up. Angling her elbow, she raised her torso and then used her bound hands to push herself up into sitting. She trembled and sweated as she leaned against the wall, flexing her painful muscles.

Her breath came in pants and gasps as she tried to find a comfortable position. She looked around, and yes, she could see better from here: the cave entrance, the cauldron, the warlock, the coat stand, and to her left, the prone body of the spirit lord. Wisps of smoke from the cauldron fire wafted upwards through a hole in the ceiling.

Once her breathing steadied, she mustered all her

politeness to extract more information from the warlock. "Excuse me, Mister Warlock Sir, but you didn't answer my question earlier, about exactly which bits and pieces of me you require. Am I allowed to know, please?"

The warlock had been glancing over at her and now seemed taken aback by the politeness of her question. It was her first small victory. "Asks us very nicely, doesn't she, yes, she does. Very polite, very nice, so do we tell her, do we?" He muttered and mumbled words she didn't catch, as though debating with himself. "She wants to know our ingredients, doesn't she, yes, she does. Our secrets, she asks, and shall we tell her? Not all of them, no. No use without all the ingredients, is it."

She listened patiently and found herself hoping that the 'bits and pieces' he required would be her hair or nail clippings, or even some skin or blood. She could survive without these and would spare them if this allowed their escape.

"Let us see now," the warlock said, and counted the items on his fingers. "The ingredients, yes, that she wants to know. From the mortal girl: a piece of the heart, a piece of the brain, a part of a lung, and most of the blood. Yes, those are the main bits and pieces. The others are smaller and less significant, but that is it in the main. Have we answered her question, have we?"

Yes, he had, but the shock of the warlock's list was sinking in. He required no replaceable items, nothing that could heal again afterwards. He meant to murder her here, to cut her open and take her apart, adding her vital organs to his potion. Having thought he might eat her, this was little different, just piece by piece, added to his human stew.

No, no, this couldn't be happening. She was set to *die* here? This had to be a nightmare. Soon, her terror would wake her up. But the sharpness of her pains told her this was no dream. There was no waking up. This was real.

But to keep her composure, she chose to deny the possibility of this, clinging to the hope of avoiding that fate. With an effort she shoved his words out of her mind, refusing to be terrorised, and swallowed hard. Calm, polite, determined, she reminded herself.

She managed to ask, "And the spirit lord, what is it that you require from him?"

Again, her reaction to his list won her a minor victory. He clearly expected raging, curses, abuse, or begging and pleading, but she was determined enough to give him none of these.

"Well, she took that rather well, didn't she? Must be cold, heartless, unfeeling, yes, she is, to take her own death so lightly. But the immortal spirit lord, yes, she asks about him. Of course she does, he's her friend, isn't he? Now the spirit lord, what does the potion require of him? More of him we need, the immortal one, yes, we do. We need all the heart, and all the brain, all the lungs, and all the blood, and a full spirit lord wing. That is what does it, yes, it does."

The warlock's answer was predictable. The details didn't matter, because the prospect for them both, for this spirit lord and for her, was that they would die here, whatever this warlock did with their bodies afterwards. And had he called this young man beside her immortal? Except it seemed he could still be murdered.

She half-wished she hadn't asked about the 'bits and pieces' but reminded herself that she needed the information. If she knew what she was facing, she was better placed to win this battle. And the politeness was paying off, since he was answering her questions.

"I see," she said, suppressing her rage into a calm and level voice. "You need to kill and dismember the spirit lord and me to add our body parts to this potion of yours. May we know what it is we're dying for? Why is this potion so important that you're willing to execute us for it?"

The warlock was gazing into his cauldron, as if considering her question carefully. She waited for if he would answer. "What are we brewing, what is this potion, so very important?" he murmured to himself. "Shall we tell her, shall we? Would it hurt if she knows, what she's helping to make? Shouldn't be a problem, should it, no, what can she do?"

He paused his stirring of the cauldron and fixed her with his sagging, piercing blue eyes. He worked his mouth, as if savouring the word he was about to say. Then slowly and clearly, he said, "Longevity."

She frowned, her mind racing. "Longevity? Some drink or potion to make you live longer? Are you sure? Is such a thing possible?"

He cackled and capered at her words. "Is it possible? Are we sure there's a potion to make us live longer?" He burst into choking laughter. "Knows all about it, does she? No, she doesn't understand at all. Must live longer, yes, we must. The valley will be destroyed if we don't stay alive, yes, it will, so we need to defend it. Must live as long as we can, to keep our magic alive, so the potions we make and continue living, yes."

She stared at him but didn't understand. What valley? Destroyed how? Defend it from what? She couldn't remember. And what did he mean about keeping his magic alive? But here was his self-justification for making longevity potions. "You mean you've tried this before, or used a potion like this in the past?"

He nodded vigorously, in his hunched, stooped posture. "Used it before, haven't we, yes, we have. Very useful, works well, doesn't it? How else have we lived so long, then, how else?"

A thought occurred to her, and she asked, "How many times have you used it, then, if you don't mind my asking?" She remembered to be polite, if it would keep his answers coming.

He paused and regarded her shrewdly. "Asks politely, doesn't she, but it doesn't matter, because we can't tell her, can we? How many times used the potion, we don't remember, do we? Many times, and many years, it is, yes."

Her mind processed this. If he'd made this potion many times to keep on living, that meant he'd killed many mortal and immortal people for their 'bits and pieces'. His obsession with longevity had turned him into a multiple murderer.

She decided this wasn't something she should say out loud, not if she wanted him to keep answering her questions. He'd turned his back on her, leaning over a workbench. She flexed her wrists to ease where the ropes cut into them, and then wanted to regain his attention, so asked the first thing in her mind. "How old are you, then?"

He turned around and guffawed. "Mustn't ask, must she, no, mustn't ask. Not polite, is it, to ask a young gentleman his age." He broke down into laughing and coughing, seeming intensely amused at being asked his age. "A young gentleman we are, and her a young lady, or so we thought her, and she asks us our age? Perhaps she fancies us, yes, she must, and wants to know if we're about her age. She wants to ask us out, to flirt and seduce us, yes, she does."

She ignored his wild musings and hilarious ramblings, because the thought of fancying him was too revolting to contemplate. As she considered other questions and topics to ask him, he shuffled around the cauldron to face her.

"How old does she think we are then, how old?" He leered at her, a wicked, testing glint in his eye, and she weighed up the options of not offending him. Would saying a lower age than she thought work to flatter old men? Or was he proud of how old he was and wanting to boast of the longevity he'd achieved?

She could delay answering no longer, and so ventured, "Seventy?"

He shrieked, and she was quickly relieved that this seemed to be not in outrage but delight. "Seventy? Seventy?" he cackled with glee. "She thinks we're seventy! So many years old, that is, yes. She thinks us an old man, ancient, decrepit, yes, she does. Seventy years old! Not the fine young gentleman we are really, no, not at all. Young and handsome, aren't we?" He passed his pale, trembling fingers over his long, greasy, grey hair, and the wrinkled skin of his face.

It was revolting to watch but she couldn't avert her gaze. There was a self-pitying note in his voice, both wistful and sad, remembering times long ago.

"Raven black hair we have," he murmured, "and bright blue eyes, and pale smooth skin, and a handsome young face, yes, and a firm strong figure. A fine young gentleman we are, yes."

She wondered what it would be like to be so old. To have lost forever your youthful appearance, when strength and good looks were never more than a memory. That had to be sad, but she refused to pity this old man after the murders he'd committed to stay alive this long.

The warlock was lost in memories, and she didn't want to distract him. But all at once, he came back to himself, realised she was watching and listening, that he wasn't musing alone. He cackled and was the decrepit old warlock again. "Seventy years old? Flattering us, she is, not telling the truth, no. We don't look a day over our four hundred years, do we?" He burst into hilarity again and turned back to the cauldron.

"Four hundred?" she burst out. "You reckon you don't look a day over four hundred years old? You've lived for *four centuries,* through using these longevity potions?"

He didn't answer. Either he didn't want to admit it, or thought he'd told her too much already.

She winced as she shifted her position, because her backside was numb where she sat on the stone floor.

Another vital piece of information was how long they had to live. "So, this longevity potion," she went on, "you need some parts for it from me and the spirit lord—"

He interrupted her. "Yes, yes, the spirit lord is the key. The immortal one, most important for longevity he is. We need the immortal heart, you see, don't we, yes, and the brain and the lungs and the blood and the wing. All must be immortal, you see, to give us long life, yes, they do."

"So, why do you need the parts from me as well, a mortal young woman?"

The warlock gave half a laugh. "Thinks she knows all about it, doesn't she, yes, she does. Understands longevity fully, does she? No, not at all, not at all." He looked up from stirring his cauldron, and she caught a glimpse in his ancient face that he enjoyed explaining this. He took pride in his knowledge, wisdom and experience, in teaching a young mortal what he knew before she died.

He straightened and drew a deep breath. "The mortal parts balance the immortal, you see, don't they, yes, they do. But more of the spirit lord we need, all of his parts, and less of the mortal girl, smaller portions, for longer life, yes, that's how it works."

She didn't understand but wanted to try. "What if you left out my mortal parts," she asked, "and put in only those of the immortal spirit lord? Wouldn't that make you an immortality potion instead of a longevity one?"

He snorted and scoffed. "Immortality potion, she says, immortality, yes, that's what she says. Understands nothing, does she, no, she doesn't. Very tricky, immortality, very tricky, perhaps impossible. We've tried, haven't we, yes, we have, but never succeeded, no, impossible. We can rely on longevity, yes, we can, stick with that. Make it we can, and works we know. Stick with longevity."

She needed to press him again on how long they might have to live. "This longevity potion, how long does it take to prepare, please? How soon will you need the parts from the spirit lord and me? Excuse my asking, but it is my life that's at stake, you see." Calm, polite, determined.

He drew in breath through the gaps of his missing teeth. "Difficult to say, isn't it, how long to make. Always different, isn't it, depends on so much, the quality of the ingredients. We've added some bits and pieces already, haven't we, yes, some blood from each."

She glanced down at her cut and bloodied arms. So, before she awoke, the warlock had extracted her blood for his potion.

"And some nail clippings and hair," the warlock went on, "and some saliva and tears and sweat. All to start the potion off. The basics of each being, the mortal and the immortal, yes, they're in already."

Her self-control cracked. "Wait a minute. While I was unconscious, you stole not just my blood, but also my hair and nails, my saliva, tears and sweat? How dare you." He had violated her, collecting these ingredients from her body. But these she could spare, unlike her vital organs.

He ignored her outburst and went on. "We'll know, won't we, when the time is right, when the mixture is ready for them, yes, we will. But only just started, haven't we, yes, so about two or three days to get the basic potion right. Yes, we'll add their parts in two or three days."

She swallowed. *Two or three days?* That was how long she had left to live. Or more to the point, that was her deadline to devise and carry out an escape plan for them.

In the valley below, Helena eased herself down the spiral stairs of Meadow Cottage. They were too steep for her, and she clung to the handrails on both sides, the firm, wooden poles that years of her grip had worn smooth. She took it one step at a time, pausing to rest whenever she needed to.

She mustn't exert herself. Stay calm, stay relaxed, she

repeated to herself, otherwise the chest pains would come. Not that she was old – fifty-one years wasn't old – but she wasn't well. For months now, years if she were honest, she'd hidden her discomfort, because she didn't want anyone else to worry. She worried enough for all three of them.

She descended a few more steps, one at a time. But how could she stay calm and relaxed this morning, when the worst thing possible had happened?

Rozabella hadn't come home last night.

The reminder of it sent a shiver through her limbs and clenched her struggling heart. No, no, she mustn't think about it. Their daughter would return to their cottage this morning and explain how she'd been kept away overnight.

Helena made it down the last few steps into the corner of their kitchen. Or their living room, or her husband's bedroom, or whatever else this downstairs room should now be called. And there was Arthur, slumped in his armchair. They'd moved a bed downstairs for him, but he slept in his armchair as often as his bed.

Helena sighed as she gazed at him. It was good that Arthur was asleep now, because no doubt, like her, the worry about Roza had kept him awake too. He'd spent yesterday evening making light of it, joking as he always did. It was his way of coping with anxiety or distress, and she knew she ought to be grateful for him keeping their spirits up. But where could their girl have got to?

She shook herself. No, don't get yourself into a worry, but get on with the jobs Roza would have done. Before tending to the animals, she needed to light the fire. Arthur would be cold when he awoke, and they needed hot water for breakfast. Sweeping the grate would wake him, but that couldn't be helped.

Helena knelt in front of their small fireplace and began to brush last night's cold ashes into the dustpan. The unavoidable scrape of metal on stone caused Arthur to stir behind her.

"Helena, is that you?"

"Yes, dear, it's me. Just preparing this morning's fire."

"And has our Roza returned from her night out on the town?"

It was predictable that this would be Arthur's next question. Of course, before she'd ventured downstairs, Helena had checked Roza's bed in case she'd crept back in the middle of the night. But the girl's sheets and blankets were untouched.

Helena tried to make her voice sound unworried. "Not yet, Arthur dear. But she'll be back soon. She's a kind and sensible lass, and knows we'll be interested in where she's got to."

"Aye, or once she's slept off the evening's revelry," Arthur went on. "It's about time she enjoyed herself away from the two of us old codgers, having a drink and a party with her friends in town. I expect she'll … spin us a good yarn … when she returns."

Helena gave the required groan. Arthur had been a weaver before he retired, and now he played a game of sneaking as many weaving references into their conversation as he could. Helena's role was to groan to indicate she'd noticed them.

But back to the worry at hand. Their Rozabella was not the sort to go drinking and partying with friends in town, and they both knew it.

Something must have happened to her.

The stab of fear that Helena tried to deny jabbed itself into her heart again. She stopped brushing the hearth to rub her chest with her hand, laid down the dustpan and stood to face her husband. If she didn't express what she thought and felt, the nagging worry would spiral her downwards into fear and despair.

Arthur's milky eyes weren't quite directed towards her. His other senses were good, but Helena found herself missing that they would ever look into each other's eyes again.

"Until she gets back, we won't know what Roza has been doing or whether anything has happened to her," she began, in as level a voice as she could muster. "I'm trying to avoid getting all het up, because there might be a reasonable explanation for why she didn't return last night."

"Who needs a reasonable explanation?" Arthur countered. "Our girl is nearly an adult and can choose to go out for an evening if she wishes. Alas, long gone are the days of our little girl whom we could keep on a leash and demand to know wherever she went."

"It's unlike her to stay out without letting us know," Helena argued. "She knows we rely on her and that we'll worry if she's late or missing."

In fact, we depend on her too much, she added to herself. Our Roza's a young woman with her future ahead of her, and we can't ask her to stay and look after her ailing parents for the rest of our lives.

"Yes, we appreciate all she does," Arthur said, "but we're not completely helpless. We can still do some things between us. Just so long as I'm waited on hand and foot, kept in the comfortable manner to which I'm accustomed."

Helena pulled a face she was glad Arthur couldn't see. Yes, she tried her best to look after them both, but Arthur couldn't manage much and so Roza did most of the physical work. Like lighting the fire, looking after their animals, and going into the forest to chop firewood.

Helena returned to the subject at hand. "Arthur, you know what Roza's like. I think last night she might have met someone who needed her help. Maybe she was coming back from her chopping and found someone in the forest who was hurt or ill. She would have helped them back to town and made sure they were all right. She's caring and thoughtful like that."

Arthur turned his face towards her, and Helena knew he was considering this. He nodded at last, with a grunt. "Aye, that's what she'd do. She's a good lass, but a bit too trusting at times. Our young damsel can't resist saving a knight in distress, can she? She'll be back as soon as she finishes rescuing whoever it is."

Helena let out a breath, turned back to sweeping out the hearth, and prayed that what she'd suggested were true.

CHAPTER FOUR

Exhaustion must have overtaken her, for she jerked awake. In her groggy state, she was disorientated, wondering where she was. Then the bonds around her ankles and wrists, and the aches in her body, reminded her. She glanced around for the warlock, but he was not in sight. The cave was quiet apart from the bubbling and simmering of the cauldron. The warlock had to be outside the cave somewhere, so she shifted position to look at the spirit lord again.

He hadn't moved but still lay awkward and crumpled to her left. Her heart twinged as she looked at him. He might be immortal, but he looked to be dying or dead. He might not die of old age, but he could still be killed. He needed help, and she was the only one who could save him.

She rested her head against the hard stone wall and tried to think. They both needed water and food. If possible, she needed to get free of her wrist bonds to drink and feed herself. She needed the freedom to move, to wash and bandage their wounds, and to feed and care for the spirit lord too.

And it was urgent. Two or three days.

She struggled against the ropes at her wrists, but it was no use, they were too tightly bound. She looked for something to cut them on but there was nothing in reach. She was too weak and sore to try anything else.

A scraping sound from the kitchen area made her look up ... and then she stared, unable to believe her eyes. The polished wooden coat stand was standing next to the cauldron. It was standing a little away from it so that its wooden feet didn't get singed by the fire underneath. And it was bending slightly in the middle, leaning forward, and reaching with one of its arms above the cauldron. There was no mistaking what she was seeing. The coat stand was using one of its hooks to hold a long spoon and stir the potion.

A sound from the cave entrance distracted her incredulous staring.

The warlock returned, carrying a bucket of water. He staggered unsteadily under the weight, slopping the water onto the cave floor. He reached the kitchen area and set down the bucket.

"Give me that," he ordered, and grabbed the long spoon from the coat stand's grasp. The warlock took over stirring the potion, but she couldn't look away from the coat stand. It tottered back from the cauldron and took up position in front of the bookcases again.

She stared at it, trying to work out how a coat stand could walk, or hold anything. It had four feet, which it seemed able to bend and lift to make a scuttling, tottering motion. The hooks at the top seemed able to twist and tighten to hold an implement. And the wooden pole down the middle seemed supple enough to manage a stiff curve.

So, what was this? An enchanted piece of furniture? A tool the warlock had bewitched to do his bidding? Being in the company of someone who worked with magic meant she needed to open her mind to fantastic possibilities.

Again, she had the feeling the coat stand was looking back at her, so she dropped her gaze. Having seen it move and stir the cauldron, she didn't dismiss as stupid any more that those knots at its top might indeed be eyes.

The warlock seemed to notice her watching the coat stand but said nothing. Never mind the enchanted furniture, she told herself. Unless she escaped this warlock's clutches, she was due to be executed here as ingredients for that wretched potion. And the first steps were food, drink and unbound wrists.

She needed to talk with him and see what he would tell

her, and if possible, for him to trust her enough to release her wrists.

"Excuse me," she said, "is the potion going well?"

"Humph," he replied. "Is it going well, she asks. How is the potion, yes, how is it? Well enough, yes, it is, but not perfect, no. Needs some more work, difficult, tricky, yes, need to think, don't we, yes."

"It is just, if you don't mind my asking, that you've said how difficult it is, and always different, and how it depends on the quality of the ingredients. Is that right?"

He regarded her warily. "Very difficult and tricky it is, yes. And always different. Always better with good ingredients, isn't it, yes. High hopes we have for this time, yes, we do. A strong, young girl, and such a fine, powerful spirit lord, yes, excellent, excellent quality ingredients."

"Is that why you're in such a good mood?" she ventured. "Because you have high hopes with your quality ingredients?"

He nodded. "Maybe the best ingredients we've ever had, yes. The promise of many more years of life this time." He looked over at her. "But perhaps she thinks we shouldn't be so happy about their impending deaths, is that what she thinks?"

"No, you shouldn't be happy about that at all," she agreed, and then went on cautiously. "But the thing is, this strong, young girl is dying of thirst and starving hungry. And the fine, powerful spirit lord is probably the same. You need our body parts in two or three days, so I presume you need us both alive and healthy until then."

A look of alarm crossed the warlock's face, as she scored another point in their battle. His greenish yellow tongue licked across his thin, cracked lips. "Alive and healthy, healthy and alive, yes, we do, for them both, yes."

Before he could say more, she pressed her advantage. "So, the less healthy we are, it isn't so good for your potion. The body parts you need from us – the heart, the brain, the lungs, the blood, and all the rest – won't be much use if we're suffering from thirst and starvation. We should have water and food, to keep our parts well until you need them."

The warlock jumped on her words, and her heart pounded to hear him agree with her. "Yes, yes, she's right, isn't she, yes, she is. The parts must be well, in good condition, yes, they must. Well-fed and healthy, right up to when we need them. With all our focus on the potion, we'd forgotten, hadn't we: look after the donors. It happened before, didn't it, they wasted away and spoiled the potion. Too few extra years we got out of them, yes."

"So, would you be able to give us some water and food, please?"

He looked at her sharply. "No more games or spilling the cups of water, that's what she's saying, yes, she is. Wants a drink and some food, for her and for him, yes, that's right. Should we give them? Yes, we must, she's right, for the potion, yes."

"Perhaps," she suggested, "since you need to work on the potion, you won't be able to look after the two of us as well. You say how tricky it is to get right, and you need to concentrate on what you're doing, so if you bring some food and drink over here, I could look after myself and the spirit lord for you."

He narrowed his eyes at her words, and she knew immediately that he'd understood her meaning. "What is that, what is she saying? Look after herself and the spirit lord, will she? How can she do that, all tied up in ropes, eh? How?"

"Yes, I see your point," she added, trying to look as if she'd only just thought of this herself. "Listen, if I promise not to try anything stupid or foolish, would you untie my wrists? I promise I will only give food and drink to myself and the spirit lord, and wash and bandage our wounds, and that's all."

"A promise? A promise?" he shrieked. "Can we trust her? The promise of a mortal girl, what is that worth, eh?"

Before he could go on, she cut across him. "Listen, please, I realise how hard it is for us to trust each other, but we need food and water, and you want us to have it too, so I don't see how else we can do this."

He was silent for some moments. His eyes flicked from her to the spirit lord, to the cauldron, and back to her again. "We need to think of the potion, yes, we do, get it right. Need to concentrate, work it out, add and adjust all the time. Make up the fire, keep it hot, keep it just right, yes. Enough to do without feeding and drinking for her and for him, yes, we've plenty to do. But can we trust her? She needs food and water, and so does he, and she could do that for us, yes, she could. But can we trust her?"

She sensed the turmoil going on inside him and decided to say no more. He seemed to be persuading himself to trust her this far. He came to his decision, and she awaited the outcome of this next battle in their war.

He picked up a cup and a jug of water and brought them over to her. Next, he loaded into a bowl a loaf of bread, a lump of cold meat, two apples and two pears. He shuffled back to her and placed the bowl by her feet. He knelt and leant over her, his horrible blue eyes only inches from hers. The sagging folds of his face's wrinkled flesh quivered as he spoke, and he slavered gobs of saliva onto his chin.

"Now, listen to us she must, yes, she must," he hissed and spat. He was trying to be threatening, but the victorious feeling welled inside that she'd won this next round in the battle. "She can eat and drink, and feed the spirit lord, and heal the wounds, but no more. She must do as we say, and not try to escape, nor attack us, as she promises. For we have spells and defences, and magic to cause pain, yes, we do, and it would turn out the worse for her, yes, it would."

"Yes, I promise," she said hastily, most concerned to get him away from her as quickly as possible. "You will see, you can trust me, I will do as you say." She held out her wrists, longing for him to get on with releasing her.

He seemed to consider he'd given sufficient warnings, for at last his long pale fingers reached for her wrist bonds. He was trembling, but untied the tight, complex knot without difficulty, and immediately backed away. He seemed nervous that his prey was partly free, but on purpose she made no sudden movements. He stood up and retreated to the cauldron, as she flexed and massaged her aching wrists.

It felt wonderful to have the use of her hands and arms again. Watched most carefully by the warlock, she reached over for the jug and cup of water, and the bowl of food. She leant back gratefully against the cave wall and gulped a full cup of water straight down. She wasn't sure whether it was because of her extreme thirst, but the water tasted exceptionally cool, sweet and delicious.

Next, she sank her teeth into the ripe pear, and the juice oozed wonderfully down her neck. She crunched her way through an apple and devoured ravenously half the loaf and the meat. She was careful to leave half of the food for the spirit lord, and was content to ignore the warlock for now, however closely he was watching her.

While eating, she examined her wounds, and although bruised and aching, she had no major gashes that were still bleeding. She needed cleaning up, and the scabs and scars would take time to heal, but all of that could wait. The priority now was to attend to the spirit lord.

She shuffled over on her backside to where the spirit lord was slumped against the wall, bringing the food and water with her. The closer she got, the worse he looked, and her heart ached to see him like this. He looked wretched.

She touched his bare arm, and was relieved to feel a

soft, gentle warmth, not the cold clamminess of death. His restrictive bonds made it a struggle, but she arranged his limbs less awkwardly, propping his back against the cave wall. His head lolled forwards and sideways, and she adjusted his position so that he could rest backwards. There was no sign of life from him; he was weak and limp, no moan or murmur, no stirring or sigh.

Then she noticed his wing. The bottom portion of the spirit lord's left wing had been hacked off. There was a jagged cut where the warlock must have removed part of it for his potion, for he'd mentioned that in his list of ingredients. She looked closer, and the lower end of the wing was scabbed closed with an ugly grey line of congealed spirit lord blood.

She wondered whether a spirit lord could feel an injury to his wing. Was it like hair, or more like a hand or an arm? She could only imagine how that might feel, so her sympathy for him was growing. How could she better care for him?

"May I remove his gag, for him to eat and drink properly?" she asked, over her shoulder.

"Yes, she may," came the warlock's reply, and she resumed ignoring their captor's presence.

She loosened the rag tied around the spirit lord's face, and he gave his first sign of response. With a low moan, he stretched his mouth and lips, clenched his teeth and tried to swallow. His mouth was too dry, so she offered the cup. The water ran down his chin and neck, but he took a drink. She watched and waited for his eyelids to open, but they didn't. Once he swallowed, she repeated giving him a drink of water, and then dabbed his chin with her sleeve.

Now to give him some food. She needed a knife to cut up the apple and pear but felt it would push her luck to ask the warlock for one. She held the pear to the spirit lord's lips, but he was too weak or unconscious to take a bite. She opened the pear with her teeth, and broke it into smaller, juicy pieces with her fingers, and fed it between his lips. He chewed and swallowed slowly, as if in his sleep. She did the same with the bread, the apple and the meat, and he ate it all eventually.

While he was chewing, she used some water to wash him with the rag that had gagged him. She ran her fingers through his tangled, knotted auburn hair, trying to comb it behind his head. She straightened and flattened his wings, as much as the bonds of rope would allow, and they folded neatly against his back. She dabbed at the wounds on his arms and legs, removing dried and caked blood, and washing away the sweat, grime and tears on his face.

With a sudden jolt, she realised she would never dare to touch the spirit lord like this if he were awake. She began to feel self-conscious about every touch of his hair and skin, and the feeding of food and water into his mouth. But he was unconscious, she told herself, and in desperate need, and only she could help him. Surely he would forgive her touch, her care and attention to his immortal body, under these circumstances?

She watched him eating. His chewing and swallowing seemed timeless, unhurried, as though immortality truly gave him all the time in the world. It was getting darker outside the cave, and the light of a candle reflected off his auburn hair, giving it gentle highlights of red and gold. As she brushed a few strands of stray hair away from his face, she wondered how this young man's body was immortal. What was it that made him so different from her mortal body, that he was immune to aging, decay or natural death? And if he was also magical and powerful, where did that come from?

His eyelashes were long and dark on his closed eyes. What colour were those eyes behind their lids? If she knew this spirit lord from before, she should remember his eye colour, but found she could not, and that troubled her. She didn't dare lift his eyelid to look.

She shifted her position, glanced up, and was shocked to see the warlock glaring at her from across the cauldron. He must have been watching every touch of hers for the spirit lord, and it looked to have filled him with jealousy. Did he remember someone once touching him like that? Was the warlock jealous of the spirit lord for being tended to by her? If so, that might be something to be careful about, or to exploit.

But first, she needed to distract him, to change the focus of his attention. It was the first thing she could think of to ask. "Excuse me," she said, "why can't I remember anything?"

The warlock was startled. "What? What did she say?"

"I'm sorry to disturb your concentration and work on the potion, but I asked why I can't remember anything."

"Oh yes, oh yes." The warlock was back to his old self again. "Can't remember a thing, can she, no, that's good, that's good. A kindness and a mercy, it is, yes, if she forgets all about the past, her old life, before meeting us. Makes it easier for her to die if she knows nothing of all she's leaving behind."

"But why can't I remember, please? Is it some spell you've put on me?"

The warlock eyed her warily. "Wants to know our powers, she does, yes, our potions and spells. Curious and interested, she is, keeps asking. But a useful spell that is, isn't it, yes, the Forgetery Spell. Wears off eventually, of course, but not for a long time, no, not for a very long time. And she doesn't have that long." He muttered and mumbled and busied himself with his cauldron.

She turned back towards the spirit lord and sighed. However he tried to present it, the warlock had used this Forgetery Spell to scramble or wipe her memories as a ploy to confuse and isolate her. His crimes and violations against her were mounting into a lengthening list. Part of her wanted to pay him back, to avenge herself on him, but that seemed too much to hope for at present. Finding a way to confound the warlock's plans, to prevent him from executing and dismembering them both, had to be her main priority. Everything depended on surviving and escaping.

But the warlock was right about the forgetting making her feel rootless and alone. She must have a past, a home, a family – parents, perhaps brothers and sisters – but if so, they were blocked and lost from her. Or had she lived in some wretched hostel for orphaned young people, or on the streets, or out in the wild? She had no idea which.

But if anyone was missing her, she had no way of contacting them. So now, if her past was lost and forgotten, then this present was all she had. Her immediate future was only this cave, the warlock and the spirit lord. And only two or three days left to live. That was what she needed to do something about. But her circling thoughts and guesses were getting confusing, and her brain was too tired. She needed to rest, to think, to take stock and refresh herself.

She couldn't stop from watching the spirit lord though. After looking at the warlock, he was a balm for her aching eyes. She remembered the warlock's putrid stench, and as she leaned forward to give the spirit lord another sip of water, she breathed deeply of his scent. It was a woody fragrance that seemed to cleanse her nostrils and lungs, filling her soul with the essence of a forest.

Here was her one and only friend, her ally and companion. Caring for him seemed a natural, as well as a necessary, thing to do. Her remaining life – long or short – was bound up with his, and for now, he was all she had.

The warlock had described this spirit lord as immortal. That he was magical, powerful, gorgeous, and now also ageless and deathless, didn't seem fair. Perhaps if she'd been unconscious, and he the one awake and alert, then their chances of surviving and escaping might be better.

But in the meantime, here she was, and their lives and deaths depended on her.

Helena shuffled through the last trees towards their corner of the meadow and heaved a sigh. She'd made it home, and before dark as well. Through the twilight, there was no glimmer of light from inside the cottage window. In his permanent darkness, Arthur wouldn't have bothered to light a candle for himself.

Helena straightened and flexed the aching muscles in her back. She couldn't decide whether her back or her chest hurt more. Her hands crept up and massaged around her heart. If she wasn't careful, she feared this was killing her. But how could she possibly stop worrying: a mother for her only child? After finishing her daughter's morning chores with the animals, she hadn't been able to sit still and wait for her to reappear. When Roza hadn't returned home by lunchtime, she'd ventured out to search for her.

It was time to break the news to Arthur. She leaned forward and picked up the handles of Roza's barrow, her axe, saw and cloak resting across the half-load of chopped wood. It had taken her all afternoon, but she'd stumbled back to their cottage from the clearing where she'd found Roza's things. At least it had been along flat forest paths, because she couldn't have managed any climbing, up or down. That was one thing she could be grateful for, that Roza hadn't gone far down the valley, or up into the hills of the Heismith Range, or she might never have discovered what had become of her.

Helena wheeled the barrow to the woodstore beside the cottage and let it rest there. Her breath was coming in shuddering gasps, as she heaved the air into her lungs, even though she felt she could never get enough of it. She needed to calm down before she spoke with her husband, for fear of alarming him even more. Shuffling across to a bench, she lowered herself onto it and closed her eyes.

A beautiful place. Picture somewhere calm and peaceful, where she'd been happy. That always helped. Soothe away those stresses and try not to think about all that threatened to overwhelm her. Roza as a tiny baby, feeding at her breast. Watching Roza as a growing girl, running and playing in the meadow.

It worked a little. But the memories were all about Roza. Now she needed to get through telling this news to Arthur, and the sooner she did that, the better. She levered herself onto her feet and rested a hand against the cottage wall, easing herself around to the front door.

"Rozabella, is that you?" Arthur's voice called out as soon as her hand lifted the latch. "Helena, are you there, are you back?"

"Yes, Arthur, it's me," Helena replied. "I'm back, I'm all right."

"What about Roza, is she with you?" Arthur asked at once.

Helena drew in a deep breath, as she closed their front door behind her. What else could she say but tell him the stark truth? "No, I'm afraid not, dear."

There was silence while Arthur's blank stare turned towards her, trying in vain to locate her. His voice lowered to a whisper. "Have you found nothing, no sign of her?"

"Let me light us some candles first," Helena said. She located a few of these, lit their wicks from the glowing embers in the hearth, and set them up around the room. At last, she seated herself in front of her husband. She needed to be comfortable before venturing into this conversation.

"I started with the nearest places where we know Roza collects firewood, but there was no sign of her there. In the end, I reached the clearings underneath the Heismith cliffs, and that's where I found her barrow, axe, saw and cloak. I brought them back with me."

Arthur licked his lips nervously. "But what about our

girl? No sign of her?"

"Well, some of the grass had been flattened. There were footprints, but I don't know enough to tell one from another."

"Why didn't she take her cloak or tools with her?"

Helena could only shrug. "I don't know, Arthur."

"So, what can we do now?"

Helena sighed. She knew it wouldn't be 'we' anyway – it would be her. Arthur didn't have the confidence to leave his cottage blind. "I think I need to go down into town. We should report that Roza has gone missing and ask if anyone has seen anything. Ask if anyone can help us with the footprints or following tracks. We need some help. We'll struggle to cope by ourselves out here on our own, let alone conduct a search for Roza."

"But who will help us?" Arthur asked. "The town guards? The Reeve?"

"Yes, I was thinking of asking them." She hesitated, because Arthur wouldn't like her next suggestion. "I also wonder whether young Jorxy might help us."

As she expected, Arthur burst out with, "What? That boy is a rascal, a troublemaker and a thief. We've always tried to keep our Roza away from him. Why would you ask for his help? Isn't he locked up for his stealing now anyway?"

Helena sighed. "No, I don't think he's locked up at present. And the reason I'll ask for his help is because he's always had a soft spot for our Roza. Through all their years in the town schoolroom together, poor Jorxy would do anything for her. He's one person who won't rest until he's found her."

Arthur bowed his head, and Helena saw a tear trickle down his cheek. No more keeping their spirits up. Her husband had also succumbed to fear and despair at last. "To think we've come to this. Relying on that Jorxy to find our precious daughter. We're done for. The Dragon might as well come and finish us off."

"Hush, no, don't say that," Helena hissed. "Don't even mention that creature. Have you forgotten that doing so only attracts him?"

Arthur shook his head but didn't say more.

CHAPTER FIVE

As darkness fell, she lay down to sleep. She positioned herself alongside the spirit lord, supposing she was protecting him. The warlock disappeared, probably into another room or area of the cave where he slept. The fire died out beneath the cauldron, and the cave was silent. She listened to a gentle rustle of leaves in a night-time breeze outside. She craned her neck to look, and saw a faint glimmer of starlight, and perhaps the moon, showing up the rough arch of the cave entrance.

She considered trying to escape. If she untied her ankle bonds, could she drag the limp spirit lord out of the cave and away? He wouldn't be too heavy, but in her current weakened and injured state, she doubted it. If the warlock left them alone the next night, that would be a better opportunity for flight, when they were better healed and strengthened. Above all, the spirit lord might wake, and it would be much easier if he could walk.

She closed her eyes, and in the darkness, she seemed to sense the form and presence of the spirit lord beside her. Was it her imagination, or did his body radiate light and warmth, even through his unconsciousness and her closed eyelids? It was bewitching. Was this more of his powerful magic, setting him far above an ordinary, mortal girl like her?

She pulled herself together. She needed to plan how to get out of here, not dwell on the spirit lord. The warlock seemed jealous at her touching her fellow captive. Perhaps he remembered a time, even centuries before, when he had had a parent, a sibling, a friend or a lover, who had touched him in a kind and gentle way. In his ancient decrepitude, was he longing for a caring, understanding, compassionate hand, a smile, a laugh, an embrace? A pang of sorrow and pity stirred in her heart for the old warlock, but she quickly squashed it again. She needed to think how to use this to her advantage – but not until the morning.

She awoke early, and it was not full daylight. There was a half-light of dawn creeping through the cave archway, and a sweeter smell in the air as if a shower of rain in the night had dampened the grass and trees outside. What had woken her was the warlock coming in, humming to himself, carrying a bucket of water and slopping it onto the floor again. He noticed she was awake.

Without a word, he fetched and brought her a loaf of bread, two hard-boiled eggs, more fruit and water. As he placed them next to her, she looked at him and couldn't help noticing that he seemed a little different. His stench was still there but significantly faded. Was she simply getting used to it? But his black robes were nothing like as dirty or frayed as yesterday. She concluded that, since he now had company, he'd washed himself overnight and changed into newer and cleaner robes for today.

She ate and drank and watched him light the fire under the cauldron and start work on his potion again. With a sinking jolt she realised it was now the next day. Her deadline of life or death was now tomorrow or the day after. How could she find out everything she wanted to know and convince him to spare them?

"Excuse me, Mister Warlock, sir." Calm, polite determined, and he looked over at her. "You said you need to make this longevity potion so you can stay alive and defend the valley. Your Forgetery Spell means I don't even know which valley you mean."

He stared at her. "She doesn't even remember her own valley. That's good, Forgetery Spell worked well, yes."

"So, are we in this valley now?" she pressed. "Is that what's outside this cave?"

"Outside our cave, yes," the warlock nodded. "We

defend everything out there." He waved an arm towards the entrance.

"Defend it from what?"

His piercing blue eyes fixed on her again. "We do not speak of it. She has forgotten the danger our valley is in. She's lucky not to remember, yes, she is. Everyone in the valley would rather not know, would prefer to forget as well. But the warlock, we know and remember, we prepare and defend, for the sake of everyone."

"So, you're not going to tell me the danger?"

"No, we won't tell her. It's kinder that she doesn't know. Better to be innocent and oblivious, yes, it is."

She gave an exasperated sigh and tried another line of attack. "You also said about keeping your magic alive, so what do you mean by that?"

The warlock's gaze was now a hostile glare. "She wants to discover our warlock secrets, and we will never tell her those," he thundered.

"All right, all right." She held up her hands to placate him. "Please forgive my curious questions, but I'm trying to understand why I need to die here."

He seemed to calm down as he regarded her. "Wants to understand the need for her self-sacrifice, of course she does. Is that reasonable, does she deserve an explanation, does she?"

She dared to press her point. "You see, if you're taking the lives of the two of us, the spirit lord and me, that implies you think you're more important than we are. That your life, when you've already lived four hundred years, has more value than mine, when I'm only young."

Her words seemed to sink in and shame the warlock, but he soon masked it with anger and offence. "She thinks us selfish, yes, she does. To snuff out her young life to add a few more years to ours. But let us ask her this: does she know magic? Can she defend this valley? When she doesn't even remember what we're facing?"

"No, of course I don't–" she began, but he cut her off.

"Then she should leave these important decisions to us older and more powerful people who know what we're talking about. Yes, she should."

"So, I need to shut up and accept my fate because you won't tell me anything?" she protested.

His blue eyes held her gaze, and she reckoned she'd scored a point against him. He drew a deeper breath. "It is sad, of course it is, that she and the spirit lord need to die for us to go on living. We wrestled with our conscience many years ago about this, before we made the first longevity potion, yes, we did. But her sacrifice is necessary, yes, it is, sad but necessary, because there is no other way."

"So, that's it? The whole explanation? It's sad and necessary, but we need to die. I can't accept that, because I still don't understand."

The warlock stepped forward. "Longevity must be paid for. A death for a life, that's how it is. A cost, a sacrifice is required to cheat Death, yes, that's what he demands. So, for us to stay alive, someone else must pay. It's sad and unfair, but necessary, because we need to stay alive, and longevity must be paid for. Now, she needs to leave us to attend to our potion."

He turned his back on her, but she sent a parting shot after him. "How much more selfish can you get? Robbing someone of their years to add to your own? So, we pay the price for your eternal youth?"

He ignored her, and she sighed.

It was time to give the spirit lord his drink and food, but she found this morning that the skin of her hands was stinging. It was painful, itchy and irritating, as if she'd been stung by a nettle or had a rope burn. She tried washing her hands, but it seemed to get worse every time she touched or tended to the spirit lord.

The warlock noticed her discomfort. "Are her hands burning this morning?" he enquired. "Irritated, itchy, are they?"

"Yes, they are," she replied. "What is it?"

He smiled to himself and shook his head. "Helping the spirit lord, she wanted to, yes," he said. "Washes him, feeds him, touches him. Can't do that without a cost, can she? No."

"What do you mean?" she asked. "Is there something in his skin that burns my hands?"

The warlock cackled. "How dare she? Her, a mortal girl, touching an immortal spirit lord. Shouldn't do that, should she, not without permission."

She was at a loss. "But how could I get his permission? He's unconscious and injured, starving and thirsty, so surely he needs my help? He would understand that, and agree to being looked after, wouldn't he?"

"Not the point, is it, no." The warlock was lecturing her from across the cauldron, seeming to retaliate for her accusing him of selfishness. "We saw her, we watched her, didn't we, yes. Not just feeding and washing him, was she, no. Enjoying it, she was. We know that look, that touch. Likes him, doesn't she, thinks him handsome."

Her shame and embarrassment rose as though she'd been found out. The jealous warlock was getting his revenge for her victories. She'd tried hard to ignore him and pretend it was just her and the spirit lord in the cave. To care for him, looking after him gently and tenderly. But the warlock had noticed it all, and she spluttered to defend herself. "Yes, of course he's handsome. He's a spirit lord. Any mortal girl would like him and enjoy caring for him."

"Humph," the warlock replied. "Still a punishment it is, yes. The hands that touch his skin and hair, they burn and itch and irritate, don't they? He knows the thoughts of the girl that touches him, yes, he does."

She snatched back her hands from the spirit lord because the warlock's words had stung her. His sleeping form seemed to rebuke and chastise her from behind his closed eyelids. She was fascinated by him and relieved to be able to touch and care for him without his knowledge. But was it true that her wonder and admiration for him had been found out? Did spirit lords have secret defences in their skin against unwanted touch, even when asleep or unconscious?

She was troubled and felt the warlock had won this battle over her. She tried to finish feeding and washing the spirit lord without touching his skin or hair at all. She touched his tunic and the ropes instead, but her stinging hands only got worse, not better.

The morning wore slowly by, and she watched the warlock pottering at his cauldron, fetching, chopping, adding and mixing ingredients. He often consulted his books and parchments and took sips of the liquid to test it.

An urgency nagged at her, that she needed to gain his trust and escape before the basic potion was ready. The first step was to gain more freedom in movement and give him more reason to trust her. Her wrists were free, but she wanted his permission to untie her ankles. Her backside had become numb, and she needed to exercise her legs.

After lunch, a growing pressure in her bladder gave her an idea. She tried to pick a time when he didn't appear to be concentrating. "Excuse me," she said.

He looked at her irritably. "What?"

"I'm sorry to disturb you," she said. Calm, polite, determined. "Now that I'm eating and drinking again, I need to, um, relieve myself. Is there somewhere here I can go to do that? I realise I need to stand and walk, but I promise I'll go and stay exactly where you tell me to. Please may I untie my ankles?"

He snorted. "Free her legs, she wants, of course she does. But she can't make a run for it, no, she can't. Wouldn't get out of the cave. She doesn't know, does she?"

She couldn't help wondering what she didn't know but

pressed on for his permission. "No, I promise I won't try to make a run for it, or anything, just relieve myself and then stay here in this corner. So, may I untie my ankles?"

The warlock considered for some moments, stirring the potion. Finally, "Shall we let her?" he said. He cocked his head sideways, regarding her. She offered him what she hoped was her most persuasive and trustworthy smile.

Her smile seemed to confuse and embarrass him, as though he hadn't seen one in longer than he could remember. Eventually he nodded. "She can untie her legs, but we warn her: we have magic and spells, and she mustn't approach us. We can stop her and hurt her in a moment, so she mustn't try. We've stopped her leaving the cave too, so she mustn't try that. She looks after herself and the spirit lord and no more. Does she understand?"

"Yes, I understand, and thank you," she said as graciously as she could. She reached for her ankles and fumbled with the ropes. The knots were wickedly tight and fiendish to untie. After a long time, she succeeded in loosening a first strand, and finally her legs were freed. It felt glorious to flex and massage her ankles and feet, and using the support of the wall, to leave the cold, hard rock of the cave floor. She stretched and bent her legs and feeling returned to them.

The warlock watched her warily, but she was careful to make no sudden movements or do anything unexpected. He jerked his head towards an alcove beyond where the spirit lord lay, and she went there and relieved herself out of sight.

When she returned, she looked down at where the spirit lord sat, propped up against the cave wall, still tightly bound. "Seeing as how he's still unconscious," she asked, "and not about to run off anywhere or do anything, please may I untie some of the spirit lord's ropes too?"

"No, she may not!" The warlock thundered with unexpected vehemence. He straightened and his eyes flashed. "The spirit lord stays where he is," he shouted, "bound with all those ropes as he is now, does she understand?"

"Yes, yes, of course," she said hastily.

She needed to change the subject, as she seemed to have upset the warlock, asking too much and damaging his trust in her. She looked around, searching for something else to talk to him about.

Now she had a different perspective on the cave, it looked worse than ever. It was more filthy, untidy and ramshackle than she could see from the floor. She looked at the polished wooden coat stand and thought that maybe it had watched her stand up.

She turned towards the daylight. She longed for the fresh air out there, or at least a change of view, and said, "May I look out of the cave entrance? I'll take a few steps over in this direction and have a look outside. Is that acceptable?"

The warlock narrowed his eyes at her, suspicion all over his face. At last, he nodded. "It would be well for her to find out what holds her in, wouldn't it? Let her touch the Barrier, and she won't get any ideas, will she? Made sure she can't escape, didn't we, with our powerful magic, yes, we did." He chuckled to himself, as though impressed with his own brilliance and skill.

She turned away. She didn't need to watch his self-congratulation. Instead, she screwed up her eyes to shield them from the brightness outside. It was mid-afternoon, and the sun was high. She hadn't known what she might find outside this horrible cave but hadn't expected it to be so beautiful.

Through the cave's arched entrance, she saw a path and grass stretching towards scattered trees. The sunlight slanted down between dappled shade, with a breeze rippling through the leaves. There were flowers in clumps around the tree-trunks, and wildflowers waving between the blades of grass. She tried to identify the trees, and while some were oak, beech and ash, others were fruiting: apple, cherry, pear, plum. The closer she looked, the more it looked like an orchard. Of course, that's where the warlock must have collected the fruits they'd been eating.

Without realising it, she'd been edging forward to get a better view of the outside. A sudden flash of blue light blinded her, a deafening crash, and an agony shot from her shoulder down through her whole body. She staggered backwards, collapsing to the floor. The warlock erupted into hilarious cackles.

"Got her, yes, got her, we did. Found the Barrier, hasn't she? Can't go outside, can't escape, she's kept safe and secure inside our cave until we need her, yes, she is. Very clever spell it is – it lets us through, but not her, no. But did it hurt? Did our magic pain her?"

She was massaging her shoulder, and the grimace on her face must have answered his question. So much for thoughts of escaping while the warlock left them alone at night. She should have realised he'd anticipated and prevented that.

"Yes, now she learns, now she understands, doesn't she? A powerful warlock we are, yes, and that's why we need to stay alive. Our magic needs to stay in the world until we can pass it on, to protect the town, and not die with us and leave everyone defenceless. It is sad, of course it is, that we need to keep her here. But she must understand that her sacrifice is necessary and has a purpose."

She looked away, unwilling to witness any more of the warlock's self-justification.

A small movement caught the corner of her eye. It was the spirit lord. He had stirred, shifted. Perhaps the light and crash of the cave's Barrier spell had roused him. Having been just her and the warlock since she awoke, now the captive, injured spirit lord was waking.

A sudden panic gripped her. After these hours – or had it been days? – of being here and looking after the spirit lord, now she would need to talk with him. Her attention for him had been secret and safe, or at least known only to the warlock. The fear arose that the spirit lord would reject her, disapprove and criticise all she'd done so far.

She swallowed hard. There was no alternative. She had no other option but to try to make common cause and friendship with this seriously injured, immortal being, who was also under threat of impending death. How would he respond to their plight?

She crawled across the cave floor towards him, ignoring for now what the warlock might be doing. She couldn't let the old man distract her from keeping her whole focus on the waking spirit lord.

She kept a short distance away as the spirit lord moaned. She didn't want to startle or alarm him when he came to and opened his eyes. But his eyelids remained firmly closed.

Picking up the cup of water, she shuffled closer. She held it to his lips, and the spirit lord responded, opening his lips to receive a drink, and swallowing it down. As she lowered the cup, her hand was trembling.

She watched and waited for him to wake. But he didn't. His eyelids remained closed. His tongue moved over his moistened lips, and he muttered. His muscles strained and squirmed against his bindings, and he groaned.

Was there any way to relieve his pain? Not without untying the restricting ropes that bound him, and the warlock had strictly forbidden that.

She tried to calm herself. The spirit lord might be distraught at his situation, at being captured, injured and held prisoner, but he would view her as an ally, surely? After all, she'd done her best for him, with untying his gag, with food, and water and washing. But she found herself nursing a desperate hope that he would be her friend. In her current situation, her one and only friend.

The spirit lord quietened down again, his mumbles lapsing into silence, his straining slumping into stillness. Maybe he would retreat into sleep again. She sat back on the cave floor and glanced towards where the warlock stood by his cauldron.

His piercing blue eyes were boring into her. Was that jealousy again? The warlock regarded the captive spirit lord for a moment and then harrumphed. He returned to busying himself with his potion ingredients.

She turned back to look at the spirit lord and jumped in shock.

His eyes were open.

He glared at her from out of black wells of hate and disgust.

She stared at him. She'd wondered about the colour of his eyes but never imagined the depths of black that now assailed her. The beauty of his sleeping face was transformed with a fury and pain that made her recoil.

She swallowed hard, and then started a move towards him.

"Stay away from me," he hissed.

She dropped the arm she'd raised. His gaze remained fixed on her, and she could see the veins throbbing in his neck.

"Um ... how are you feeling?" she ventured.

"What do you care?" he snapped.

In her nervous dread, she couldn't have imagined a worse response, or such hostility from the waking spirit lord. Tears stung the back of her eyes, because she'd been trying her best for him. "It's ... that ... I've been trying to look after you while you were unconscious."

"You ... you touched me?" he spat.

She could no longer hold his gaze and looked down. How could she explain to him so he would believe her?

"I ... I had to give you a drink of some water, and feed

you some bread and fruit, and wash your wounds…"

He turned away from her, wriggling so his back was to her. "Don't you dare touch me ever again," he snarled over his shoulder.

The hurt inside made her angry too. "Fine. I'll stop helping you then." She turned her back on him as well. But inside, she was desolate. This wasn't how it was supposed to go. They were meant to be allies and friends, united against the warlock in their need to survive and escape.

Perhaps she needed to give him time. He'd only just awoken and discovered his predicament. He needed to adjust to finding himself a prisoner, and bound, and injured. Once he'd calmed down from those shocks, she'd be able to reason with him, wouldn't she?

But time was the one thing they didn't have.

A chuckle from the warlock disturbed her thoughts. She glanced up and her anger surged. It seemed that nothing made the old warlock happier than seeing his two captives arguing. He was grinning and nodding, as though with delight at the sharp exchange between her and the spirit lord.

She hated him more than ever. Wasn't it enough that he'd captured and intended to kill them, without tormenting and gloating over them too?

She sighed. If the spirit lord wouldn't talk to her, there was nothing for her to do. She curled up against the wall of the cave, wrapped her arms around her knees and stared at her scuffed leather boots.

CHAPTER SIX

It was time for the evening meal, and the warlock brought a jug of water, two cups and a tray of food over towards her. There was two of everything: small loaves of bread, eggs, slices of ham, hunks of cheese, and apples. The warlock laid them down with another chuckle, as though to say: I dare you to try and feed him, and I'm going to enjoy watching you fight again.

She glanced at the spirit lord. He turned his head and looked at the food over his shoulder. He must be hungry, if not starving. She had to try. She picked up the tray and held it out towards him.

He scowled at her and turned away. Maybe he wasn't as starving as she thought. Perhaps he could survive without food for longer than mortal humans could.

She lowered the tray again, poured herself a cup of water and helped herself to the food. She took no more than her fair share, half of what the warlock had supplied them. The old man was chuckling away to himself at the antagonism between his prisoners in their corner.

Once she finished her food, she was determined to feed the spirit lord. She wouldn't let his meal go to waste uneaten. She would avoid looking at him, just get the food and water inside him. She dragged the tray across the cave floor until she was beside him. At least, since he was still bound, he couldn't get away from her.

Waves of anger and hate radiated from him, but she ignored that. She knelt next to him, filled a cup with water and lifted it to his lips. He turned his head away.

"Aren't you thirsty?" she asked.

He didn't reply.

"The water is here. You need to drink. It isn't poisoned

or anything. Your arms are bound, so I'm trying to help you."

"I'm not taking anything from you," he snarled.

She lowered the cup, taken aback. "Why not? Why won't you accept my help?"

"You're working for him. You're his slave and accomplice."

She couldn't help it. She laughed with relief, finally understanding his antagonism. "Don't be ridiculous," she said. "I'm his prisoner too. Just like you."

His eyes widened to stare at her but remained black with anger. "Then why am I bound, and you're free to move around?"

"Um … well, I woke up first. I persuaded the warlock to untie me so I could look after us. He needs us alive and in good condition."

"As I said: you're his slave and working for him," he sneered.

"No, it's not like that," she said quickly. "It's in our interests to be alive and in good condition too, isn't it?"

The spirit lord didn't reply. She offered the water again, but he turned his face away.

"You must be working for him," he said. "You were there when he captured me, weren't you? You were the bait in his trap for me."

His words jolted her with surprise. Her mouth dropped open, and she knelt up straight. "You remember us being captured?" she gasped. "I don't remember a thing."

He narrowed his eyes at her, and she could tell he didn't believe her.

"It's true," she said. "I can't remember anything, not even my own name. The warlock said he used a Forgetery Spell on me, or something."

The spirit lord's black eyes regarded her, as though assessing, appraising her.

"Rozabella," he said at last. "That was the name you

told me. Roza for short. With a 'z'."

As soon as he said this, it connected in her memory. Yes, that sounded right.

"Roza," she said. "Yes, I remember now. With a 'z'. Thank you." It felt good to know her identity, like she'd become a person again. "But is that all I said about myself?"

"You told me you're seventeen."

She smiled at him. "Roza, short for Rozabella. Seventeen years old, yes, that's me, thank you."

He grunted. She offered the cup of water to the spirit lord again, and this time he hesitated. "You said it isn't poisoned, so I want you to drink some of it first to prove it."

Roza rolled her eyes. His suspicion exasperated her, but she duly took a sip. When she offered it again, this time he accepted it. She tipped it up, and he drank it all down. As good as it was to know her own name, it was better to think he was willing to accept her help. That they might yet be allies and friends against the warlock.

"Your food next," Roza said, and started in turn to put pieces of bread, ham, egg, cheese and apple into his mouth. "Before we were captured," she said, "did you tell me your name?"

"I did. In your tongue you can call me Kerenzi," he said as he chewed.

"Kerenzi," she repeated, "right. And the warlock called you something like a spirit lord. Is that what you are?"

"I am. Master of the spirits of the forest. Your legends give me the title of spirit lord."

She stopped. For a moment she couldn't believe she was feeding a piece of boiled egg into the mouth of someone from legend, a master of forest spirits. However, she made sure not to show her awe and went on. "What was I doing when we were captured? Where were we?"

Kerenzi stopped chewing and regarded her. "You really

don't remember anything, do you?"

Roza shook her head.

"You were chopping firewood in a clearing," he said. "I came and talked to you and the warlock surprised us."

Roza frowned. "Why was I chopping up firewood? Did I live near that clearing? Was I doing that for myself, or for someone else? I can't remember."

Kerenzi shrugged. "No idea. I can't answer any of that. All you said was you had to, because everyone needs to store up firewood for the winter."

"No mention of parents, family, home?"

He thought for a moment. "Not that I can remember."

A pang tugged at Roza's heart. No answers to her questions about her origins or background then. So, she'd been chopping firewood. Had she been doing that willingly, to help the rest of her family? Or were they harsh and cruel to her, ordering her to do all their hard and menial work for them? She wished she knew.

She wondered how to ask whether the two of them had been friends, without sounding desperate. She decided on, "Did the two of us meet just that once?"

He shook his head, and her heart leapt with hope. When he swallowed his mouthful, he said, "Twice," and her fantasies of friendship with this gorgeous spirit lord were dashed. "I appeared to you briefly a few days before."

She tried not to look crestfallen. In between giving the spirit lord pieces of cheese, Roza absent-mindedly rubbed her itchy hands up and down her trousers.

Kerenzi noticed it. "Why are you doing that?" he asked at once. "Are your hands sore, irritated?"

She decided that an immediate and honest apology was the best approach. "Yes, they are, and I'm sorry. The warlock explained that those who touch the skin of a spirit lord without his permission are cursed with painful, itchy hands. I had to touch you, to try to feed and wash you, and I didn't know about the curse, and I was only trying to help you, so I'm sorry."

For the first time, the corner of the spirit lord's mouth twitched into a smile. Her insides squirmed at how attractive that was. "The warlock told you," he said slowly, "that your hands itch and hurt because you touched my skin? And I was supposed to give you my permission before you did anything like that? Even though I was unconscious?"

Roza nodded, but she knew from his expression there was something she didn't understand. "Why, what is it?"

Kerenzi sighed. "The warlock lied to you. It isn't my skin that irritates your hands, it's these wretched ropes. They're made from Bindweed, which is terrible stuff. It suppresses the magic of the being it binds. These ropes keep me in physical form, instead of reverting to invisible spirit. They drain my magic and hurt me wherever they touch my skin. Trust me, the pain and irritation in your hands is nothing compared to what they're doing to me."

Roza stared down at the spirit lord's bindings. Now she examined them closer, the grey fibres of the ropes were covered in cruel barbs and tiny spines. Was it these that had got into the skin of her hands? Her relief from the shame of touching the spirit lord without permission, changed into anger at what the warlock was doing to them both. Where the ropes touched Kerenzi's arms, legs and neck, there were red welts on his skin.

"I'm sorry this has happened to you," Roza breathed. "Now I understand why the warlock wouldn't let me untie your ropes. But I promise you that none of this is my fault. I'm not his slave, or working for him, or the bait in his trap for you. I would never help the warlock do this to anyone."

Kerenzi's eyes now had flickers of dark green in them to soften the black, and they made Roza think of shadows under the trees. "I think I believe you," the spirit lord said. "And I'm sorry about your hands. There's nothing you can do to relieve them until the spines work themselves out naturally."

They lapsed into silence, and at length Kerenzi finished eating. Roza decided she needed to say something to the warlock when she delivered their tray of empty bowls back to the table.

The warlock watched her closely as she stood up and carried the tray over. He wore a self-satisfied smirk, because he must have been listening to the conversation between his captives.

Roza's anger burned, and she was surprised at the vehemence in her voice as she spoke. "You are a cruel man and a liar. You kidnap the spirit lord and me, inflicting agony and fear on both of us. You wipe my memories and lie about the Bindweed ropes stinging my hands. You're selfish and jealous, you're a bully, and a coward and an evil man. You should be ashamed of yourself." Her words came out bolder than she expected, spitting the last sentences at him.

For a moment the warlock seemed taken aback, almost as though he accepted her rebuke.

But then he straightened and stepped over to the cauldron. He dipped in a cup, drew out some steaming liquid and took a sip. The meaning of the warlock's action seemed clear: you can say what you like, but I have all the power here, and I'm going to chop you up and add you to my potion.

Roza stood glaring at him across the cauldron, all her muscles tense, as he continued to taste the cup of his magical liquid.

But as she stared, she couldn't help noticing things. When the warlock had stepped to the cauldron, he hadn't shuffled. He stood straighter, not hunched or stooped. His grey hair had streaks of black in it and didn't look so greasy. Even if he had some magical way of washing the grey out of it, he definitely didn't look as ancient, decrepit or revolting as he did before. Was his longevity potion starting to take effect? But he hadn't added any of their vital organs yet.

What was going on?

Helena eased back on the reins and slowed her horse Poppy's walk to a stop. Her heart was pumping too fast, and she needed to get her breath back. Riding in the cart, downhill just as much as on the flat, took it out of her. She needed to be calm and so closed her eyes, drawing the deepest breaths she could manage. Picture a peaceful, beautiful place, she repeated to herself. It began to work.

"Are you all right, madam?" came a voice. "Do you need some help?"

Helena opened her eyes. A young man in a town guard's uniform was peering at her. "Oh, um, yes, thank you." The young guard stepped closer to her cart, and she smiled at him. "I'm a bit breathless after the ride in the cart," she explained. "Is it all right if I sit here and rest for a minute?"

She'd paused within sight of the gate into Albany and the young guard must have noticed her and walked over. Beyond him she saw the gateway in the town's wooden palisade and the handful of guards on duty there today. The afternoon sun was lowering towards the western mountaintops behind her, but still warmed this part of the valley.

"Of course, take all the time you need," the guard replied. "But shall I lead your horse to the gate for you?"

Helena managed a nod, handed him the reins, and leaned back. It was easier not to have to control Poppy. The guard clicked his tongue, and the horse stepped forward on the beaten earth track, pulling her rickety cart to the gateway. She rested a hand on her chest, massaging it and hoping no one noticed. Her breathing steadied.

"Aren't you Helena, the town Judge?"

She looked up. They'd stopped at the gateway, and an older guard in a sergeant's uniform was regarding her, frowning.

She sighed. "Yes, sergeant, I am Helena, and I used to be the Judge, until my health prevented me from serving. I've come to town because I've an urgent and important matter that I need some help with."

"How can we help you, Judge Helena?" the sergeant said. "You served the people of this town for many years. How is your husband – I'm sorry I forget his name?"

She smiled. "Thank you, sergeant. I'm grateful to hear that my work in the town hasn't been forgotten. Arthur is not so well, I'm afraid, because he struggles to cope with his blindness. He remembers too much of the things he can no longer see. Still, we manage as best we can."

"And what about that strapping daughter of yours, Rozabella? She's not with you today?" He grinned, and Helena noticed the smiles of the other guards. Roza was liked by the young men of the town, so perhaps her popularity could help and save her now.

"No, she isn't, and that's why I've come to town. Rozabella has gone missing. Have any of you seen her in the last two days?"

At once the smiles of the guards became frowns of concern.

"What do you mean by 'missing'?" asked the sergeant. "When and where did you last see her?"

"Two days ago," she replied. "She was chopping logs in the forest and didn't return at dusk. I found her axe and saw, her barrow and cloak in a clearing but no sign of her. Has she come this way into town?"

The sergeant looked round at his guards, but they were shaking their heads. "No, I'm sorry, Helena, none of us has seen her. But I'll send word through the guards in case there's any news, and let you know. I'll also inform the Reeve because I'm sure he'll want to know and help too."

She nodded her thanks to the sergeant. "I'm staying at the Mermaid Inn tonight if anyone needs to find me. But there's someone else I want to see first."

To the puzzlement of the guards, Helena pulled the reins to turn Poppy to the left, drawing her cart along the track outside the town's protective palisade. The ride was bumpy, and she smelled her destination before she saw it.

Outside the town on this north-western side lay Albany's rubbish ditch. In a deep cleft between the palisade and where the valley rose into the surrounding mountains, fires were always burning to consume the town's refuse. Helena wrinkled her nose at the acrid stink of the smoke and pulled Poppy to a stop. Because she'd found the boy she was looking for.

Jorxy was a thin boy with red-brown hair in ragged clothes, a year younger than her Roza. He was sitting on the bank high above the ditch, throwing stones at targets among the rubbish. His aim was good, because Helena heard each missile result in a clang of metal, or a smash of pottery, as the boy took pleasure in destroying what lay below.

But finding Jorxy here saddened her too, because too often she'd picked up the pungent smell of the rubbish ditch smoke on Rozabella's clothes. That meant her daughter had chosen, against her parents' instructions, to spend her free time hanging around out here with this boy.

Jorxy must have sensed her gaze, because he looked around and leapt to his feet when he saw her. The lop-sided features of his face meant he was bullied by the other boys as ugly. He stormed up to her cart with predictable anger.

"You! Are you spying on me? I ain't done nothing wrong. Leave me alone."

"Calm down, Jorxy. I'm not spying on you or trying to cause trouble—"

"I don't have to listen to you. You had me locked up.

Or have you forgotten that, Mrs Judge Helena? I hadn't been stealing—"

It was her turn to cut him off. "I'm not here to debate your guilt or innocence, young man. I'm here because I need your help."

Jorxy's ugly face creased into a sneer. "You? Need my help? I ain't never doing nothing to help you."

Helena heaved a deep breath. Arguing with this boy was upsetting her, and her heart couldn't take much more of this. "All right. I accept you might not want to help me. But what about our Roza? Will you do something to help her?"

His hostility looked less certain. "What about Roza? Why does she need my help? And don't order me to leave her alone. She sees me because she wants to. So there."

Helena held up a placating hand to try to stem the boy's anger. "Yes, Roza needs our help. She's gone missing and we don't know where she is." Her voice broke as she said this.

She repeated to him what she'd told the guards at the gate and Jorxy narrowed his eyes as though trying to detect the lie and trick in Helena's words.

"Why come and find me?" Jorxy asked. "What help can I be? Those others, your town guards, are better at searching."

"I came to find you, Jorxy, because we know you like our Roza. We thought you'd care about what has happened to her. That you'd be someone who wouldn't rest until you found her and brought her back safely."

Jorxy took a step closer, so he was almost hissing in her face. "You're right there, Mrs Judge. There's nothing I wouldn't do for my Roza, and don't you forget it."

"Thank you, Jorxy. We hoped we could count on you, and if you manage to find her, we'll be forever grateful, and all will be forgiven."

He leaned closer, making Helena retreat into her seat.

"I don't need your thanks or forgiveness, Mrs Judge. I'm doing this for Roza. Not for you."

Jorxy turned and stomped past her, up the lane towards the gateway.

"I'll be at the Mermaid Inn tonight, but returning to our cottage in the morning," she called after him. "And I can show you the clearing where I found her things." But he had already disappeared along the path.

Helena's heart was thumping enough that she wanted to wait before making the effort to turn the cart and leave, but the rubbish ditch smoke was catching her throat. She pulled on the reins and would rest once she reached the Inn.

CHAPTER SEVEN

The following morning, the warlock left the cave again. When he came back, Roza understood that outside lay not only the orchard of fruit trees, but also the source of their eggs, milk, meat and grain for bread. In the warlock's absence, the polished wooden coat stand was in charge of the potion, giving it an occasional stir with the long spoon.

Roza assumed the coat stand might have ears to hear them, as well as eyes to watch, so she and the spirit lord spoke together in whispers. They sat side by side, their backs against the cave wall, Roza being careful not to touch the Bindweed ropes and make her itchy skin worse.

She told Kerenzi what she'd learned so far, that they'd been captured for their body parts to be used in the longevity potion. To her surprise, the spirit lord nodded at this.

"My people have been going missing for years," he said. "Every few decades a wood nymph, dryad, sylph or naiad would disappear, never to be seen again. Of course, I knew of the warlock, and wondered about his unnaturally long life, but he's a powerful and dangerous man to confront. An enemy with Bindweed nets is not to be tackled lightly, and we had no proof that he was responsible."

"And you never found any trace of your missing people?" Roza asked. "Because their remains must be buried somewhere near this cave?"

"I think that's right. And now he's got you and me. He'll be especially pleased to have a lord of the immortals this time. But it's a barbaric thing to consider, repeated murder to keep yourself alive."

"When I first awoke," Roza whispered, "the warlock said he'd need our body parts in two or three days. By now, that means today or tomorrow. It's now urgent that we find a way to escape because I refuse to be his next victim. I've been trying to think of a plan but haven't come up with much."

Kerenzi turned to look at her. With their faces so close, Roza noticed flecks of a brighter green within the spirit lord's dark eyes. "You have hope," he murmured, surprised. "We're in a desperate and impossible situation, and yet you're still determined to live."

"Of course," Roza replied, with a twitch of a smile at him. "Perhaps it's the mortal in me, that we only get a brief span of life, so I object to it being cut even shorter."

Kerenzi smiled back, and this was what Roza had hoped for. A bond between them, a friendship forged in a bleak situation and the shared desire to escape and live.

"I've been trying to gather information," Roza went on, "about the potion, and how long we've got. I've also worked hard to earn his trust, by being calm and polite, accepting my fate. And one of us being free of ropes must improve our chances."

"All very nice for you," Kerenzi complained, "but I suppose I agree. I'm not sure what else we can try."

"How about if I unfasten your Bindweed ropes while the warlock is out of the cave?"

Kerenzi shook his head. "I'm sure he'll have thought of that and put a spell in place to prevent it. You can try now, if you like, but it will make your hands burn again."

Roza examined the bindings and knots, then braced herself for the pain and itching. She started on a knot near the end of a rope, trying to touch it with only the tips of her fingers. She loosened and began to untie it, but the rope slipped back under her hand. The knot was fastening itself again. She tried with a different binding, but the same thing happened.

Kerenzi shrugged, saying, "I thought as much. He had to make sure I couldn't be released to attack him or escape. I told you this Bindweed is terrible stuff, but it's perfect for keeping me prisoner."

Roza leaned back against the wall, refusing to despair until they considered all their options. "What about anyone from outside coming to rescue us? I might have family or friends who have missed me and started a search."

"Yes, they might," the spirit lord replied. "But they don't know what happened to you or where you are. How can we let them know we're here?"

Roza had no answer for that. "Okay, what about your people? You said they know about the warlock and where he lives. Won't they come from the forest to rescue their lord and master?"

Kerenzi let out a cold, mirthless laugh. "The chances of that are even lower than your parents happening upon this cave with the Emperor's whole army behind them."

She was puzzled. "Why won't any of your people want to rescue you? Don't they respect or care about you?"

Kerenzi sighed. "It's not a question of respect or care. The wood nymphs, dryads and others do most of what I tell them when I stand over them to make sure they do it. We're an independent lot and value our space and freedom. But risking themselves to save me so I can return to rule over the forest? Not a chance."

Roza hesitated to ask but wanted to understand the ways of the spirit lord's people if she could. "You must be important to them for keeping order in the forest. Doesn't anyone care enough to miss you and want to help?"

Kerenzi's answer was dry and sardonic. "Oh, they'll care enough to notice I've disappeared, but the last thing my people want is for me to be rescued and return."

It crossed Roza's mind that Kerenzi might be a cruel or unpopular leader of the forest spirits but couldn't think of a subtle way to ask this. So, she settled for, "I don't understand. Why don't they want you back?"

The spirit lord shifted himself to face her better, and

again Roza enjoyed being so close to him. "I see I need to explain what it's like to live as immortals," he began. "Among mortals, you expect your parents and leaders to age and retire or die, to be replaced by a younger generation. You wait your turn, and in time you get the chance to be Town Reeve or other important jobs, inherit a house or business, or whatever you want. As immortals, we don't get that turnover. There's no natural wastage, what I think you call 'filling a dead man's shoes'."

"Yes, I understand how that's different, I think."

"So, among my forest spirits, my disappearance is the best opportunity for hundreds or thousands of years. Anyone wanting to become lord and master themselves has had to wait for something disastrous to happen to me. Right now, they'll be secretly celebrating my absence and competing for the right to succeed me. So no, they won't send out a search party to rescue me."

It saddened Roza that the spirit lord's people were so ruthless and selfish, but perhaps that explained his weary acceptance of his fate. She wanted to continue with their escape options, and so asked, "What else have we got, then? Could we sabotage the warlock's longevity potion?"

"What would that achieve? He can always start it again and keep you under tighter control next time."

"It might buy us some time," she suggested.

Kerenzi nodded towards the coat stand giving the potion an occasional stir. "Hasn't our wily old warlock left that thing guarding both us and his precious potion?"

"What do you make of this coat stand, then?" Roza asked. "Can it hear as well as watch us?"

"It's under an ancient enchantment," Kerenzi replied. "I've never seen anything like it."

"While the warlock's out of the way, shall I see what I can find out?"

The spirit lord shrugged and nodded, so Roza got to her feet. As she expected, the coat stand swivelled to watch her. She stepped towards it and said, "Hello."

She cringed at the absurdity of addressing a coat stand, but persevered. She stayed out of touching or grabbing range, so as not to alarm it. If it could even be alarmed.

"Can you hear me? Can you understand me?"

The coat stand lifted the long spoon away from stirring the liquid and straightened. It edged sideways to come between her and the cauldron, in definite potion-guarding duty. The knots in the wood looked more like eyes than ever, but there was no sign of ears or a mouth.

"If you can hear and understand me, please nod your top slightly – your top hooks – to say 'Yes'."

To Roza's amazement and delight, the upper section of the coat stand inclined a little towards her.

"Can you speak at all?" she tried. "If 'No', then shake your hooks to the left and right a little."

This time, the coat stand's top moved left, right and back again.

Roza turned and grinned at Kerenzi, but then froze. The warlock's silhouette was framed in the cave entrance.

"What does she think she's doing?" the warlock thundered, stamping into the cave. "Get back in her corner she must, yes, or it will be the worse for her. We must punish her for this."

"No, wait, listen," Roza protested, hurrying back to the spirit lord. She chose an abject apology to try to soothe the warlock and restore his trust in her, when she'd stretched the limits of her freedom. "I haven't done anything. I didn't mean anything by it. I was just curious about your amazing, enchanted coat stand–"

"It's not so amazing," the warlock grunted, putting down the basket of eggs he was carrying. "And she mustn't distract it from stirring the potion."

"No, I'm sorry, I didn't mean to–"

"Standley, get back to the bookcase," the warlock ordered, and snatched the long spoon away from the coat stand's hooks.

"Wait a minute," Roza said. "You called it, 'Standley'? It has a name? 'Standley', very good, I like it," and she beamed at the warlock.

For an instant, Roza thought the corner of the warlock's mouth twitched upwards, almost smiling back.

"I think that's great," she went on before he could reply, "calling your enchanted coat stand 'Standley'. I didn't realise you had such wit and humour too." She sat down next to Kerenzi, hurrying to be out of the way and no trouble at all before the warlock followed through on his threat to punish her.

The warlock scowled, busy with stirring the potion again. But underneath that, Roza felt sure he'd appreciated her compliment. Instead of a setback in his trust of her, they'd almost shared a moment of amusement.

Roza glanced towards Kerenzi and mouthed, "Phew." The spirit lord smiled at her, and her insides warmed.

The minutes passed, and the warlock seemed to forget about punishing her. He was tasting his potion more often now, lifting ladles of it to smell and examine and sip.

With a clutch of dread, Roza remembered that her execution might be today. How would the warlock do it? Would he knock her unconscious again, like that BodyCrusher spell, or whatever it was called, he'd used before? However this monster did it, every hour brought that moment closer. She needed to distract herself from her panic.

"Kerenzi," she asked, "how come you remember more than I do? You knew our names, and about when we were captured, so didn't the warlock use the Forgetery Spell on you like he did on me?"

"No, he cast it on me as well, but it didn't work so effectively. There might be two reasons for that. First, I have my own magical power, a magic resistance, which protects me a little even when I'm trussed up in Bindweed.

And secondly, I have rather more memories than you."

Roza gazed into the spirit lord's eyes and remembered she was speaking with someone immortal, who lived unthinkably many years compared with her own short, mortal life.

"When you've lived as long as I have," Kerenzi went on, "we develop complicated ways of remembering all we want to. You're only seventeen and so don't have much to remember. The Forgetery Spell cleared out your few memories easily enough but struggled to make any headway against my vast store of them. And you short-lived mortals don't notice or remember much of what's going on around you anyway."

Roza opened her mouth to protest but didn't want to start an argument with the spirit lord. They lapsed into silence.

She glanced towards the warlock and noticed that, for a change, he didn't seem to be listening to them. Previously, he'd scowled over her care for Kerenzi or gloated over their arguments. Roza watched him for a while, although hiding that she was doing so.

Soon there was no doubt: the warlock was distracted. He wasn't working at his bench, chopping up ingredients. He'd stopped adding to, stirring or tasting the potion. He let the fire die out under the cauldron. Maybe that infernal liquid needed to cool and settle before the next stage.

But instead, the warlock kept pulling down books from the shelves and flicking through them, as though searching for something. At other times, he sat on a stool, gazing out of the cave entrance, towards the grass and trees outside, a faraway look in his eyes. But Roza couldn't fathom the expression on his face.

Her words of last night came back to her mind, when she'd called him a cruel man and a liar, who should be ashamed of himself. Had her words struck home, causing him to stop and think about what he was doing to them?

Was that too much to hope for? Or was he merely waiting for his potion to be ready for their contributions?

Later, the warlock brought out and placed on a workbench a large mirror and examined himself in it. Like much else in the cave, the mirror was old and dusty, the frame tarnished, and the reflective surface spotted. But the warlock was leaning forward, touching his face, absorbed in his own reflection.

Later still, she looked up to see the warlock gazing fixedly at her. Their eyes locked before she looked away, embarrassed. Why was he staring at her?

As though he'd been discovered watching her, the warlock stirred himself and jerked back to the present. He grunted and stood up.

Roza kept her eyes down, remembering his threat of punishing her for disturbing Standley. He walked over to them, and she had to look up when he stopped, towering above the two of them on the floor.

Was this it, then? Her moment of execution? A desperate anger surged within her that she wanted so much to run, to escape, to live, be free.

"There may be a way we can avoid killing her," the warlock stated. "We need to test it with some fresh blood from them both. Will they supply it willingly, or must we make them unconscious and extract it by force?"

Roza swallowed hard and glanced at Kerenzi, who was glaring up at the warlock. Part of her slumped with relief that her hour of death had not yet come. For now, their executioner wanted no more than blood. She almost refused the demand at once, determined to make the potion as difficult as possible to complete.

But he could extract the blood anyway, and she didn't want to be made unconscious. What did he mean about avoiding killing her, or was this just another of his games? She remembered the plan to gain the warlock's trust. If they agreed, would he trust them more, or could she request some favours in return?

"Yes, we agree to supply some blood for you," Roza answered for them both. She sensed the spirit lord's face jerk towards her, and the heat of his outraged glare warmed the side of her face. "But I ask to extract the blood carefully and properly myself, with water, bowls, bandages, and a sharp knife." She didn't meet the warlock's eye as she said this last. Would he object to supplying her with something she might use as a weapon?

"Of course," the warlock replied. "She means no hacking and slashing at their arms, leaving scabs and scars, like we did before."

Roza glanced up at the warlock's face in amazement. Not only had he agreed to the knife, but the curve of his mouth was almost a smile, like he was joking or teasing them. She was at a loss to know what to make of this.

"Does she request any other concessions in return for her willingness?" the warlock asked.

She couldn't believe this either. It had to be some new trick their captor was playing on them. But she couldn't see the catch, and so her mind raced through what she could ask. She didn't dare ask about untying the spirit lord again, because that had been refused so firmly. What else did she want?

"Um … I'd like to be able to go outside, please," she ventured. "Could you remove the Barrier spell from the cave entrance, so I could go out into the daylight, on the grass and among the trees?"

Again, she didn't meet the warlock's eye as she asked this and chewed her lip over whether she'd pushed her request too far.

"Yes, we think we could allow that," the warlock replied. "Anything else?"

This time Roza had to stare up into the warlock's eyes to believe what she was hearing. But she detected no trace of deceit in his calm, open face. He was being nice to her.

It was as though she wasn't his prisoner, and not about to be murdered and cut into pieces by his hand. If she wanted him to trust her, that seemed to be working, but she wasn't about to trust him.

"And … and…" – what else could she ask for? – "I want to know your name."

As soon as this came out of Roza's mouth (and she had no idea what prompted the request), embarrassment welled up inside her. It was such a stupid, trifling thing, and this was confirmed when the warlock actually laughed. Not the cackle or chuckle of before, but a proper belly-laugh by someone finding a statement genuinely funny. Roza's shame prevented her from looking anywhere near catching the spirit lord's eye.

The warlock calmed himself and said, "The requests will be granted, but the blood first." He turned away and started gathering in the kitchen what was needed to collect the blood.

"What the hell are you doing?" came Kerenzi's angry whisper as soon as the warlock was busy. "You want to know his name? What difference will that make? And yes, I'm sure you want to go outside and enjoy the lovely grass and trees, but what about me? Why not ask something that will make my torture even a tiny bit bearable?"

The spirit lord's anger and sarcasm stung Roza and put her on the defensive at once. "If you must know," she spat back, "I considered asking to untie you, but didn't risk it because it was refused so firmly before. And I want to look outside, not for a lovely walk, but so that *when* we both escape from this cave, we'll know where we are and how to reach safety. And in case you've forgotten, our plan was to build trust, and knowing his name might help him to respect us as people. So there."

Roza stood up and walked away before Kerenzi could answer. But she was trembling as she neared the kitchen, waiting to receive the bowls, water, cloths and knife for the blood. The spirit lord had magnified her embarrassment, and she hated their arguments when they were supposed to be allies and friends in the cause of survival and escape.

"The spirit lord first," the warlock said, as he handed her a tray. It had two bowls, a jug of water, a pile of cloths, two small cups for the blood, and a sharp-pointed knife. Roza didn't look at him as she took it and carried it back to their corner.

"I'm so pleased that you and the warlock are getting along so well," Kerenzi resumed his sarcastic tone as she knelt next to him. "Friendly, first-name terms will be so nice as he chops you into pieces and boils up your heart and brain."

"Shut up," Roza snapped. "I'm trying to get us both out of here alive, and I'm sorry you can't see that."

"Oh, yes, very kind," Kerenzi sneered. "Shall I help by pointing out exactly where to insert the knife to cut out my heart? Ow!"

Roza had washed the spirit lord's arm and now stabbed the knife point into a vein a little harder than she needed to. The immortal silver-grey blood oozed down the knife and into the waiting cup, while Roza concentrated on what she was doing and ignored Kerenzi's jibes. The spirit lord turned his arm to make it difficult for her, but she grabbed and held it tight against the Bindweed ropes. He moaned and cursed under his breath, but she didn't let go until she'd filled two-thirds of a cupful.

She placed the cup carefully on the floor before washing and tightly bandaging the spirit lord's cut. "Thank you so much for being such a kind and gentle nurse," Kerenzi hissed, as she prepared to stand up.

Roza's patience snapped. "Listen to me," she hissed back, and realised she was pointing the sharp knife at him. "I am trying my very hardest to save both our lives, so if you have any constructive suggestions, instead of snide and sarcastic comments, I'll be very pleased to hear them."

She stood up before he could say anything more and carried the cup of the spirit lord's blood over to the warlock's kitchen table. Instead of watching her, the warlock was preoccupied with examining himself in the mirror again.

Roza remembered that she'd noticed last night the changes in his appearance. Had he noticed it now too?

She shrugged and returned to their corner. Kerenzi looked to be sulking, curled away from her, cradling his bandaged arm.

Roza steeled herself to cut her own arm, placed the knifepoint against her vein, and stabbed. It hurt. A lot. She gritted her teeth, determined not to cry out, concentrating on watching her precious lifeblood dribble its way down to fill the warlock's cup. The irony struck her of doing this to assist a cruel and lying enemy, while causing an argument with her fellow sufferer and supposed friend. She sighed, wishing their situations were simpler or for someone else to tell her what to do.

Her cup was three-quarters full of her precious deep red liquid, and she struggled to knot a bandage around her own arm. She was hot and shaking from the wound but tightened it enough to stop it bleeding further. She washed her arm and the knife and gathered everything back onto the tray. She couldn't exactly hide the knife without the warlock noticing it was missing.

Roza carried the tray back to the kitchen and placed it on the table. She waited while the warlock put away the knife and then lifted the cup of her blood over to the workbench with the mirror. The spirit lord's cup remained exactly where Roza had placed it.

The warlock sat again on the stool in front of the large mirror. Without even looking at Roza, he lifted the cup of her blood to his lips and drained it all down in successive gulps.

CHAPTER EIGHT

Roza stared at the warlock in shock, the feeling growing inside her that something was very wrong here.

"Hang on a minute." She stepped forward, only to find her way blocked by Standley the coat stand, tottering between them. "What the hell are you doing, drinking my blood like that?" She was nearly shouting. "That was supposed to be for the potion. And instead, you sit there and gulp it all down. It hurts to stab my arm, you know, so I'm not bleeding my precious lifeblood just to provide you with a drink. What's going on? Are you some sort of blood-drinking vampire as well as a warlock?"

"It's all right, Standley." The warlock's voice was calm, almost soft. But he didn't look up from studying his own face in the mirror. "And if she'll wait a few minutes and sit down at the table, we'll explain everything to her."

"And stop calling me 'she' and 'her'," Roza yelled. "I'm standing right here. Talk to me and call me 'you' instead. While you're at it, call yourself 'I', and not 'we' as well."

She hadn't intended to attack the warlock about the way he spoke, but it burst out in her anger, confusion and fear. She stepped back, and Standley the coat stand did too. Roza calmed herself with some deep breaths, remembering that self-control might be needed to manage their escape. The warlock had offered to explain everything to her, and that was a promise worth waiting for.

Roza moved back around the kitchen table and sat on one of the stools away from the warlock. He was still touching and examining his own face in the workbench mirror. She didn't look back towards Kerenzi, still annoyed at his comments while taking the blood.

At last, the warlock looked away from his own

reflection and stood up from his workbench stool. Roza studied him as he came to sit across the kitchen table from her. She remembered now that a few days ago his blue eyes had been sunken, bloodshot, staring from sagging folds of skin. Now the face around his eyes was still lined but much smoother, healthier. He offered her a broad smile, and now she saw that his teeth were no longer greenish, but ivory coloured.

Was this the same man who had been the ancient warlock of days ago? It must be, because she'd been here all the time and noticed the small changes and improvements to his appearance. She wouldn't describe the man sitting opposite her now as ancient, but maybe old, or even middle aged. And in the cauldron next to them, the longevity potion remained incomplete. What was going on?

"She asked for our name," the warlock began, but stopped. "You asked for my name," he corrected himself, and Roza was pleased to notice the use of 'you' and 'my'. The ancient warlock of a few days ago could hardly have managed a clear conversation like this. "It's been many years since anyone has been interested enough to ask us that, so my name is Philoe." He held out a hand for Roza to shake, but she didn't budge. He might be all friendly and trusting now, but she wasn't convinced.

"We understand that you are Rozabella," Philoe the warlock went on, dropping his hand, "known as Roza for short, and that the spirit lord is Kerenzi."

Roza nodded. She had no idea where this was leading but concluded that sitting and listening might be fruitful.

"Next, she asked us to remove the exit Barrier spell from the mouth of the cave so that she can walk outside. Excuse us for a moment." The warlock rose from his stool and strode to the mouth of the cave. Extending his arms, he looked to be taking down and folding away a large sheet. A few blue sparks and fizzes crackled around the cave mouth as he did so, but once he'd finished, the way to the outside looked as clear as before.

Roza narrowed her eyes. She hadn't been able to see the exit Barrier spell before, so could she trust that it had really been removed? She could test that shortly, but in the meantime the warlock seemed willing to talk and explain, so she would listen first. Kerenzi and Standley were also following the warlock with their eyes, and she was sure they'd be listening to the conversation too.

Philoe sat down opposite her again and waved an arm towards the daylight outside. "Please feel free to enjoy a walk on the grass and among the trees whenever you wish, Miss Roza."

Roza's eyebrows rose. This was surreal. The tone of this conversation suggested that their roles had reversed. She had sought to gain the warlock's trust, but now this Philoe was trying as hard as he could to be willing, friendly and persuade her to agree to something. These changes were dizzying but her instincts were suspicious, and she remained on guard, watching for the trick or the catch.

Philoe placed his hands on the table surface. "And finally, she asked – you asked – what the hell I was doing drinking your blood like that." He gave her a grim smile. "No, I am not a vampire, and I don't normally drink human blood. I needed to test something, to make an experiment, so that we could be sure."

"Be sure about what?" Roza blurted out, her curiosity overpowering her resolve to remain silent and listen.

He drew a deep breath. "When we first met, we had a conversation about how old you thought I was. You were kind enough to say I looked about seventy years old. Would you still agree with that assessment?"

Roza gave a slow shake of her head. They were approaching the heart of the matter: how did the warlock have a younger appearance. "I guessed at seventy because I didn't want to upset or offend you. If I were honest, I'd have said nearer your figure of four hundred years."

Philoe nodded. "You thought I looked older than a mortal human has any right to be. But what about now? Would you still say four hundred, or seventy, or what? And please be completely honest because this is vitally important."

Roza stared at the warlock opposite her and shook her head again. "No, I wouldn't guess you're four hundred any more, or even seventy years." She appraised his face, hair and posture. "I'd say more like old or middle-aged, in your fifties or sixties, perhaps."

Philoe beamed. "Exactly. So, she agrees with us. She saw me examining myself in the mirror just now, and I think I look much younger than I did a few days ago. We want to be sure that this isn't some illusion, some trick of the mind or eye, but that someone else considers us younger too."

"But the potion isn't complete," Roza said. "So how has this happened?"

The warlock held up his hand. "We'll come to that in a moment. First, I want to explain that I don't just *look* younger, I actually *feel* younger. We can stand up straighter, instead of being hunched or stooped, so my back is stronger. We can breathe easier, instead of all that coughing and wheezing. Our point is that these changes are not just on the surface, in our appearance. They include our internal organs and general health, such that we feel younger too. Would she agree with us that all the signs are that we don't just *look* younger, or *feel* younger, but that we *are* younger? All the accompaniments of old age have been removed. Our aging process has not just been stopped, but reversed, and taken us back to being a younger man: middle-aged, in fact, instead of ancient. Would you agree?"

Roza gave a slow nod. "Yes, I agree. That is how it seems to me too."

"Excellent." Philoe clapped his hands together. "If these are the facts, then we need to discover the explanation. You must understand, Roza, that we have spent much of our long life studying how to live longer, to avoid death, to become younger. There are three things required for that: the desire, the power and the method. Because longevity is complicated, would you like me to explain what we mean in simpler terms?"

Roza realised she'd been frowning, struggling to understand this, so with relief she said, "Yes, please."

"Well then, suppose we want to dig a large hole in our garden," Philoe began. "It begins with our desire to have the hole, deciding where to dig it, how big and how deep. We can visualise and plan it all we like, but that doesn't achieve our hole for us. The next thing we need is the power: we need the strength in our arms, and in all our muscles, to be able to dig it. Is she following us so far?"

Roza nodded. "So, you have the desire and the power for it. What was the other thing?"

"The method. In the case of digging a hole, the method is the spade. We need something to dig with. We need a tool, an implement, something that will translate the strength in our arm muscles, and the desire in our heart, into creating the actual hole in the ground. The process needs a means, a mechanism, a channel to turn the desire and the raw power into a physical reality."

Roza was frowning again. "Yes, I think I understand that. But how does it relate to the process of longevity then, to being younger?"

"We have the desire for it in abundance," Philoe replied. "That has never been our problem. And all my life I have studied magic to acquire the necessary magical power. In the case of longevity, the strength in the muscles corresponds to the ability to wield magic, to harness and bend the powers of nature, of the spiritual and magical realms, of the Universe, to my will."

"You have the desire and the magical power, and until now your method has been the potion?"

Philoe's eyebrows rose. "Very good. I see she might have an aptitude for this. Yes indeed, up to this time, we have always used a longevity potion as the means and mechanism for translating our desire and magical power into the end result of living longer. But it is a method that is almost impossibly difficult. We spent decades learning how to make this potion. And each time it requires us to kill people: a mortal and an immortal for their body parts." He grimaced. "We hope you understand, Miss Roza, that we have never done this lightly. We have regretted it every time, but it has been necessary. It is the only way."

Roza heard Kerenzi snort behind her, and she was equally unimpressed. "I don't think your regrets, your 'never doing this lightly', make much difference to the people you have killed, Warlock Philoe. I don't agree that it is ever 'necessary' to commit murder."

The warlock looked down at the table. "We accept your rebuke, Miss Roza. We are willing to discuss the morals and ethics of what we have done at another time. Because today we need to explain to her that the longevity potion has been necessary, and the only way for us to live longer. Until now."

"Yes, what is different this time? How are you managing to become younger without a completed longevity potion?"

"That is precisely the question I have been asking myself for the last day or two," Philoe replied. "We have been considering all the elements involved to try to understand this and have come to only one conclusion. Firstly, our desire is the same. Our will and need to live longer are just as they have always been."

"What about Kerenzi, the spirit lord?" Roza asked. "Is he more magically powerful than the lesser immortal beings you've used in the past? Has he made the difference?"

"She is correct that he is a greater spiritual being than the mere wood nymphs, dryads, sylphs or naiads we have captured and butchered in the past." He said this with a look of distaste on his lips. "But remember that he adds power to the process, and not a method to it. He might have stronger magic than others, and when added to our own, we make a formidable magical force. But we still need a method, a mechanism, a means to achieve being younger, and that is what has stumped us. Until now."

"What do you mean, 'until now'? Do you have an answer to what is making the difference?"

"Yes, Miss Roza, we do. The only conclusion we can come to is that the difference in making us younger today is something to do with you."

Roza stared at him as a chill shivered down her spine. "Me? But I haven't done anything. And I can't do anything. How can the difference this time possibly be something to do with me?"

Philoe held up his hands to calm her. "For the last two days I have been sipping and tasting this potion with your blood in it. There are other ingredients too, but the blood from you and the spirit lord are the most potent I have added so far. I wanted to test whether it was yours or Kerenzi's that was making the difference, so I drank yours first. I observed myself in that mirror before, during and after drinking the cup you kindly provided, and I saw my face change before my own eyes. The difference this time is not because of the spirit lord, but because of you."

Roza couldn't believe this. "There is something in my blood that has some magical power?"

Philoe shook his head. "Not a magical power, no, but a longevity method or mechanism. They are different. Remember it is my magic that provides the power for it, but now it seems that you yourself are some sort of means or method for longevity, instead of needing to use a completed potion."

Roza couldn't stay seated and jumped to her feet. "This is ridiculous. How can I possibly be a method for making you younger?"

"Please sit and listen because this is most important. And if it is true, it will save your lives."

At once, Roza lowered herself onto her stool again.

"I understand your scepticism, young lady. I felt the same way four hundred years ago when my warlock mentor suggested I had an aptitude for magic. It requires a change in mindset, a new outlook to consider oneself proficient in magic. But Rozabella, this afternoon I encourage you to have an open mind and to consider it."

"But I'm just a mortal girl," Roza protested. "I wish I could remember my background, but I can't. Have I ever cast any spells or met any magical beings like warlocks or spirit lords before? Or was there something magical in my family history for me to inherit it?"

"I regret now that my Forgetery spell robs us of answers to these questions," Philoe replied. "However, I believe my suggestion to be a possibility and expected that you would need persuading of it too. So, I would like to suggest a further test, to either confirm or reject this theory of mine. It will be another experiment to see if you, on your own, can make me a little younger again."

"I'm not giving you any more of my blood to drink, if that's what you mean." Roza's finger was jabbing at him across the table.

"No, I wouldn't ask you to," Philoe reassured her. "It won't hurt or injure you at all. It will involve nothing more than you holding my hand. Would that be acceptable?"

Roza considered this. A few days ago, holding this man's hand would have been disgusting and repellent. He wasn't as hideous any more, but had he proved himself any more trustworthy? Was this the trick and catch, that some new spell of bewitching or entrapment required a physical touch? Perhaps she should test whether Philoe had kept his word in removing the exit Barrier spell first.

"I need to think about this," Roza said. "It's a lot to take in. You said I could go for a walk outside the cave whenever I want, so I'm going to do that now." She stood up from her stool at the kitchen table.

"Of course." Philoe stood up too. "Let us show her around what we have here."

Jorxy paused on the forest track, waiting for Judge Helena to catch up with him again. Roza's mum was making her way along the path through the trees at a measured pace, supporting herself with her stick. Jorxy didn't mind too much, because making himself go more slowly, and stopping from time to time, made sure he didn't miss anything.

He'd met her at Albany's Mermaid Inn that morning at a time when he thought she should have finished breakfast, but still had to wait over an hour for her to be ready. Then came a slow and awkward ride on her horse and cart from town up to her Meadow Cottage on the edge of the forest. Jorxy was used to physical discomfort in the bumps and lurches of the cart and needing to guide the horse from the hard wooden bench seat. The awkwardness was because he and Judge Helena were enemies and only doing this for Roza's sake.

As soon as they arrived at the cottage, Jorxy had wanted to set off to search the forest clearing at once, but Helena had insisted on showing him where to go. And that included her needing a rest first, and some food, and to see to Arthur, before starting their walk through the trees.

Now at last Jorxy was following the wheel marks of Roza's barrow towards where she'd disappeared. He was also making sure to recognise the shape and imprint of her boots wherever the ground was soft, so he could look out for anything else in or near the clearing. Jorxy prided himself on being good at noticing things, watching out for the small details that others missed. It was invaluable for picking pockets and breaking into houses, but he'd never admit that to Judge Helena.

"It isn't too far now," she said, catching up with him, and absent-mindedly rubbing her chest. "Thank you for coming out here and doing this for our Roza. We do appreciate it, Jorxy."

He rolled his eyes at her and set off again along the track, his eyes constantly sweeping the ground from left to right and back again. But it seemed that Judge Helena wanted to strike up a conversation with him.

"I hope you don't mind my asking," she went on, "but why do you and Roza meet at the town rubbish ditch and spend your time out there? It seems a dismal, stinking place to me."

Jorxy paused and looked at her. "You really wanna know?"

Helena nodded. "Since you're a friend of our daughter's, I'd like to try and know you a little, to understand what's going on in Roza's life."

Jorxy snorted. "Don't bother. I ain't worth getting to know, and you'll never understand Roza either."

But Helena was still looking at him. "Please," she said, "I'd like to try."

Jorxy shrugged and continued walking, noticing that she tried to keep pace with him now. "We meet at the rubbish ditch because it's on her side of town and people leave us alone there."

"But what do you do there? Just sit and talk?"

Jorxy gave her a sceptical look, to say, I'm not telling you what we do. But after a silence, he said, "We throw stones at the rubbish. It's good for improving our aim. And I keep an eye out for items brought in that someone might want."

"You salvage items from other people's rubbish?" She

had a look of distaste on her face.

"There's no need to look all disgusted," he retorted. "You'd be amazed at things you rich people throw away. Things that us with less to our names might want or pay for. So, I provide a public service, I do. I rescue stuff before it's destroyed and help it find its way to new and happy homes. For a small price."

Helena was frowning. "How do you do that, then? Do you have a stall in the market, or something?"

Jorxy scoffed. "No, of course I don't have a stall in the market. What, you think I got that sort of money? No, when I find something someone might want, I supply it to a market trader who could sell it on for me. With a few coins coming my way."

"What about stolen goods, then?" Judge Helena's voice had recovered its hard edge. "Is that what you do with items you burgle and thieve?"

Jorxy stopped dead and rounded on her. "I knew it. I may be poor, but I ain't stupid. You're trying to catch me out. You don't wanna know or understand me at all. You only want more evidence to have me locked up again. I ain't talking to you." He stalked off along the path.

"Jorxy, I'm sorry, please, wait." Her voice came after him. "I shouldn't have said that. Please slow down again so I can keep up."

Half of him wanted to keep walking and never speak to her again. But this was Roza's mum, and if he had the chance of winning her onto his side, it had to be worth a try. Right now, she needed him, and he might never have a better opportunity to get in her good books. He made himself stop and face her. But his anger was still burning.

"You rich people don't understand at all, do you? What it's like to be poor. What it's like to be starving hungry and have no food in the house. What it's like to live in a shack with a mum and dad, and four brothers and two sisters, and have to fight for everything you need." He pointed a finger at her. "Your Roza never had to put up with any of that, did she? No, she can have everything she needs, don't need to share it with no-one, and her mum and dad have proper jobs as a judge and a weaver, bringing in a tidy bit of money I don't doubt. It's not fair, I say, and all you do is lock me up for trying to feed myself."

Judge Helena was staring at him, and she swallowed before she spoke in a softer voice. "No, I don't know what it's like to be poor. But I'm not well, and Arthur is blind, so neither of us are bringing in any tidy bits of money any more. In fact, we can hardly even look after ourselves and must rely on our Roza to do lots of things for us. So yes, we've tried to give our daughter the best life we can, but our current situation is hardly fair on her either, is it?"

Jorxy couldn't restrain his sarcasm. "Oh, so you've noticed, have you, that your darling daughter don't feel as free as she'd like to be with what she does with her life? That she might feel a bit trapped in looking after the two of you so she can't even think about doing nothing else? Oh yeah, she plays the part of the dutiful daughter, because you're kind and grateful to her, and – to her credit – she truly cares for you both. But that don't stop her wishing she was free to make her own choices and go where she wants in life. Understood all that, have you?"

Helena was staring at him, her face stricken, but Jorxy couldn't resist pressing the point further while he had the chance. He took a step closer to her.

"Yesterday, when you told me Roza was missing, you know what my first thought was? That she'd finally done it. She'd gathered her courage and run away from home at last. She was finally taking her fate into her own hands, leaving you two behind, and heading off to make her own way in the world. Did you consider that, did you?"

Helena seemed to sag, clutching her heart, and stumbled backwards. She reached for a tree trunk to support her, and Jorxy leapt forward to catch her before she fell. He managed to guide her onto a mossy mound where she could sit, lean back against a tree and rest.

Part of him felt bad that he'd attacked her so ruthlessly with the truths she didn't want to hear. But she'd asked to know and understand what was going on.

"Are you all right, Mrs H?"

Her eyes were closed. She drew a deep breath and then nodded. "Just a bit of chest pain. My heart's not very good, you know, and it doesn't help if I'm anxious and worried. Like now."

Jorxy moved to sit beside her on the ground. "We can rest here for a bit if you need to."

She opened her eyes and looked at him. "Thank you, Jorxy." She hesitated and then asked, "Did Roza say anything to you about running away?"

He shook his head. "Not recently, no. We joked about it, ages ago, but I think she'd have told me if she was planning this."

Helena looked relieved, and they sat together in silence for a while. Jorxy couldn't help adding to himself that he'd have run away with Roza if he could. If she would have him. If she'd let him go with her.

At length he said, "You asked to try to understand me, Mrs H. If you mean that, I'd better tell you this. We agree that life is unfair. It's not fair that I'm poor, or that you're ill, or that Roza must look after you. All I try to do is make life a bit fairer, taking things from those who have too much and sharing them with those who have nothing. That changes the balance between rich and poor, don't it, making the sharing out of everything more equal all round."

Helena gave a snort and moved to stand up again, so Jorxy helped her to her feet. The look in her eye was Judge Helena again. "Don't give me that stealing from the rich to give to the poor nonsense. You steal from anyone to keep for yourself. Well, I'm not surprised you've invented a way of justifying your stealing to your conscience. But I need you to answer me this, Jorxy. Have you ever stolen anything from Arthur or me? Or would you?"

He held her gaze. "No, I ain't stolen nothing from you, and I won't neither, for Roza's sake."

"Good." Helena took a couple of steps further along the forest path.

"Except..." Jorxy wondered whether he could make a deal with this woman. She'd turned to hear the exception, so he ventured his best roguish smile. "Except ... maybe, if I can ... your daughter's friendship?" And her love, he added to himself.

Helena's face hardened and she seemed to be searching for how to say what she thought.

"I mean, I know you think she can do better than me," Jorxy went on, "but that's not for you to decide, is it? Can we agree to respect and follow what Roza decides about who she wants as friends?"

Helena was gazing at him. "I appreciate that you've been honest with me, Jorxy. I'm very glad we've had this chance to talk today, to understand each other better. I begin to see why Roza might want to spend so much time with you."

Jorxy nodded. This was about as much respect and acceptance as he was likely to get, so he was grateful for that. He tilted his head as he regarded her. "Don't you wonder why Roza likes to spend her time with me? Because I got you to thank for that too."

She frowned and looked bewildered. "Why would you thank us for that? We haven't done anything to encourage Roza to see you. The opposite, in fact."

Jorxy couldn't help grinning. "And that is exactly my point." He folded his arms. "When it comes to the law, Mrs Judge, haven't you noticed that as soon as you ban something, or forbid people from doing anything, then that's precisely what they want to do? There's something inside us that objects to being told what to do. It makes us want what's forbidden."

Helena was nodding. "So as soon as we discouraged Roza from seeing you, that only made her want to meet you all the more."

His roguish smile was back. "I never understood it really, but it seems many girls like us bad boys more than the squeaky-clean ones. So long as that works in my favour, I ain't complaining, am I?"

"Hmm," she mused. "Parents like to think they understand their children, but they never do, do they? Not completely anyway."

Jorxy started to move along the path again. "But this don't matter unless we can find her again. It seems someone has gone and stolen our Roza away from both of us. Are you ready to help me find her?"

For the first time, Helena gave him a warm and genuine smile. "I'm glad we have you to look for her, Jorxy. I was right that you won't stop searching until you bring her back to us."

Jorxy noticed that his fists were clenched. "And if it's true that someone's taken her away from us, then heaven help them when I find them. I'll make it clear what I think of them. Come on, Mrs H, let's search that clearing."

CHAPTER NINE

Roza had wondered whether the warlock would let her wander outside on her own, and supposed she had to accept the restriction of his company. She reminded herself that this still fulfilled her plan of gaining information and of winning the warlock's trust. She could decide what to do with the information later.

As she walked towards the cave's arched entrance, Kerenzi the spirit lord called out, "Enjoy your lovely walk in the fresh air and sunshine."

Roza decided it was high time to be sarcastic back. "Thank you very much. I'll try my best to enjoy it. Shall I tell you all about it afterwards?" The spirit lord scowled at her as she turned away towards the daylight.

It was late afternoon now, and the diagonal sunbeams cast a warm glow across the mouth of the warlock's cave. The closer she got, the more Roza squinted her eyes and shielded them with her hand, after the gloom inside. She approached the point where the exit Barrier spell had thrown her backwards, and so stretched out a cautious hand and edged forward. She didn't want to be hurt like that again.

Beside her, Philoe chuckled, but he didn't seem to mind her caution. Soon Roza was sure she'd passed the line of the spell and began to relax, believing it had genuinely been removed. She stopped, closed her eyes, and let the sunshine warm her arms and face. She also filled her lungs with the clean, fresh air. It hadn't been too stuffy inside the cave because it was open to the outside, but the difference now was a gentle breeze across her skin.

She opened her eyes and walked forwards. From the cave mouth, a path led across a wide expanse of grass, dotted with widely spaced clumps and rows of trees. The grass was almost a meadow: close-cropped in places, but in others filled with wildflowers and long grasses. To her left, a waterfall fed a stream that flowed away beside the meadow.

Roza eased her hands into her trouser pockets and walked at a meandering pace. Philoe accompanied her, but he seemed content to let her wander with her own pace and direction. This wasn't the guarded walk of a prisoner, but the company of a guide, close enough for her to ask him questions if she wished.

She turned right and strayed between the groves of fruit trees, enjoying the springiness of the turf under her boots after the hard stone of the cave floor. Then she turned back to look towards the cave. The opening where the warlock held them captive was at the foot of a low cliff, with a hillside rising further above it towards lofty mountains. The thought came to her that she ought to recognise those heights if she lived anywhere around here. They did seem vaguely familiar, but maybe she'd always looked at them from a different perspective before.

Roza stopped and stared, a chill running down her spine. Looking more closely, the cave entrance and hillside above it resembled a skull. The cave was like a gaping mouth, jagged and ravenous. Above it, hollows and shadows in the rock face looked like empty eye sockets. The sense of death amidst all this beauty was overwhelming. Roza shook herself. The warlock's cave of death was a correct description, if this was where she, Kerenzi, and so many others, would meet their end. She looked away.

To the right of the cave mouth, the waterfall caught her eye, and she walked in that direction.

Over the top of the low cliff, a stream fell in rocky steps and ran away to tumble into a pool in a stony basin beside the grassy meadow. The gushing waters formed a fine mist in the air before the stream continued its course off between the trees. Roza stopped at the water's edge and let the mist wash her face.

Philoe came to stand beside her. "This supplies all our water for drinking and washing. It's clean, and I like the taste of it." He chuckled to himself. "I remember you liked that I named my coat stand 'Standley'. Well, I call this stream and waterfall 'Torrence'. Get it?"

Despite herself, Roza smiled back. "As in 'torrents' of water. Very good."

A narrow stone bridge spanned the stream as it bubbled and frothed away from the waterfall pool, and they crossed this. On the other side was where the warlock kept his livestock. There was an enclosure for pigs, a run for chickens, and a small grassy field with a few cows and sheep. Beyond these there looked to be fields of grain, which Roza guessed supplied the flour for the bread.

"Are you ready for the names of the animals?" Philoe said with a sideways smile.

"Go on, then," Roza grimaced, "do your worst."

"Well, I call the sheep 'Shearer'. And the cows are 'Dairy', because they supply all our milk, cream and cheese."

Roza groaned. "And the chickens?"

Philoe pointed to each of them as he named them. "Boil, Scramble, Poach and Fry."

"After what you can do with their eggs," Roza nodded, rolling her eyes.

"And the pigs are Ham, Bacon, Gammon and Pork."

Roza thought about this. It seemed surreal that she was having this friendly conversation with the cruel and lying old warlock who was her kidnapper and tormentor. It was time to remind this Philoe of his vicious crimes against her and Kerenzi, so she turned to face him squarely. "So, the pigs are somewhat more committed to their names than the chickens are. They must give of their own flesh to provide your food, whereas the chickens only sacrifice the eggs they produce, and live on to lay more eggs for you to cook tomorrow." She held Philoe's eye as she said this next part. "A bit like the spirit lord and me, when you ask us to donate our vital organs to your potion instead of our blood and hair."

The warlock couldn't hold her gaze and looked away. Roza turned and walked back over the stone bridge.

She noticed that beyond the cave mouth from where she now looked at it, a faint path ran off across the grass and into the trees. She explored along this and heard Philoe following behind. Soon the trail had passed beyond the many clumps of trees, and what Roza found on the other side took her breath away.

A vast panorama opened in front of her. She saw now that the ground on which she stood – the cave in its low cliff, the meadow and trees, the waterfall and stream, the fields and animal pens – were all on a large plateau atop a much higher cliff. The faint path she had been walking along ran over the edge and down a very long slope, sometimes zig-zagging back and forth, until it disappeared from sight below her.

Before her lay a wide, green bowl of a valley, surrounded by forests and mountains. The slopes to her left and in front rose to dizzying heights of ridges, shoulders, and snow-capped peaks for as far as her eyes could see. To her right, two shoulders of the mountain range plunged to form a narrow gate and pass out of the valley, with a wide open plain visible beyond.

On the valley floor sat a town. Roza saw at once that it outstripped the description of 'village', as the streets and houses stretched in a maze of lines across the valley. In the town centre were larger, three-storey buildings, clustered around an open market square. The town was surrounded by fields and farms, orchards and barns, and wood smoke hung in the air from many chimneys.

Philoe had caught up with her and stood beside her. "This is the valley and town of Albany," he said. "Do you remember anything of it?"

Roza looked again, and if she thought hard enough maybe there was something here that reminded her of it being her hometown. But she couldn't be sure. If anything, her gaze was drawn more to the surrounding forests than to the town itself.

Philoe was waiting for an answer, so she said, "No, nothing at all. Thanks to you. And if I must die here then I suppose that at least it's a beautiful enough place for it."

The warlock sighed. "Yes, it's a beautiful place to live, and I'm very glad you like it too." He hesitated, and then said, "We regret now that our Forgetery Spell eradicated your memories, so please accept our apology and forgive us for that."

Roza snorted. "You ask me to forgive you for wiping my memories when you're about to cut me open and add my vital parts to your cauldron? My letting you off that smaller crime hardly seems to matter in the face of the much larger one, does it?"

"Rozabella, please listen to me because this is very important." Philoe drew a deep breath and laid a hand on her shoulder to turn her to face him. She knocked away his hand but stayed facing him.

"No, I don't want to kill you, Roza. This is what I want to explain to you this afternoon. Until now, the longevity potion has been my only and necessary way to live longer. But look at me. I'm younger already. If I'm right, and there's something about you that's making a difference, then I don't need the longevity potion any more. My life has already been extended, without cutting anyone open or adding their vital parts to my cauldron. I don't need you or the spirit lord for that now."

Roza stared at him. "Do you mean we're no longer your prisoners?"

"No, you're not. But I would ask you please to consent to return to the cave and confirm what's going on here. I think it's vital to discover the truth behind how I've suddenly become younger." He held out an arm to invite her back along the path towards the cave.

Roza hesitated. Part of her wanted to run away, to escape this evil man and his horrible cave and flee down the cliff path into the safety of the town. Two things stopped her. Firstly, the thought that Kerenzi the spirit lord remained tied up with Bindweed in the cave, and their plan was to ensure they both got away from here alive and well. Secondly, her curiosity was piqued. She couldn't deny that the warlock seemed genuinely younger in every way, and even the remote possibility that she had something to do with it was too intriguing to ignore.

"I'm going to sleep on this," she said. "I'll have a think, and let you know in the morning."

Philoe nodded. "Thank you."

As the sun lowered in the sky behind them, Roza turned and led the way back through the trees and towards the cave. Philoe's inhabited cave looked different now, coming back to it from the beauty outside. Yes, it was still cluttered, and full of old and dusty things, but it also had something of a homely quality to it. It looked 'lived in', and some cleaning and tidying could transform it.

Kerenzi turned away from her, clearly not wanting any report on how beautiful it was outside. Part of her wanted to tell him at once that the warlock might no longer need their body parts for his potion, or to keep them as prisoners, but what did that mean? Did she have Philoe's permission to untie Kerenzi from the Bindweed now? She wasn't sure and wanted to know more before trying to explain their new situation to him.

As she lay down on the rock floor of the cave that night, Roza's mind was reeling. If she really was free now, what would she do? She had no memory of her life before waking up in the cave, and therefore no knowledge of anything to go back to. Did she have parents, brothers or sisters? A home or work? She supposed she could go down into the town and see if anyone recognised her or had missed her and was looking for her. What had Philoe said the place was called – Albany?

Or maybe she didn't have anyone or anything down there. She might be an orphan, a drifter, a poor beggar. In which case, this was an opportunity for a fresh start. She could leave the valley, explore the world, and find a new beginning somewhere else. But then what did she have to offer? No skills or abilities as far as she was aware, except perhaps being young, willing, and strong enough. What was she supposed to do? She couldn't decide.

But when she wondered about her background, she considered the evidence of her own body and clothes. Apart from the injuries and abuse of the last few days, she didn't look skinny, tattered, or badly cared for. That was an encouraging thought, that she might previously have been well fed, washed, and properly clothed. Maybe she had a loving home, parents, and family, who were missing her now and starting a search.

All this swirled around inside her mind as she lay awake inside Philoe's cave. It was too much to think about. It could wait until the morning.

Early the next morning, Roza went for a brief stroll outside to be sure of what she'd decided. Philoe was standing in front of his kitchen workbench and turned to face her as she entered the cave. Roza walked past Standley the coat stand and straight up to the warlock. For once, she was glad of her height, that she could look him full in the eye as an equal.

Without giving any warning of what she was about to do, she raised her arm and smacked the warlock as hard as she could across his face.

With lightning speed, Standley the coat stand was behind her, pinning her arms to her sides with its painful hooks. Her own palm stung at the impact, and a red weal sprang at once across the warlock's cheek. Philoe's eyes blazed with outrage at being struck, and he looked about to hit her back.

Roza had no way to avoid his retaliation, because Standley held her defenceless in its vice-like grip. All she could do was yell at him. "That was to pay you back for all the pain and fear you've inflicted on the spirit lord and on me."

Philoe's clenched fist halted in mid-blow. The vicious glare in the warlock's eyes evaporated and was replaced by guilt and shame. He stepped back and lowered his arm. "It's all right, Standley, you can let her go. We deserved that, and she has the right to pay us back for what we've done to her."

The coat stand released her, and Roza rubbed her arms where Standley's hard hooks had bruised them. Having made her point, she stomped over to the kitchen table and seated herself on a stool.

"Good slap," came Kerenzi's voice from behind her. "But you should have kneed him between the legs as well."

Philoe was massaging his slapped cheek as he came and sat down opposite her. She was pleased to see that this cruel and arrogant warlock now looked abashed and less certain of himself.

"Now then, Mister Warlock Philoe," Roza said, "you say you want to perform another test or experiment on me. One that doesn't involve my blood. I need you to explain exactly what you want to do, and what will happen."

Philoe nodded, seeming keen to move quickly away from their confrontation and onto his experiment. "Of course, Miss Roza. I want to discover whether you have the gift to make something younger by touch alone. And if this works, I hope it will convince you that this ability does indeed come from you."

He laid his hands flat on the table surface, turning them over so that the palms faced upwards, and then back again. "Look at my hands, Roza. Examine them carefully, and notice the lines and wrinkles, the blemishes on the skin. I have warts and callouses, some scars and moles from centuries of use and aging. I suggest we try to make these younger too. Would that be acceptable to you?"

"It might be," she replied. "Explain exactly what I need to do and what is going to happen."

"You will need to touch my hands, to hold them. And do you remember what I said about longevity needing the desire, the power and the method?"

Roza nodded.

"Well, I have the desire for my hands to look younger, and I hope you do too." He gave her a tentative smile.

She shrugged, so he said, "It is important, Roza, that you want this to work as well. Your desire needs to be channelled into this exercise, so that we work together in partnership to see if this will succeed. Because the other elements – the power and the method – one will come from each of us. I will provide the power, and you will supply the method."

Roza frowned. "I don't understand. What do you mean?"

"When we hold hands, I will provide the magic, the strength, the energy to perform the task, which will be channelled through your gift and ability to make things younger. Remember what I said about digging a hole, when the arm muscles exert their strength through a spade to move the dirt? In this case, I will be the arm muscles, and you will be the spade."

Roza pulled a face. "That doesn't sound very flattering. So, I'm a spade. Just a tool, an implement to be used by you to achieve what you want? That sounds like you're exploiting my gift."

Philoe looked sheepish. "Yes, I'm sorry, that's not very flattering, is it? Perhaps I should have found a better analogy. But the point is that it's an illustration of working together. The arm muscles by themselves can't dig the hole, and neither can the spade on its own. It's only by working together that the project succeeds. It's only since you arrived in this cave, with your unique and remarkable gift, combined with my magical energy and experience, that we've achieved me becoming younger. We need to understand this wonderful collaboration, how it works and what it might produce."

The warlock stopped. His excitement had been bubbling over in his words, and Roza found herself suspicious of his enthusiasm. But what if this did work? What if they discovered together some way of making a person younger, wouldn't that be an important and powerful thing?

Roza nodded. "All right. Do you expect I will feel anything?"

Philoe beamed. "Excellent. Yes, you will feel the magical energy coming from me, so please try to channel it back down into my hands. Are you ready?" He stretched his hands across the table. "Remember what my hands look like now, the signs of age on them, so that we can compare them afterwards."

Roza drew in a deep breath, and decided it was time to get this new experiment over and done with. She reached out and grabbed his hands, examining the skin under her fingertips, the wrinkles and callouses. Then she closed her eyes to avoid needing to look at him or what her hands were touching.

It didn't take long before she felt something, an unmistakeable tingling in her fingertips, which spread to her palms. It felt like a trickle of energy coming from him, out of his hands and into hers, travelling up her veins, her nerves and her bones, washing over her skin. Her arms grew warm, making her skin prickle and all her hairs stand on end. The goosebumps made her shiver as the trickle strengthened into a stream.

From her shoulders it flowed into her heart. She began to feel hot and sweaty, as though this energy was filling her up. Was this his magic, his power and strength, giving her what she needed to accomplish something wonderful?

And in that moment, she knew.

This.

This is what she wanted to feel again and again, as often as she could.

This strength, this power, this magic, she had to have it. She'd never felt so strong, so energised. She was buzzing, at last able to control her own destiny.

Then she remembered she was supposed to be doing something with it. Before this inflow of energy caused her body to explode, she tried to think about turning it around. It needed to go back, down her arms and into Philoe's hands. She shifted her focus away from her own swelling heart and tried to send the energy into the flesh under her fingertips.

It must have worked because Philoe squeezed her hands tighter as though he felt something too. Roza tried to channel her desire: I want the warlock's hands to become younger too, in the appearance of the skin and right down through the flesh, to the joints and bones. I want this to work, to discover whether I have this power to help people, to change their lives for the better.

She lost track of whether it was only a few minutes, or perhaps longer, before the inflow of magical energy through Philoe's hands began to lessen. She was emptying herself of that invigorating power, but kept her eyes closed until she could be sure their experiment was finished.

It was Philoe who loosened his grip first. He released her hands, so Roza opened her eyes. The warlock was turning his hands over and back on the table-top, staring at them. Roza looked too.

They had changed. It was unmistakeable. Some of the scars were still visible, and the marks where the warts and callouses had been, but they were lessened. And the skin was smoother, on both front and back, with fewer lines and wrinkles, stronger, fresher, *younger*.

Philoe looked up at her, unable to grin any wider, the tears spilling down his cheeks. He let out a whoop and jumped to his feet. He looked ready to burst with excitement as Roza stood up too. She couldn't believe that she'd accomplished this, but the evidence was right there in front of her, in his younger-looking hands. Fresh from the feelings she'd just experienced, her awe at the power of magic mingled inside her with a giggle of delight.

Philoe almost danced around the table and looked as though he wanted to hug her. She shrank back, but then he flung his arms around her shoulders.

They remained like that for only a moment until Roza pushed away from her this man she hardly knew. This man who also possessed the one thing she now wanted more than anything in the world – magic.

He let go of her too but rested his hands on her shoulders. His *younger* hands. The tears were still streaming down his face as he grinned at her.

"For four hundred years I have been searching and hoping for someone like you," he said, "and I can hardly believe it. Miss Rozabella, I do believe that you are a spade."

She couldn't help but grin back and spread her arms wide. "So, I am a spade. I'm a spade!"

CHAPTER TEN

If the two of you have quite finished your little love-in over there, someone needs to explain to me what the hell is going on." Kerenzi's voice boomed across the cave and Roza had forgotten that the spirit lord was even there.

She and Philoe sprang apart, and the warlock turned away to tidy the bowls in the kitchen. Clearly, it wasn't going to be Philoe explaining anything to the spirit lord. Roza agreed it would come better from her anyway, but this wouldn't be easy to explain.

She stepped across to where the spirit lord lay against the wall, still trussed up in his Bindweed ropes. He looked weaker and paler than ever, his head sagging on his neck, the red welts angry on his arms and legs. But the look in his eyes made Roza quail, as the deep black wells of hate were back, with a flicker of scarlet fire.

She sat down cross-legged in front of him. How to begin – with the good news first? "I'm pleased to tell you, Kerenzi, that the warlock no longer needs our body parts for his longevity potion." She ventured a smile, but it wasn't returned.

The spirit lord grunted. "I'm supposed to be happy about that, am I? That this murderer has graciously decided not to execute us today? Has he admitted his guilt in capturing, imprisoning, threatening and maiming us in the first place?"

"Um, well, I don't know. But it's good news, isn't it, that our lives are going to be spared? That we can both get out of this cave alive?"

"That depends," Kerenzi spat, "on what punishment that villain is going to receive for what he's done to us. What were the two of you doing over there?"

Roza hesitated. This was harder to explain. "Well, it turns out I have some sort of a gift, an ability to make people younger. It was working on the warlock through my blood in the potion, but we've confirmed it just now. Haven't you noticed how he looks and stands and walks better now, like a middle-aged man?"

Kerenzi looked across to where Philoe was working in the kitchen and scowled. "Not really, no. I can't see much difference at all. But then, you mortals all look the same to me: always decaying and falling apart."

Roza was taken aback at this. "You can't see much difference? But he was ancient when I first woke up here, and now he doesn't look more than middle aged."

Kerenzi narrowed his eyes at her. "You woke up before me, so how can I know how he looked when you first saw him? But have you forgotten he's a warlock? Don't you think he can create illusions to make you think he's younger?"

Roza was disconcerted by this. She was used to trusting the evidence of her own eyes and didn't like to think anyone could fool or trick her like that. "But why would he do that? He's trapped us here and could carry on with using our body parts in his potion. Why create illusions of looking younger if that means setting us free unharmed?"

"Unharmed?" the spirit lord bellowed. "Do you call this unharmed? Tied up with vicious Bindweed ropes, cut and slashed to extract my immortal blood, and worst of all, having half my wing hacked off?"

Roza had forgotten about the wing. She looked down at her own arms and reckoned she would recover completely from this ordeal, with only a few scars to show for it. All that had been done to her would heal, and the trauma of the last few days might be forgiven in time. But what about the spirit lord?

"When you are released from the Bindweed ropes, will your magic come back? Your cuts will heal, but is there no way to regrow a wing?"

"Regrow a wing?" Kerenzi let out a mirthless laugh. "If I cut off your hand or foot, can you make a new one pop out of the end of your arm or leg? No, of course not. Yes, I will recover from the Bindweed, but it will take some time. And that is not the point. This warlock deserves to suffer after what he inflicted on us, and we are the ones to ensure he receives the punishment that is due."

Roza didn't know what to say to that. Justice demanded that Philoe pay a penalty for his crimes, but where would that end? Could they lock up a powerful warlock in the town prison when he could use magic to escape whenever he wished? Wasn't it more constructive to use his magic to help others, to protect the town, until he made amends with good deeds for the evils he had done?

Kerenzi interrupted her thoughts. "You say you've confirmed you have a gift of making people younger. How did you discover that then?"

"Well, we held hands across the table, he sent his magical energy to me and I channelled it through my gift to make his hands younger. After a few minutes his hands had lost most of their warts, callouses and wrinkles." Her voice still contained the wonder and joy of a few minutes before.

"You mean you've been helping him?" Kerenzi thundered. "This man kidnaps you and ties you up. He cuts your arms for your blood and threatens to kill you. And you repay him for this by giving him exactly what he wants? He's been murdering people for centuries to stay alive, and you surrender and hand him what he asks for on a plate?"

"The point is," Roza shouted back, "I've helped him so he doesn't need to murder people any more. Including us. And no, of course I didn't help him willingly to begin with. He captured me and took my blood without any of us knowing what it might do. But now we've discovered my gift, with a bit of magical power alongside me, we could achieve a lot of good things, such as helping others who are suffering with old age."

Kerenzi was staring at her. "He's bewitched you, hasn't he? He's put some sort of charm or enchantment on you to make you say and do exactly what he wants. Wake up, Roza. This man is a cruel, evil, lying villain, and you've fallen squarely into his trap. I despair of you mortals. I hope the Dragon comes and takes you all."

Roza couldn't listen to this any more. She jumped up and ran out of the cave entrance. Her limbs were still shaking and her stomach churning when she slowed to a walk among the trees outside. It was late morning, with the sunshine coming and going between intermittent clouds.

What could she believe? Kerenzi's words had stung her deeply. Was she such a naïve and innocent girl that she could be taken in by lies and illusions so easily? But if she could no longer trust her senses, what her eyes and feelings told her, then what could she believe? She had entered an unknown world of magic and power and had never been more out of her depth. Did rare and remarkable abilities exist, such as making people younger, against all the accepted laws of nature? And could such a gift ever appear in someone like her, an ordinary mortal girl from some non-descript town?

Her wanderings across the grass brought her to the stream and she stopped and watched the waters for a while. "Hello, Torrence," she murmured, looking up towards the waterfall. She gave half a smile. It all came back to the character and qualities of Philoe the warlock. Here was a man of intelligence and wit, who gave funny names to his animals, a coat stand, and a waterfall. Was he inherently evil, or had something else made him do all these dreadful things in his past?

Roza started walking again, following the bank of the stream away from the cave. She continued until it reached a cleft where it toppled over the edge of the cliff to cascade down to the valley and the buildings of the town below. A large boulder stood near the cliff edge, and she climbed it to perch on the top. The rush of the water was soothing, and the mist of the spray made her wrap her arms around herself for comfort. She stayed like that for a long time, as the sun inched its way slowly westwards across the sky above her.

Philoe had been old, or even ancient. What must that be like? How would it feel to have lived so many years, and be mortal, and therefore to know you are dying? Roza had never thought much about death. She was young enough to consider it too far away to think about. But then she'd been threatened with death over the last few days. Had she feared it? Willing to do whatever was necessary to escape and survive? Yes, she had. Was that what it was like to live as an old person, then, with this constant fear of impending death closing in on you? Could that make you desperate enough to do unspeakable things, such as butchering innocent victims to keep you alive? Once Philoe knew how to do that, would the temptation to make each new longevity potion be too great to resist?

Roza shivered. The afternoon was getting cooler, but as she looked down at the town, she was sure of one thing. She was glad to be young. And if her gift could relieve the miseries of the elderly, or remove their fear of death, wasn't that something worth exploring and sharing?

And then there was magic. If the townsfolk below knew how wonderful it felt to wield magic, they would be thronging up here to the plateau to learn it. More than anything, she wanted to feel that power again. She'd never experienced such exhilaration or ecstasy before. A door into a whole new world had been unlocked, and she was desperate to throw it open and explore all that lay beyond it. How could she feel it again, and learn to use it? Could she persuade the warlock to teach her?

Philoe was waiting for her outside the cave entrance when she arrived back. Not an angry, impatient waiting, but a concerned, caring one. He looked relieved to see her. "I was afraid the spirit lord had upset you enough to make you run off down the path," he murmured. "Can I say something more to you before you go to sleep this evening?"

Roza nodded, and he indicated a wooden bench among the trees. They sat at opposite ends of it.

Philoe drew in and let out a long breath before speaking. "I don't know what you plan to do next, Rozabella. I can understand that you want to go down into Albany and find any family and friends. You need to know what life you had before I captured you and obliterated your memories."

Roza glanced across at him. He looked sad, genuinely remorseful at what he'd done to her. Part of her wanted to reassure him, that she could rebuild her life. She could go back to where she'd been before with no lasting damage done. She wanted to say that she understood how old age and a fear of death could drive a man to do desperate things. The other part of her felt sad and lonely too. What if she had no life of any meaning to go back to? If she had no family or friends who missed her, or searched for her, what would she do?

"How long have you lived here on your own, Philoe?" she blurted out. She hadn't meant to ask it, or to interrupt whatever the warlock wanted to say, but once she'd said it, the words seemed to hang between them in the early evening air like a first gesture of her trying to understand his situation.

"Oh, um, too long," Philoe replied. "I became a novice here as a young man when the warlock before me was still alive. He mentored me for many years, teaching me his magic until his death. So, it's at least three hundred and fifty years, I suppose."

"And have you had much company during all those long years?"

"No, not much actual company," the warlock admitted, "only … victims."

Roza shivered and spoke again quickly. "But you've had your animals, and Standley."

"Yes, but they're not the same as human company, are they?"

"You mean, animals that can't speak at all, and a coat stand who can only manage 'yes' or 'no' answers, isn't much of a conversation?" She offered him an understanding smile, and he returned it with a grateful one.

"That's right, Miss Roza. In fact, when you started to speak with me in the cave, and were polite and curious, that was the first proper conversation I'd had in very many years. I'd forgotten how good that felt. And from time to time, you even offered me a smile. Then watching you care for the spirit lord reminded me how human beings are supposed to relate to each other."

She stared at him. Here was an old man who had been not only mortally afraid of his own death, but intolerably lonely too. With the magical power he wielded, could she understand how that might tempt him to be selfish, bitter and cruel?

"I owe you many apologies, young lady," he went on. "I've been on my own for so long, I've forgotten that other people have feelings. I've fallen out of the habit of thinking about anyone other than myself at all. I'm sorry. So, my selfishness and thoughtlessness ended up making me cruel and abusive to the very person I've been waiting for all my life – a source of longevity."

Roza's mouth fell open. "You've been waiting for me all your life?"

Philoe's voice sounded nervous now, and the next words came out in a rush. "So, you've brought me to what I wanted to say to you, Rozabella. I'd like you to consider staying here with me, so that we can explore more about your gift."

Part of her already expected this request, but her heart still gave a small leap at the confirmation he was as curious about it as she was. Now that this warlock had discovered her rare and remarkable gift, of course he'd want to explore and develop it. If she could learn all about it from him, that would widen her opportunities to help others too. And the prospect of feeling magic again was far too tempting and powerful to resist.

And yet, she ought to check what she was leaving behind. Her life might not have been of any consequence before, but she could check about that before committing to anything here. She looked across at him, as he studied the grass between his feet. He looked afraid of being refused and rejected, bracing himself for disappointment.

He'd been waiting a minute for her reply to his nervous invitation. "Thank you, Philoe," she said, making him look up at her. She gave him what she hoped was an encouraging smile. "That's a big decision to make, and I've got much to think about, but I will seriously consider staying here long enough to explore this ability I seem to have."

Philoe's face split into a grin of delight. "You will?" he squeaked, his voice much higher than normal. "That's wonderful. Take whatever time you need and ask any questions you like before you decide."

He stood up and walked back into the cave. Roza remained on the bench for a few minutes as the first stars came out before following him in. And after she lay down in the dark to sleep on the cold stone floor, she dreamed of being so full of magical power and energy that it overflowed and changed the world.

Jorxy was running back along the forest track towards Meadow Cottage as the late afternoon daylight was fading.

He had something to report to Roza's parents at last.

Yesterday, when he'd finally reached the forest clearing with Helena, he hadn't had time to search properly before night fell. Roza's mum had returned to her cottage before him, needing to look after her husband and their animals. Jorxy had found plenty of flattened grass, and Roza's wheelbarrow tracks, but he'd needed better light to be sure of not missing anything.

This morning, he'd returned to the clearing at first light and scanned every blade of grass and bare inch of earth as closely as he could. It was four days ago now that Roza had disappeared, so after this time there was a limit to how much the ground could tell him. But working outwards from the clearing in all directions, he'd finally spotted the tell-tale clues that indicated something.

He reached the cottage and gasped some deep breaths before knocking on the door and entering. Arthur was in his armchair, and Helena at the counter in the kitchen.

"I found something," he blurted out, before they could even ask.

Arthur gripped the arms of his chair and Helena laid down her chopping knife.

"I worked outwards from that clearing, looking for anything unusual. There wasn't much I could see for certain, except some animal tracks. But then I found some boot prints that definitely aren't Roza's."

"Where?" Arthur demanded, his milky eyes not quite looking at him. "Which direction did you see them, and which way were they heading?"

"Now that's the thing," Jorxy replied. "They were east of the clearing. Which means towards the edge of town, or towards the plain. And in a stretch of mud, I found these same boot prints in both directions: leading towards the clearing, and also away from it. And they could be about four days old."

"So, what does that tell us?" Helena asked. "That

someone definitely went and met her there?"

"Sounds like it," Arthur agreed. "But who? And what happened when they met?"

"The other thing I noticed," Jorxy butted in, "there was no sign of Roza's boot-prints with those tracks. So, I don't think she left with him. I say, 'him' because those boots look large, and so more like a man's than a woman's."

He saw Roza's parents turn towards each other, and Arthur muttered something that sounded like 'bastard'.

"That doesn't mean the man … um … did away with our Roza," Helena insisted. "She might have been taken ill, and he found her, and needed to carry her down to town…" Her words faded away, as though failing to convince even herself.

"I lost those boot tracks at the spur that comes down from the mountains," Jorxy went on. "That ridge is too rocky to show any tracks. I want to continue the search on the other side of that ridge, which means doing so from town. It's too far from here. From town I could leave by the warlock gate and go up the farm tracks to see what I can find."

Helena leaned heavily on the kitchen counter. "Thank you, Jorxy. You've given us the only piece of news about our Roza that we've had for days. And this confirms something else I've been thinking, Arthur. You and I need to move to stay in town for a while. I can't keep looking after us, and the animals, and everything else Roza used to do for us. If we can find someone to tend to the cow and chickens here, we could stay at the inn. We need to be there, if that's where Jorxy is searching, so we can hear any news as soon as there is any."

Arthur seemed to sag into his armchair. "I don't want to move. You know how much I rely on knowing where everything is here, to feel and find my way around." He sighed. "But if you think this is best, dear, then we can go."

Jorxy had little understanding of how difficult this might be for the old couple, but he had one idea. "My older sister, Joidi, could come here and look after your cow and chickens for you. She'd love that because she's mad about animals."

Helena smiled and nodded.

"I'll run down to Albany now and come back up here with Joidi first thing in the morning," he went on. "Then if the two of you will be ready to leave by then, I'll help you with moving what you need into town." He would leave the rest of their domestic arrangements to them because his mind was now consumed with following this possible lead to find Roza.

CHAPTER ELEVEN

By the time the cool light of dawn was filtering in through the cave entrance, Roza had already compiled a list of questions and conditions to present to Philoe. When the warlock appeared from his inner cave sleeping chamber, she allowed him to attend to his morning chores first. In fact, she helped him by bringing in two buckets of water from the pond while he gathered eggs from the chickens.

Kerenzi was still sulking and furious as she fed him his breakfast. She decided not to discuss their situation with the spirit lord until she received some answers from Philoe. When the warlock sat down at the table for his bread, boiled eggs and bacon, Roza joined him. She could tell he was itching to hear whatever she wanted to ask.

"I have some questions for you," Roza began, after swallowing a chewy crust.

"I hoped you might," he said, with a nervous smile.

"Kerenzi the spirit lord, what will happen to him?" She asked this knowing that the bound figure behind her was listening to their every word.

"He is also free to leave this cave whenever he wishes."

"He is furious and vengeful towards you," Roza cautioned, holding the warlock's gaze.

Philoe sighed. "I know. And with good reason. So, we need to be careful as we release him from the Bindweed and consider under what terms he will leave here."

Roza nodded. "Secondly, the potion. What will you do with it?"

Philoe shrugged. "Pour it away. I have no need of it any more, so we could carry the cauldron out to the stream and let it flow down into the valley."

A thought occurred to her. "That potion has my blood in it," Roza mused. "So, if anyone down in Albany drinks from the stream, do you think the much-diluted potion will have any effect on them?"

Philoe chuckled and said, "It might, you know. They'll probably put it down to having a particularly good day and feeling well and vigorous that morning."

Roza smiled. "Next, I'd like my memories back, please."

The warlock's face fell. "Alas, you ask for something I'm unable to give you. Memories are fragile things, so easy to break but so difficult to put back together. I regret that I've robbed you of your previous life, but I promise they will return in time. There is no spell that reverses the effects of the Forgetery, only the natural healing of your mind. I'm sorry. However, there are things that will help: returning to familiar places and spending time with people you know will re-establish the mental connections."

"I guessed that might be the case or you'd have offered to help me remember. But that links with my next request. I'd like to go down into Albany and see if anyone knows me. I need help to re-discover where I live, my family and friends, before I make any final decisions about my future."

"Of course," Philoe replied. "I'd be happy to come with you for that visit, if you'd like me to. I can introduce you to those who run the town to see if they've had reports of a young woman going missing."

"You know those who run the town?" Roza asked, before realising that of course he would.

"Oh, yes," Philoe said, with a casual smile. "They ask for my advice about things and rely on me to provide Albany with some protection against external threats."

Roza frowned. "We mentioned those before. What kind of external threats does Albany face?"

Philoe stared at her. "Ah, yes … you don't know."

"No. I'm the one who's lost her memory, remember?"

The warlock coughed and busied himself with his breakfast. "It's not something we like to think or talk about. There's a widespread belief that even speaking about the danger brings it down upon us. Like saying the name of the thing summons it against us."

"You mean like when Kerenzi mentioned a Dragon?"

"Hush, hush, hush." Philoe looked panicked. "Yes, that's exactly what I mean. Let's talk about something else. Anyway, I think the people of the town are quite proud to have a friendly warlock at their disposal. Anything else you wanted to ask me?"

"Um, I was thinking while I lay on the cave floor last night that I might quite like a bed?"

Philoe clapped a hand to his forehead. "How remiss of me. I've been so long without human company that I've forgotten any manners or kindness. I'm sure there's spare furniture in my storage chambers and we shall get something out before tonight."

"Thank you." Roza went back to eating and noted with pleasure how many times Philoe had referred to the two of them as 'we'. It was only a little thing but made her feel less lonely. Maybe that was why the warlock had taken to addressing himself as 'we' during all those long years.

And there was one last question she wanted to ask. Roza gave him what she hoped was a persuasive smile. "There's one other thing, until I can think of anything else. If I'm staying here for you to explore my gift, I'd like you to teach me how to use magic myself."

"What was that? What did she ask?" The sudden change in the warlock's face was alarming. "She wants to learn our secrets and powers, she does." It was as though Philoe had become the hideous ancient warlock again, even speaking like before. "No, we refuse to teach her, and she shouldn't have asked."

Roza was appalled. All at once, her dreams of feeling

magic again were slipping through her fingers. "Why not? Why won't you teach me magic and why shouldn't I ask?"

"Warlocks never share their secrets. Our magic powers are known and kept by our fellow warlocks alone."

"Well, how did you learn it, then?" Roza demanded. "And how does anyone become a warlock anyway?"

Philoe sniffed. "A warlock may enlist a group of novices, and in time choose a worthy apprentice from among them. That is what happened with me. My predecessor as warlock enrolled a class of novices from the town of Albany, and after a long and rigorous training, I was selected as his apprentice as the one with the best aptitude for magic and most worthy as his successor."

"So, appoint me as your apprentice, and then you'll be allowed to share all your so-called secret powers with me."

"It is not her place to ask," Philoe insisted. "Asking to learn magic implies a greed for power which is a wrong attitude in an apprentice. Being a warlock is such an important and responsible role that it needs to be matched with a proper attitude of service so that the magical power is not misused."

Roza fired up at once. "So that magical power is not misused? You mean like kidnapping and imprisoning innocent people? Hurting, threatening, and tormenting them? Chopping them up into longevity potions? Does that count as misusing magical power, or is that somehow a 'proper attitude of service'?"

Philoe looked stricken. She refused him the chance to defend himself and pressed home her attack.

"After all the wrongs you've done to me, Mister Warlock, you owe me a lot. Don't forget that I've made you younger too. Thanks to me, you've got decades of life back and can enjoy being middle aged again. So, in return, the very least you can do is to make me your apprentice and teach me your magic. Otherwise – and let me be clear about this – I also refuse to stay here for you to explore my unique and remarkable gift. Got it?"

Philoe opened and closed his mouth a few times. Then murmured, "You make some good points, Miss Rozabella. We will consider your suggestion and in due course let you know whether we might be willing to share our warlock secrets with you."

"I should think so too."

The rest of their breakfast passed in uncomfortable silence. When they finished, Roza asked, "What's first?"

Philoe drew in a deep breath. "The most difficult. The spirit lord."

They stood up and cleared away the breakfast things. Roza edged towards the corner where Kerenzi lay bound, as he had done for days now. He looked weaker and paler than ever, but his gaze assailed her with defiance and betrayal.

"He's going to release you now," Roza said, but her smile at him wilted like a breath before a storm.

"That's exceedingly good of him," Kerenzi sneered. "And has he graciously consented to release you from his spell of bewitchment?" The spirit lord was still in his sarcastic mood.

"I'm not bewitched," Roza protested. "I can think perfectly clearly and make decisions for myself." She earnestly hoped this was true.

"In which case, I trust you've made the sensible choice to escape this villain and his dreadful cave and accompany me down the path to the town."

"I … I haven't finally decided yet. Yes, I'm going to visit Albany soon to see if there are family and friends who have missed me, and what sort of life I might have had there."

"Ah, yes, the convenient loss of memory. Very convenient for the warlock, I mean, while he tries to charm and entice you into staying here with him. Has he fed you stories about how you might be an orphan, no family or friends to search for you, and what a privilege it would be to explore your supposed gift with him?"

"No, he hasn't said anything of the sort." Although Roza conceded she'd had those thoughts herself. Was the warlock capable of planting such ideas in her mind? She didn't know, and wished her decisions weren't so confusing.

Philoe came to stand beside her, wearing thick leather gloves. "I'm going to unbind your legs now, spirit lord," he said. "Then we'll help you to stand and walk outside."

"You are so kind and considerate, my good warlock," Kerenzi goaded him. "I think I'll give this establishment a glowing recommendation when I get home."

Roza bit back the retort on her lips. Kerenzi had suffered grievously at this man's hands, but his bitterness shocked her. She tried to think how it would be if she'd lost a hand or a foot during these days, and how deep her desire for revenge might run. It wasn't pleasant to think about. Was there anything she could say or do to stop these two men detesting each other?

Philoe had untied the leg bindings, and Kerenzi said, "A pity you didn't offer Rozabella the gloves to wash and feed me earlier. You could have saved her such a lot of pain and irritation."

Roza wished they could get this over. Kerenzi's presence and attitude had become pure poison.

The spirit lord flexed his leg muscles, and Philoe stepped back. Kerenzi was still bound from the waist upwards, but the warlock removed himself from the possibility of being kicked.

Roza and Philoe moved to Kerenzi's sides and each grasped a wrist and shoulder, Roza being careful to avoid holding the ropes if she could. With difficulty they levered the spirit lord to stand on his feet. His knees buckled and swayed, but the two of them held him up. Roza had the impression he was leaning more towards her than the warlock.

Kerenzi bent his legs again in turn, as though to ease their numbness, but then stamped hard on Philoe's foot. "Oh, I'm so sorry, how clumsy of me. The Bindweed has such a terrible effect on my muscle control, you know."

Philoe was cursing under his breath, making sure to hold the spirit lord at arm's length from now on.

"Lean on me," Roza instructed him, and grasped him around the waist. Her whole arm was against the Bindweed now, but if this got the job done then she would live with the consequences of it later.

Together they managed an awkward shuffle towards the cave entrance where Kerenzi made a point of blinking in the sunshine, breathing deep of the air, gazing at the trees and grass, the clouds in the sky, and all the other things she'd been enjoying, but he hadn't.

"Come on, Kerenzi, please can we get this over with," Roza muttered. "Anyone would think you didn't want to leave. Let's get you away from here before he changes his mind."

The spirit lord consented to moving a little quicker, and before long he was hardly leaning on Roza at all but walking freely on his own legs. He'd been exaggerating his weakness. Philoe led the way, staying out of reach.

They'd turned right out of the cave along the path skirting the meadow until they reached the cliff edge where the path descended towards the valley and town. The morning sun was bright, and the air still and clear.

Here they stopped and the warlock faced the spirit lord to address him. To Roza's surprise, Philoe bowed low.

"Kerenzi, spirit lord of the forest, I regret now that I captured you. I apologise unreservedly for having bound you, imprisoned you, taken your blood and wing, and for otherwise ill-treating you. I ask you to accept my apology and to leave here in peace."

Roza willed Kerenzi to accept Philoe's contrition, but

he was having none of it. "You only regret my capture," he sneered, "because you found a way to get what you want from the girl. If she hadn't been duped into helping you, you wouldn't hesitate to plunge a knife into my innards and dice up my entrails for your cauldron. Your apology is hollow and cynical. You only say this because you fear my wrath and revenge. And rightly so, because I will never forgive you for this."

"I feared you would say this," Philoe replied, "so I have taken steps to protect myself after your departure. Once you have left this plateau you will never be able to return here. I have placed enchantments that will block you from approaching nearer than a mile from my cave."

"You say I will never be able to return here," Kerenzi mocked. "Such arrogance from one so limited. 'Never' is too grand a word for a mere mortal to use. 'For as long as you live', you mean. All your spells and enchantments will cease on the day you die, which I pray will be soon."

Philoe turned to her. "Roza, can I ask you to untie the spirit lord and then escort him down the path until he is a mile from the cave? My enchantment will force him to go, but I'd rather one of us saw him safely departed."

"Yes, of course."

The warlock turned back to Kerenzi. "I must also insist – no, that's too demanding a word – I beg and plead with you that you promise never to harm Rozabella for as long as she lives."

Roza met Kerenzi's gaze as he turned to look at her. For an instant she remembered those eyes shining with the greens and yellows of a meadow on a summer's day. And a darker green like holly, sprinkled with the silver of starlight. She wished they could be like that again, instead of the black and fire of fury and hate.

"I hold nothing against the girl," Kerenzi declared. "She cared for me, and I suppose it is thanks to her that I retain my life. I consider her mistaken and deluded, that you have enchanted and bewitched her, but that is between the two of you. I would not think of harming her, but to prove I am a better man than you, warlock, I give you my solemn word and promise, Rozabella, that I will never harm you for as long as you live."

Philoe took off his gloves, handed them to Roza and stepped back. She sighed and put on the gloves. The Bindweed knots came apart more easily now and stayed undone once released. Soon the dreadful grey ropes lay piled on the ground, their barbs hungry for their next victim.

Kerenzi stepped away from them and stretched his arms. His wings unfurled behind him at last, the sunshine tracing rainbows through them. But Roza's gaze couldn't avoid the ugly silver-grey gash that chopped his left wing short.

The spirit lord pointed an accusing finger at the warlock. "Because of you, warlock, my flying will never be the same again. And I use the word 'never' correctly. That you have caused me an everlasting injury makes you worthy of a horrible and lingering death. I curse you, Philoe the warlock. I pray that the Dragon will find you and you will learn the meaning of justice and judgment."

"Stop," Philoe ordered. "Do not say that name."

"What?" Kerenzi laughed and raised his voice. "Dragon? Dragon?" He cupped his hands around his lips and bellowed into the skies, "Come, Dragon, come. The town of Albany deserves your attention. Come, Dragon, come!"

The warlock flew into a rage against the spirit lord, pummelling him and shoving him onto the path down the cliff. "Stop it, silence, stop!"

Kerenzi threw him off and Philoe landed awkwardly on the grass. Roza leapt between them, grabbed the spirit lord's arm and pulled him away. He didn't seem able to stop her. Kerenzi stumbled forwards and she guided him onto the downwards path until the warlock was out of sight.

They trudged downwards side by side in silence for a few minutes. The spirit lord seemed to be pushed and forced to keep going by the warlock's spell. She'd hoped they might be friends and allies against their imprisonment, but now it had all ended in hatred, revenge and cursing. In a last attempt at companionship, Roza took hold of his hand and clasped it as they walked. Kerenzi didn't object or shake her off, which surprised and encouraged her.

"Why did you do that?" Roza asked. "Say that name. Why did you risk bringing destruction to Albany?"

Kerenzi's laugh was without warmth. "You mortals are so petty and limited. The edge of your world is one small town, and you think your happiness is bound up in its safety."

"But if … it … comes, then your forests will suffer too. Don't you care about your own wellbeing and that of your people?"

"We have our own protections. The creatures of powerful magic know better than to trouble each other."

They went in silence again until Kerenzi stopped. "We have reached a mile from the cave, so I am not compelled forwards any more." He turned to face her. "It is not too late, Rozabella. You have not made any final decisions or committed yourself to him. Come with me now. Walk on down this path, and not back, and you can discover a better future for yourself. One without illusions, bewitching, cruelty or lies."

Roza bit her lip and twisted her fingers together around his hand. "I don't think I am bewitched by illusions, but I will remember what you've said. And in turn I hope you will remember that not everything in that cave was dreadful. We had friendship and companionship in adversity for a while. Call it a mortal weakness if you must, but we consider such small things to be precious."

Kerenzi gazed at her, the black of his eyes melting into dark blue and purple. She felt self-conscious about standing so close to him, holding each other's hands. She looked down.

"You're remarkable," he said. "Always looking for hope and kindness in the midst of tragedy and pain. But you have a weakness: you trust people too easily, even when they don't deserve it. I fear that your naivety, your innocence and generosity of spirit will be your downfall. You won't remember this, but when I first spoke with you in that forest clearing, I said there was something special and different about you. Something in your spirit I'd never seen before. I realise now it was your gift that I saw."

With that, he leaned forward and kissed her on the lips. She was so surprised that it was a moment before she pushed him away. But she still tasted him on her lips.

"Yes, I will always remember you, Rozabella," he said. "And you will see me again."

With that, he let go of her hand, turned and jumped skywards. His wings beat the morning air, but unevenly, so that he leaned and veered to the left. He rose until Roza's shielded eyes could no longer make him out against the brightness of the sky. She touched her fingers to her lips, drew a deep breath, and then turned and walked back up the dusty path.

CHAPTER TWELVE

Philoe was waiting for her when she reached the top of the path. "Everything all right?"

Roza nodded. She certainly wouldn't mention the kiss. It still bewildered her. What had that been for? To thank her for saving his life? It hadn't seemed like that because his attitude was far from thankful. Perhaps it was a game that immortals played with mortals: toying with their affections, teasing them with the hint of a love they could never hope to reach. If anyone had the powers and looks to charm a mortal girl's heart, it was that spirit lord. She'd never be kissed by anyone so gorgeous again.

"We need to be careful now," Philoe was saying as they walked back along the path towards the cave. "And not just because of the spirit lord and his threat of revenge. But also because of what Kerenzi shouted as he left here. When we get the chance, I need to fill in your absent memories in that regard."

They reached the cave, and Roza felt it empty without the spirit lord's presence. What had Kerenzi done to her? Only minutes ago, she'd been wishing him gone because of his poisonous sarcasm and hatred. How could she be missing him? She shook herself. She refused to allow that gorgeous, arrogant, vengeful creature to stir up her feelings.

She needed something else to do, to keep her occupied and distract her thoughts. "What's next, Philoe?" she asked.

"A bed for you," the warlock replied. "We can't have you sleeping another night on the cold stone floor."

Outside it began to cloud over, with a cold wind and then rain, so Philoe and Roza spent the afternoon finding a bed for her in the storerooms at the back of the cave, placing it in one of the spare cave chambers that could now be her bedroom, and fitting it out with a mattress, pillow, sheets and blanket.

From that day onwards, Philoe started to clean and tidy up the cave. Roza spent much of her time outside, helping at the animal pens, carrying water and exploring the fields of wheat and grain. She also spent hours either sitting or walking along the edge of the clifftop, gazing down at the valley and town below, but she didn't leave the plateau.

Her sleep on the bed at night gradually became more comfortable, from an anxious mind waking her up in a sweat, to sleeping through without nightmares. She was reassured by the warlock being unfailingly polite, kind and considerate towards her, even arranging to be occupied inside the cave for a few hours while Roza had a welcome wash in the pool, her privacy guarded by Standley.

It was after breakfast following her first night in her bed when Roza asked about the next of their jobs. "The potion?"

The warlock was busy clearing the ash and other remnants of the fire from underneath the cauldron's legs. "Yes, but the cauldron is heavy, so it will need all three of us."

"Three?" Roza asked, and then followed Philoe's gaze towards the coat stand.

"Of course, Standley," she said, walking over to it. "How could I forget you? Please forgive me as a mortal girl that I'm not used to such magical or enchanted things."

The coat stand inclined its top hooks forward into a nod.

"I should imagine you're pretty strong but not all that supple," Roza went on. "Is that right?" Standley nodded again.

She surveyed it, with its circle of hooks around the top,

and more around the middle – she supposed these were for walking sticks. "You know, Standley, I've been thinking of you as an 'it', as I might any other coat stand. But I reckon you're more of a person, so may I refer to you as a 'he' instead?"

There was a twitch, as though a shrug, and then another nod. Roza imagined to herself that Standley was pleased about this but couldn't explain why. The coat stand didn't have a mouth to smile or anything. Maybe the lines in the wood around the knots for his eyes had crinkled up a bit. Yes, she decided, that was what she'd seen. Then she shook herself for pretending that a coat stand could be pleased at being called a 'he'.

"Come on then, Standley," she called, "time to get to work."

The three of them arranged themselves around the cauldron and gave it a first lift. Philoe was right: the thing was very heavy. It was not just the weight of the cast iron, but also the liquid inside it. They tried to find comfortable and effective handholds around the rim but managed to totter only some steps each time. And it was the humans rather than the coat stand who needed the rests.

But they managed it in successive efforts, out of the cave entrance and across the grass to the stone bridge over the stream. The most difficult stage was then lifting it on to the bridge parapet ready for tipping over the edge. Standley's strength was the most useful here, taking the cauldron's weight while Philoe and Roza raised it higher. At last, it was in place and ready for the warlock's longevity potion to be tipped away.

Philoe turned to her and said, "I vow and promise to you, Rozabella, that this will be the last of these that I will ever make. You have made me younger now, and if you're willing to do the same again in the future, then I'll be pleased to accept that. But if not, then I will grow old and accept my end with a mortal's death. I'm grateful to have had four centuries of life and can reasonably ask for no longer than that. From now on I refuse to threaten or extinguish the life of another for the sake of my own longevity."

Roza faced him squarely. "Philoe the Warlock, I will hold you to that."

Standley's hooks took the cauldron's weight while Roza and Philoe angled it to dispose of the potion downstream. The liquid was a dark purple, flecked with silver and white, as the waterfall's foaming waters bore it away out of sight. Once the cauldron was empty, they rinsed it out with buckets of water from the pool.

Good riddance, Roza thought. Although a longevity potion might be a miraculous magical creation, its cost was too high, and the world could do without extra man-made sources of fear and death.

Carrying the empty cauldron back inside was much easier. When they sat down at the table for lunch, Roza said, "You were going to fill in my ignorance about the threats Kerenzi was making as he left."

Philoe sighed. "We need to be very careful, because the creature the spirit lord mentioned has very powerful magic. It is widely believed, and with good reason, that even the mention of the creature's name has the effect of a summoning charm. To avoid this danger, the people down in the town of Albany refer to him as 'The Emperor'."

Roza's eyebrows rose in surprise. "Is he really an Emperor, then?"

"Yes, he is," Philoe answered. "The valley and town of Albany lies in the territory of the Earl of the Plains, namely Lord Vallance of Gorge City. He in turn is a vassal of the Emperor, who rules over the vast Sapien Empire. But his reign is one of fear, rather than of justice. For centuries he has collected tribute from all the Empire's towns and cities, calling them 'taxes', to pretend they are legitimate. But it's nothing more than extortion, of course."

"Don't we receive anything back from our Emperor, then? What about peace and security – could he claim he provides those for Albany and the plains and everywhere else?"

"Only if you call living in constant fear of his visits being secure and at peace. No, I'm sure he claims he protects us from invasion and lawlessness, but it's hard to think of anything worse than his tyranny and despotism."

"You mentioned 'tribute for centuries'. Has Albany been paying these tributes or 'taxes' to the Emperor through all your long life?"

Philoe pulled a face. "No, we haven't, and that's our problem. Not every town has a warlock to protect it, and over the centuries I've managed to buy Albany some time. The Emperor seems to respect me, or at least some of my powers, and over the centuries I've negotiated deals with him, to persuade him to turn elsewhere, to distract or delay him. But this means that by now the town of Albany owes our Emperor over three hundred years' worth of overdue taxes."

"Three hundred years' worth of taxes?" Roza was incredulous. "How much gold and silver does that amount to?"

Philoe's face was grim. "The amount is almost beyond reckoning. Needless to say, it's more than all the treasure, buildings and land in the whole valley. Even if we all sold ourselves to him as his slaves, we couldn't make up the total amount that is due. Hence our fear that if our Emperor comes to visit, then we're finished, destroyed, dead. He threatened last time to lay waste to the whole valley to serve as an example to all the other towns in his Empire. And he could do it too, with nothing I or anyone else could do to stop him."

Roza swallowed. The thought of leaving Albany and the valley to seek another life elsewhere had returned and now held great appeal. But what if she had family or friends here? This town must have been her home, and the thought of abandoning it because of a tyrant and bully was hard to bear. "Can we talk about something else?"

"Yes, of course." Philoe looked relieved. "I've been checking in my parchments and tomes to see if I can discover anything at all about your gift for making people younger. And you'll be pleased to hear that I've found some vague references."

"You have?" Roza brightened. "You mean someone else has had this gift before, or written about it?"

The warlock shook his head. "There is no definite case of your gift in any of the histories. Nothing more than hints, legends, and myths. It's hard to exaggerate how rare it is. You might be the first person in the whole history of the world to have your gift."

Roza gulped. It sounded nice to be special, but to be this unique might bring unwanted attention or danger.

"The legends give it a name, this gift and ability of yours. It's called Rejuvenate. The ability to make younger, to return to youth, to restore something to how it was before. Does that sound better than being a spade?"

Roza laughed. "Yes, it does. I like it. I have the gift of Rejuvenate." She rolled the word across her tongue.

Philoe was tapping his chin. "I've been thinking about that analogy I used, about a spade and arm muscles digging a hole. I don't think I got it right. With your gift of Rejuvenate, it's more like mortals being buried at the bottom of a deep pit or trapped underground by a cave-in. We're all condemned to die, with no way out. Your gift of Rejuvenate – your spade – gives us the chance to dig our way out of being trapped. Or think of yourself like a long ladder, giving us the ability to climb out of the deep pit. Through Rejuvenate, we can escape death, or at least delay it, to live for longer and longer. I don't want you to think of your ability as no more than a tool, an implement, a mechanism. Your gift is a lifeline, a rescue, a liberation, a salvation."

Roza's mouth had fallen open, and a chill washed over her skin. "That sounds like … um … a large responsibility for a seventeen-year-old girl to shoulder. But I don't get it. What's the big deal about being younger or living longer anyway? Why is it so important to everyone? Can't we all accept that we're mortal, live out as many years as we get, make the most of the time, and then die content with however long we've had?"

The warlock's eyebrows rose. "So says the seventeen-year-old girl. Believe me, young lady, the older we get, the nearer to death we are, the bigger the deal it becomes. Even if our lives have been hard, they always seem preferable to the unknown terrors of death. If life is always better than death, then we try to hold on to it for as long as we can. You youngsters think you'll live for ever anyway, but as it dawns on us that we won't, the more desperate we become. Trust me, for anyone middle aged or older, it's a big deal."

Roza shrugged. "All right. So, it's an important gift, and it sounds as though it lands me with an awesome responsibility."

Philoe nodded slowly. "Yes, I agree that it does. And I'm afraid that isn't the end of it. I need to alert you to the probable dangers inherent in your gift." He sighed and waved a hand towards his bookcases. "In the pages of our legends and myths, the tales of Rejuvenate have become muddled up with places and things as well as people. There are stories about an Elixir of Life, or a Fountain of Eternal Youth, and so on. Whether a person with your gift was behind these, we'll never know. But the point is that Empires have gone to war to possess them. Nations and peoples will do anything to gain access to a way to cheat death, to make themselves immortal." He pointed to where the empty cauldron stood. "You've seen already what I was willing to do to prolong my own life. Imagine what will happen if your gift and ability becomes widely known."

The chill on Roza's skin had deepened to freeze her bones to the marrow. Philoe's soft voice now sounded to her like a sentence of doom. She felt small, and weak, and desperately inadequate and afraid.

The warlock reached across the table and enclosed her trembling hand in his. "This is why, Rozabella, I offer that you can stay here. I can give you some safety and protection, hiding away from being known by the world. I can use my magic to defend you. Together we can explore your gift and seek to understand it, its range and depth, so that you are equipped to make your own choices about your place in the world."

Roza nodded and whispered, "Thank you." The option of hiding away in a cave for the rest of her life suddenly seemed like an excellent choice. Her ideas about wanting to help others and take away their fear of death were revealed as impossibly naïve. Had her youth and inexperience underestimated what greedy and selfish people would do to possess and control her ability?

"All right," she said at once. "We will keep my gift completely secret until we're ready to reveal it. That way I will be safe. No one else knows about it except for you and me, do they?" As soon as she asked this, she knew it wasn't true.

Philoe was shaking his head. "Unfortunately, Kerenzi the spirit lord also knows about it. You told him so yourself."

A thrill of horror gripped Roza's limbs. "We shouldn't have let him go. We should have kept him here so he can't tell anyone about it."

"Listen to yourself, Roza," Philoe urged. "You're talking about imprisoning someone here because of what he knows. We mustn't do that. And calm yourself because I don't think Kerenzi will spread the news far and wide.

He is an immortal, and the prospect of becoming younger or living longer means very little to him. It will hardly register as interesting to him. He is going back to his people, to the forest spirits, who are also immortal, and likewise indifferent to mortal obsessions with aging, longevity, and death. He will hardly wander into Albany's Market Square and announce to everybody that the path to immortality can be found in a cave up in the hills."

Roza slumped in relief. "You're right, thank goodness for that. In fact, I'm not sure Kerenzi even believed that I have this gift of Rejuvenate. He told me that you've bewitched me with some enchantment, and your looking younger is all an illusion anyway."

Philoe tilted his head to the side. "Do you think you're bewitched or enchanted, Miss Rozabella? Is what you see in my face all an illusion? The fact that I can now carry a heavy cauldron across the grass to the stream? Could I have done that when you met me?"

Roza forced out a laugh and said, "No, of course not."

But the laugh was forced because a thought had occurred to her. What if Kerenzi had been speaking the truth and Philoe was a liar? The spirit lord had doubted that the warlock was much younger, so was that all an illusion, an elaborate fabrication to persuade her of something? And Philoe had wiped her memories, and told her tales to frighten her, about the Emperor, and about what people might do if they discovered her gift. The effect had been to convince her to stay and hide here – and wasn't that exactly what the warlock wanted? If she had this gift, then she could keep him young forever, just like he'd been doing with his potions. And now at last he had a teenage girl for company. Was there anything sinister in that?

Roza told him she wanted some time by herself to think and went off into the trees for the afternoon. She'd intended at some point soon to make a trip down into

Albany to locate any family and friends. Would that be wise if she was trying to keep herself and her ability secret? And so, her thoughts revolved in circles, with hope, loneliness, doubt, fear and confusion chasing each other until darkness fell.

Leaving Helena and Arthur to finish their unpacking at the Mermaid Inn, Jorxy jogged across Albany's town square. He said hello to a few market traders at their stalls, and then slipped into the alley between the tavern and the schoolroom. This led to the little-used warlock gate on the south side of town. He slowed as he approached the guardhouse at the opening in the stockade and raised his eyes.

He wasn't as familiar with this side of town as he was with the north and west, where the rubbish ditch was. Here, the warlock gate gave access to farm tracks and lanes, that led to fields, barns and paths into the woods. More importantly for him, there were trails up into the hills, including to the other side of that mountain spur he'd reached from the forest clearing where Rozabella had gone missing.

"Hey, Jorxy, what you doing here?"

He snapped out of gazing up at the mountains to see his older brother, Rufus, strolling towards him. Jorxy had known he was on guard duty here today, and he wanted something from him.

"Searching for Roza, course, what else? Got any food?" Helena had insisted he share some of their breakfast at the inn, but if he was going up into the hills for the day, Jorxy wanted something he could take with him.

Rufus gave him a knowing glare. "Always after my rations, you are." The position of town guard meant he was provided with enough food for each shift, which made him the best fed of Jorxy's family.

"Don't share it, then," Jorxy complained back. "Here I

am, helping you out with your duties, finding a missing townsperson, and all I ask is a biscuit to help my search."

His brother grunted. "You ain't searching for Roza to help us find a missing person. It's because you fancy her, and she's your only friend. Or have her parents offered a reward for finding her? If they have, I'm finding her first."

"No, they ain't offered no reward, and if you must know, Roza is the best of my many friends. So, you helping me or not?"

Rufus narrowed his eyes at him and then turned away to fetch his food bag from the guardhouse. When he returned, he fished around inside it and handed Jorxy the smallest of his allotted biscuits. "Where you looking for her, anyway?"

Jorxy stowed the biscuit away in his pocket for later. "Roza disappeared in a forest clearing over there," he waved an arm to their right, vaguely south-westwards. "I found boot tracks heading through the trees and up onto this spur of the Heismith mountains." He indicated the massive shoulder of bare rock and cliff in front of them. "I'll see if I can pick up the tracks on this side of the spur. So, what's on this side of the valley?"

"Nothing at all," Rufus moaned. "It's the most boring guard duty ever. A few farms, tracks, barns, fields, sheep. It beats me why anyone is supposed to guard here. Almost no one ever comes in or out. Never mind 'warlock gate', it should be called 'deadly boring gate'."

"Why's it called 'warlock gate', then? What's that about?"

His brother shrugged. "Well, legend and rumour has it there used to be some ancient warlock living up in the mountains somewhere. Two of us are supposed to guard this gate to make sure no unauthorised visitors, only messengers from the Reeve, ever go up there to disturb him. But no one ever sees or hears of him, so I doubt it's true. It's just another of those stories mothers tell their naughty children to get them to behave."

Jorxy's face cracked into a grin. "Oh yeah, I remember that. Did mum ever tell you those? Go to bed now or the old warlock will come and get you."

"Yeah, well, the other guards told me that if you follow the tracks into the mountains without permission you meet a gruesome and painful death at the hands of the warlock. But I bet that was just to scare the young recruits. So, if you meet a grisly end up there, don't come back and complain I didn't warn you."

Jorxy chuckled. "Thanks for your brotherly concern. Where does this warlock live anyway, so I can avoid his hideous lair?"

Rufus shrugged. "No idea. But the Reeve must know if he's sending messengers up there. You'll be all right so long as you stick to the lower slopes. I guess the tracks of Roza's abductor – if that's what you found – will run across these fields south of town and then away to the plain."

Jorxy stiffened. "Don't say that. Roza will be fine. I'll find her and she'll be okay. She has to be. I better get on with the search. Thanks for the biscuit."

"See you later. Good luck."

Jorxy trotted through the warlock gate and started along the farm track towards the mountain spur.

CHAPTER THIRTEEN

The next morning, Roza wandered off to explore more of the plateau, this time in the direction of the grain fields. She crossed Torrence by the stone bridge, passed the animal pens, and started off across the fields. She marvelled at how the rows of corn, barley, oats, and wheat stood in such straight lines that she wondered whether Standley had planted them. If the warlock had been so ancient and decrepit until recently, would the enchanted coat stand have undertaken all these menial and physical tasks for him?

On their southern side, the fields were bordered by rising hill slopes, where a few of the warlock's sheep grazed on the tussocky grass. The slopes rose into the cliffs and shoulders of the Heismith mountains encircling the valley of Albany, with the lines of occasional paths making their zigzagged way up to the summits and passes.

Roza's wandering steps began to climb, and she found herself heading towards a vast spur of the mountain which formed the western edge of the plateau. She was breathing hard and sweating by the time her path led her to the ridge, where she was surprised to come across a bench-like stone shelf beside the way. As she lowered herself gratefully onto it, she saw at once why this seat was here.

The view from the stone bench encompassed a vast panorama of the whole valley. Below to her right she looked down on the plateau: the fields, the animals, the grass and orchard, with the sparkling line of Torrence running off to its waterfall over the cliff. In front lay the whole town of Albany, surrounded by its wooden stockade, except on the east where a stone wall defended the valley in the direction of the plain. She could see the straight line of the highway as it plunged through the cleft in the eastern mountains until it faded into a haze of distance on the plains.

But most breath-taking of all were the mountains. From down on the edge of the plateau, she'd been looking up at the ridges and peaks. Here she seemed to be among them, on their level, with the snows and eagles no more than an arm's length away.

Roza lowered her gaze from the mountain tops to the forests that clothed their slopes. Was her home out there somewhere in the middle of this? It had to be, but where? Again, she felt her eyes drawn more to the surrounding forests than to the town itself.

Then a feeling of unease struck her. Where did that come from? It wasn't a memory, because those weren't coming back. But when she thought of home, or of any family she might have, there was a definite impression of something unsatisfactory or restrictive about it. She couldn't put a finger on anything specific, which was maddening, but it surprised her to feel anything at all about her past, that it might not have been as she would have wished. It hadn't been horrible or cruel, just a bit sad. The negative impression continued to niggle and irritate her.

Having recovered her breath, she stood up to look around more easily. Then she noticed something. Looking down the mountain spur, a small figure was walking across the hillside far below her. She squinted to see, and decided it looked like a boy searching for something, because his head was down, scanning the ground. She wondered whether to call or wave, but decided he was probably too far below to see or hear her anyway.

Then a movement in the corner of her eye made her look down to her right, where another figure was climbing up the path towards her. From the black robes, it had to be the warlock, and besides, who else was up here? She smiled to herself at the thought of Standley tottering or scuttling his way up a mountainside but conceded that she wouldn't put anything past the abilities of that amazing coat stand.

Roza heard a call, and the warlock shouted, "Do you want to be alone, or can I come up?"

She thought for a moment and then called back, "Come." There was always a plethora of questions that her mind had devised to ask him. She returned to sit on the stone bench until at last the warlock joined her, and then she let him catch his breath.

"Warlock Philoe," she said, "Kerenzi the spirit lord said you captured us in a forest clearing where I was chopping wood. Where was that, then?"

The warlock pointed down the side of the mountain spur to their left. "It was down there, although I couldn't point out the exact clearing from up here."

Roza gazed down at the treetops below her, and at the fields and meadows that lay between the forest and the town, and mused, "So I guess my home must be somewhere near there."

"I'm sorry, but I can't answer that."

"It's a long way from down there to up here on the plateau, so how did you drag our bodies back to the cave after you surprised us? You were so ancient and decrepit then, I can't see how you managed it. Or did Standley help you?"

Philoe's eyebrows rose, and he gave a small smile. "Aren't you forgetting something? I am a warlock, Miss Roza. I have magic to help me."

She tilted her head to look at him. "What magic did you use to do that, then? Which spells or enchantments?"

The warlock narrowed his eyes at her. "Always she wants to discover our secrets and powers."

Roza pointed her finger at him. "Are curiosity and enthusiasm also forbidden to a warlock's pupils? Aren't we allowed to have a thirst for knowledge and understanding?"

"Curiosity and enthusiasm are good attributes," Philoe answered, "but a little knowledge can be a dangerous thing when not tempered by an attitude of service."

Roza rolled her eyes at him. "So, I guess we come back to that same question I asked you before. Are you, or are you not, going to teach me your magic?"

The warlock let out his breath, and said, "I have thought about this carefully, and on the condition that you remain here for me to explore your Rejuvenate gift, I have decided that I could enrol you as a novice."

Roza pulled a face. Novice didn't sound nearly so exciting as being an apprentice, almost like she was a little girl again. "So, what's involved in being a novice, then, as opposed to being an apprentice?"

"A novice is at the very first stage of training," Philoe explained. "You are a beginner, a learner, a trainee. By the time you become an apprentice, you are expected to take over in the warlock's absence. You are nowhere near that stage yet, so if you agree, you will become my novice."

"Didn't you say that when you were a novice there was a whole class of you from Albany? Will you look for other novices to learn alongside me, or will it be just me? I want to know whether in due course I will have competition for the position of apprentice or not."

Philoe seemed to bristle with discomfort. "You are full of demands, Miss Roza. You need to learn your place. It is entirely up to the warlock to decide on matters such as these, and she should be grateful that we are willing to accept her as a novice at all."

It was Roza's turn to become indignant, and she jumped to her feet to face him. "I should be grateful? I need to learn my place? Yes, Mister Warlock, my place is as your most recent victim, kidnapped, blasted unconscious, dragged away, bound and gagged, tortured painfully, threatened with dismemberment and death. You are the one who should be grateful I'm willing to talk to you at all instead of fleeing to find my home."

"Yes, Rozabella, we agreed that I am in your debt which is why I am willing to enrol you as my novice–"

"And what is more," she interrupted him, "you've wiped away my memories, so my last seventeen years are lost to me. And in contrast, I've been willing to use my gift to help you gain decades of extra life. You owe me so much, Mister Warlock, that from where I stand, I'm in the position of demanding whatever I like from you."

They glared at each other in silence. Roza standing facing him, her fists balled at her sides, Philoe tense on the stone bench.

The warlock looked away first and he leaned back on the bench. "Miss Roza, please sit down. We need to be able to communicate with each other better than this."

She willed herself to relax her muscles, jamming her hands into her pockets and stepping back to perch on the other end of the stone shelf. "I suppose you have a point. You mean that novices and warlocks aren't meant to spend their days shouting at each other."

"Exactly. The teacher and learner relationship needs to include openness, honesty, and trust. I accept and admit that I have wronged you grievously. I have apologised to you already and I say it again. Roza, I am sorry for all I did to you. In trying to make amends, I am willing to teach you my magic. If it comforts and encourages you, I fully expect that in due course you will become my apprentice, but that is still a long way ahead down the road."

"Well, that sounds better. But I'd still like to know whether you'll look for other novices."

Philoe shrugged. "I may. But only if someone from the town shows particular aptitude for magic. In the meantime, it has occurred to me that someone with your unique and powerful gift should have her own source of magical power to be able to exercise it. It would seem perverse if the Universe has given you the means to rejuvenate people, but not the magic to make it effectual. In other words, you need within yourself all three aspects of rejuvenating people: the desire, the means and the energy."

Roza was nodding. "Yes, that makes sense, thank you."

"So, I need to ask you, Miss Rozabella, to be willing to forgive me for what I've done to you. We can't have you bringing up all my recent crimes again and again every time you want something from me. Yes, I wronged you, and yes, I'm sorry, but if I am to teach you then we both need to know that you are trying to forgive me. I'm not saying we should forget it completely, but we need to determine, through an act of will, to leave it behind us. Can you try to do that?"

Roza gazed out across the valley. Inside she nursed the bitter knot of anger and resentment from her time bound, tortured and humiliated on the cave floor. She'd vowed and promised herself to pay him back for that. She'd managed to escape with her life, and Kerenzi the spirit lord had survived too, and was now free. The wounds and memories she had were relatively minor and would heal. Could she let those go?

And what about this offer of starting off down the road of magical education and training? Could she possibly receive a better invitation than this? She remembered again those sensations of magic flowing through her body, filling up her heart, and knew she desperately wanted that again. After all, how many young people down there in the town of Albany might long and yearn to become apprentice to the wise and powerful warlock, and learn the mysteries of magic and spells from him? This had to be the best offer she would ever receive in her life.

It felt like a momentous decision. As though here and now, she was choosing the entire future direction of her life. Would she hold on to her bitterness, run away from the ancient, cruel, and lying warlock, and seek to return to her unknown former life, whatever that was? Or could she forgive the hurts, accept that Philoe was changing away from his recent self, and embrace the exciting possibilities and adventure of a life of magic? Did the future opportunities outweigh the evils of the past?

Yes of course they did. They outweighed them by loads.

And in that moment Roza felt her heart soften. She would no longer nurse a heart as stone-hard as this bench, of anger, resentment and fear. No, she would choose forgiveness, excitement and learning instead. If that meant her heart was now of flesh, and vulnerable to being hurt again, then she would risk that. It was a price worth paying.

At last, Roza turned to face the warlock who was watching her patiently from the other end of the stone shelf. How could she put into words for him all she'd been thinking?

She smiled.

And that was all she needed to do. It was a warm, genuine, excited smile, and Philoe seemed to melt with relief.

"Yes, Mister Warlock Philoe Sir, I am going to try to forgive you. I've been thinking that a fear of death might make older people do unspeakable things to try to stay alive. The spirit lord and I escaped with our lives, and the wounds I suffered will heal. Kerenzi might think and decide differently, but I choose to stay and learn magic from you."

Philoe clapped his hands together, beaming. "Excellent. Now, if you'd like to, there's a small ceremony to admit you as a novice."

Roza felt her eyebrows rise. "And ... that entails what exactly?"

He chuckled. "Relax, it's nothing difficult. But I'm supposed to take your hand."

She reminded herself that starting this magical journey would involve any number of new and possibly unsettling experiences, and she needed to be willing and open-minded enough to learn them. And she had held hands with him before, when she rejuvenated them.

They shuffled closer together on the stone shelf, and Philoe enclosed her right hand in both of his. "If you agree to my question at the end, please reply, I will."

Roza nodded, and Philoe cleared his throat. "Miss Rozabella of Albany, by the authority of Irvine, the Master of the Warlocks, I, Philoe, Warlock of Albany, do hereby admit you to the role and position of novice. Will you devote your best efforts to learn all that I will teach you, and accept my instruction and guidance in the ways of magic?"

She couldn't help but grin as she declared, "I will!"

Philoe bowed his head to her.

"When do we start?" she burst out.

Philoe laughed. "Patience is also a good thing, and a necessary attribute for a novice, Miss Roza." He stopped and held her gaze. "But I would say we've made an excellent start on our teaching and learning relationship today, wouldn't you?"

Roza smiled back and couldn't stop herself. "So how did you get my and the spirit lord's bodies up here to the plateau from that forest clearing?"

He gave her a sideways look. "She is a persistent and unstoppable one, isn't she? All right then, once you were unconscious, and the spirit lord was disabled by the Bindweed net, I used a Lightenment spell on you both. That made your bodies light enough for me to pull them after me with no more difficulty than if you were bags of air. Happy?"

"Yes, thank you. Lightenment spells will be very useful, then. But why didn't you use one of those on the cauldron instead of us struggling to pour away your potion?"

"Ah, well spotted, my young novice. Because there are rules about combining potions and spells. We can mix different spells – such as BodyCrusher or Bindweed with Lightenment – but not Lightenment with a Longevity Potion, because otherwise the spell effects can be unpredictable. For example, the potion could have floated out of the cauldron and into the air before we could tip it away."

When they were silent for a moment, Philoe said, "Surely you haven't run out of questions for me already?"

Roza shook her head. "There is a rather important one. What are we going to say happened to me? It's only you, me and Kerenzi who know the truth about the kidnapping and captivity here, and when we go down into town, they'll want to know where I've been."

"Ah, I see your question. It will seem awkward if I've acquired a novice by force and by wiping her memories."

"We could say I hit my head while chopping in the forest."

"And that I found you?"

"And since my blow to the head affected my memory, I couldn't remember who I was or where I lived. You took pity on me and brought me up here to look after me until my memory returned or we could otherwise find out if I have a home and family."

"That is kind and gracious of you. You turn my acts of cruelty into kindness and compassion, which is more than I deserve."

Roza beamed at him and stood up. "I think that's what forgiveness is supposed to be about. And besides, we must all do our bit to make us warlocks look good."

With a sly smile at him, she started back down the path.

CHAPTER FOURTEEN

The following morning, Roza woke early, itching to start learning about magic. In fact, it had filled her dreams with a tingling excitement.

As soon as Philoe emerged from his sleeping chamber, she accosted him. "When can I have my first magic lesson, then? Today?"

He stretched and yawned. "And good morning to you too, my young novice." He tilted his head at her, considering. "I like your keenness and enthusiasm. Yes, I think we can begin today. But chores and breakfast first."

Roza never imagined feeling as energised as she did that morning, as they ate and saw to the animals.

"What are we going to do, then?" she demanded as soon as they'd finished.

"We are going to talk," Philoe replied.

She tried not to feel too disappointed, but this sounded like an enormous and boring let down.

"There are things you need to know and understand as we begin," the warlock went on. "You are curious enough that I think you'll find it interesting. I propose we go somewhere where we can sit and look over the valley."

Roza didn't want to delay the lesson by climbing back up to the stone shelf on the mountain spur, and so suggested the overlook at the edge of the plateau where the stream ran over the cliff. Once they were there, she made herself comfortable by sitting cross-legged on the boulder, while Philoe paced up and down beside it as they talked.

"The first lesson for a novice," the warlock began, "is to consider a basic question. I need you to open your mind and your heart to new, exciting, and potentially confusing possibilities. You must forget the ways in which you regarded yourself and life and the Universe and embrace a new outlook. Are you ready to do that?"

It wasn't hard for Roza to forget her old view of herself and life, since she had so few memories, but decided not to mention this fact again. "I am ready," she said. "What's the basic question?"

"The first question for us to address is this: where does magic come from? What do you think?"

"I've no idea. Why are you asking me? I thought you were supposed to be teaching me this stuff."

"Miss Roza, we need to start with where you are. We must discover what you think and know about magic already before we move on to the facts and truth about it. So, I ask you again, where do you think that magic comes from?"

"Again I say, I don't know. I suppose a few people are born with it. You said something about having an aptitude for it, so my guess is that a small number have the potential to develop an ability to use magic."

Philoe smiled. "Very good. I'm glad you've been listening to me. You are right that some people have minds so closed and preoccupied with the mundane and material world that they could never learn to use magic. They have little curiosity or imagination to ponder or consider the mysteries of the Universe. But the number with the potential to develop magical ability is somewhat larger than you think. I'm convinced that most people could learn magic if they set their minds to it."

"Most people? So having an aptitude for magic isn't all that special?"

"Ah, I didn't make myself clear enough. Most people could learn a little magic if they set their minds to it. With an enormous effort, and after long study and training, they might possibly manage a few most simple and basic spells. There is a range, a spectrum of magical potential, and the process of training novices is to discover their aptitude."

"So, if a warlock has a class of novices," Roza asked, "like when you were trained, is he or she looking for the one with the best magical aptitude to become their apprentice?"

"Very good, Miss Roza, and exactly so. The training of novices is designed to gauge the breadth and depth of their magical potential. This is what I will try to assess with you. In these current circumstances, I am willing to have a class of just one novice – you – because I don't need to compare you with anyone else. I will judge your potential based on my experience with all the other novices I have ever seen or worked with in the past."

Roza chewed her lip. "That sounds a bit daunting. Like I might fail, or something. Can you tell me how I'm doing so far, seeing as how I have this amazing and unique magical gift of Rejuvenate?" She'd been hoping that her secret ability might prove her to be automatically qualified to become the apprentice.

Philoe smiled at her. "You are doing very well, young lady. You are curious, enthusiastic, and have already shown a quick grasp of some principles. And what is more, you managed to receive my magical power, channel it through your gift and return it to rejuvenate my hands. Yes, I have high hopes that you will prove suitable, but that does not mean we can cut corners with your training."

Roza nodded. It was enough to get there in the end, even if magical training took a while.

"Now, to return to my original question," Philoe went on. "Where does magic come from? I have a very short answer for you, and a very long one. I propose to give you the short answer first."

She chuckled. "That makes sense."

"Where does magic come from? Short answer: it is a mystery."

"What?" Roza exclaimed. "You're joking. After all this,

you're telling me that the source of magic is so mysterious that even you warlocks don't know? I hope your long answer is better than your short one."

"I am not joking. I need to make clear to you that no warlock, not even the Master of the Warlocks, knows magic fully and completely. There are limits to our wisdom and understanding, and our first step in magical education is to acknowledge that our human capacities are finite. Some aspects of magic are forever beyond us, such that we always have grounds for humility, wonder, reverence and further seeking. Do you understand that?"

"All right, I understand. Don't get too big-headed about our magic because it will always be more powerful and mysterious than we can hope to box it up or nail it down. What's the second and longer answer?"

"Patience, my enthusiastic novice."

When Roza gave him a withering look, the warlock continued.

"The second and longer answer to where magic comes from is one that you will ponder for the rest of your life. As soon as I say this, it will dominate your thinking, your meditations, your training, your practice, your studies for the rest of your days. Are you ready for this?"

Roza rolled her eyes at him. "Hurry up and say it."

Philoe cleared his throat. "I'll say this as simply as I can. Magic flows from beauty."

Roza's jaw dropped. She hadn't expected that. "What? Beauty. Magic flows from beauty. I hope you don't mean that magic flows from gorgeous boys and pretty girls, otherwise I've had it."

Philoe smiled. "You are correct, young lady, that beauty is far more than physical attractiveness. In fact, the rest of this first magic lesson of ours will be devoted to examining what beauty is. Please tell me something that you consider to be beautiful."

Roza said the first thing that came into her head, mainly

because she was gazing at a vast panorama of them. "Mountains."

Philoe the warlock turned to gaze out at the peaks surrounding the valley as well. "Very good. What is beautiful about them?"

Roza hesitated. "Um … they're huge, and majestic, and solid, and heavy–"

"You're just listing adjectives about them," Philoe interrupted. "What makes them beautiful to you? In your mind and heart, what is the beauty of mountains?"

Roza thought about that. She wanted to give him a really good answer. "I love it that at different times of day, the changing sunlight picks out different light and shadows and colours on the mountains. There's always something new to see with mountains, as though you haven't seen them before."

To Roza's relief, the warlock looked impressed. "Excellent. Name something else you find beautiful, please."

She looked down to where the stream Torrence tumbled over the edge of the cliff beside her. "It is beautiful to me the way the sunlight picks out the colours of the rainbow in the fine mist and spray of a waterfall. The water is constantly moving and changing, and yet the colours in the spray seem timeless and eternal."

Philoe nodded. "Next, something other than nature, please."

This floored her. She'd been about to say the fragility and short life of a flower in a meadow. What else was beautiful? "Um … a painting?"

"A painting of what?"

She was about to say a country landscape, but then realised this would be too close to nature. So, she blurted out, "A person."

He gave her a sly look. "Are you back to your handsome boys and pretty girls again?"

Roza had been thinking of a youthful, attractive person in a painting, but denied it. "Not necessarily. It could be a painting of an older and weather-beaten person that captures their character and experience."

The warlock's eyebrows rose. "Very well, we'll come back to people in a minute. Can you think of anything beautiful that isn't nature or people?"

Roza was stumped. While she was racking her brains, Philoe suggested, "How about music?"

"Oh, no, I'm not musical at all," she said at once. "Can't play anything or sing a note. Forget that one."

"No, I'm sorry, Roza, but we can't forget music. There is so much to learn from it: melody and tunes, harmony and discord, rhythm and pace, structure and sequence, volume and tone. I see we'll need many extra lessons to explore the intricacies of music."

Roza swallowed hard. Oh no. She was mortified that Philoe had discovered one important aspect of her magical education where she was severely lacking. Would this jeopardise her chances of becoming an apprentice, just because she couldn't hold a tune? She wanted to change the subject quickly.

"What about friendship and love?" she asked. "Aren't they beautiful?"

"Now we're back to people again," Philoe answered, "but all right, let's talk about friendship and love. Tell me something beautiful in relationships."

"Like in a family, where parents sacrifice something important to them for the sake of their children, or the other way around." As soon as she said this, the feeling struck her again of dis-satisfaction with the previous life she couldn't remember. Why had she said, 'the other way around'? A child sacrificing something important for the sake of their parents? How often did that happen, and had that been her situation, because life in families shouldn't be like that, should it?

But Philoe was replying to her, and she'd missed what he said. "Are you listening to me, Roza? I said, what sort of sacrifice?"

"Oh, um, things like money, to provide schooling for them, and to care for them when they're sick. To provide opportunities, and freedom to choose, and things like that."

"So, there is family love. Other examples?"

"Having a best friend, someone your age. A brother or sister, or friend from the schoolroom. Someone you've grown up with and known for years. Someone who understands and accepts you, where there's honesty and trust and laughter and sharing your dreams." The more Roza described this, the more she felt an inner ache that she'd had a best friend like this. Had she?

"So, family love and friendship," Philoe was summing up, "and of course there's also romantic love and sexual attraction, but we won't spend time on those last two this morning."

Roza was relieved about that.

"I've given you enough to think about for one morning," Philoe went on, "so we'll leave it there for now. Before next time, please contemplate different examples of beauty." And with that, the warlock strode away back towards the cave.

The lesson had ended rather abruptly. The thought occurred to Roza that the subject matter had suddenly become uncomfortable for the warlock. Was he embarrassed?

He was a middle-aged man, and she was a teenage girl. Was it right that the two of them stayed together? What would anyone in the town think when they found out? Philoe had never implied anything romantic or sexual between them, but – since recognising her gift – he'd behaved entirely properly, like a gentleman. Just because they were male and female, with an age difference between them, did that prevent them from having any sort of friendship? No, they could be friends, and colleagues, and work together, and study magic, and live out their lives in the same place, without anything else complicating their relationship, couldn't they?

Roza sat on the boulder and gazed out over the valley, thinking, until her legs and hips became stiff and numb, and she got down. As she stretched, she surveyed the fields far below her and spotted again a small figure working his slow way across the ground.

It looked like the same boy she'd seen before on the mountain spur. Could it be? And he still seemed to be searching, scanning the ground in front of him and on either side. It suddenly occurred to her that this boy might be looking for her, the missing seventeen-year-old girl from town, looking for boot-prints or tracks for what had become of her.

She couldn't work out how she felt about that. A warm feeling, that she was missed, cared for, wanted? Or sad, that she'd lost all her memories of her family, friends and her old life, and how could she recover those again?

She shivered, turned away, and wandered through the trees of the orchard for a while instead.

Helena made her slow way across Albany's town square, supporting herself with her stick in one hand, and leaning on the arm of a girl from the Mermaid Inn. It wasn't far from the inn to the Town Hall, but these days she needed the help more than ever. She scowled at herself for walking like an old woman, but Rozabella's continued absence was making her heart the worst it had ever been.

Her progress today was also slowed by the number of townsfolk who recognised her, wanting to stop and talk with her, hear about Arthur, enquire after Rozabella, and so on. She reminded herself that they meant well, and the more people who kept an eye out for her missing daughter the better. But the Reeve was waiting for her, and she hated to be late for an appointment.

She thanked the maid from the inn once the girl had helped her up the Town Hall's front steps, and no sooner had she tottered into the building than she was conducted into the Reeve's office. Late as she was, he was waiting for her, but he showed no sign of impatience. He was an older man with thinning silver-grey hair, and he looked to have put on weight around his middle.

"It's been too long since we've seen you here in town, Judge Helena," the Reeve greeted her with a handshake. "Your health is as good as it can be, I hope?"

Helena seated herself as soon as she could release the Reeve's hand and before being invited to. Her breathing was becoming laboured, and she needed to get this over with.

"No, my health is not good, I'm afraid, and Arthur struggles to cope with his blindness, but thank you for letting me see you and for asking about us."

The Reeve moved to sit behind his desk, his good humour seeming to evaporate into sympathetic concern. "Not at all, this town owes you much. I was so sorry to hear the news about your Rozabella, so what more can we do for you?"

Helena sighed. "It's the very worst thing to happen. You can guess how much Arthur and I depend on our daughter to look after us. She's such a good girl: strong, capable, willing, not complaining. We would struggle without her, but I feel guilty that a girl her age is confined to caring for her ailing parents. It's over a week now since Roza went missing. She was chopping logs in the forest, and I found her axe, saw, barrow and cloak in a clearing, but no sign of her. Arthur and I can't conduct a search, so we've told the town guards about this. And we've enlisted one of Roza's schoolroom friends to help us find her."

The Reeve was frowning. "I can't believe that your

Rozabella could just disappear. Because what could have happened to her? Has she come into town? We will continue to search everywhere in Albany for her, and yes, of course, dispatch guards and trackers to the forest to search for her."

"Thank you," Helena murmured, "but I'm afraid we've tried everything we can think of, with little success. Roza's friend, Jorxy, said he found tracks leading eastwards from the clearing where Roza disappeared, but hasn't found anything more. To be honest, I've come to you because we're feeling desperate."

There was a silence between them, and Helena watched the Reeve's face. He was staring into the polished surface of his desk, but his eyes were unfocused, seeing miles away. He seemed too lost in thought even to remember she was there. Helena cleared her throat, and the Reeve gradually raised his eyes.

"My apologies, Judge Helena, please forgive me. I'm sorry I'm distracted, but it may prove fortuitous that you've come to me today. I've received some news, and it's almost too dreadful and terrifying for me to grasp. Here you are, asking for my help, when the circumstances dictate that I'm sitting here in desperate need of your help too."

Helena's heart gave a disconcerting jolt. The Reeve's words — for the first time in a week — diverted her thoughts away from her own troubles. What did he mean by 'too dreadful and terrifying to grasp'? She registered now how drawn and worried he looked, and it wasn't about her daughter. "What news is this, and what help could I give you?"

He let out a long breath and lowered his voice. "Before I answer that, may I ask you a question? Have you become desperate enough about your missing Rozabella to consider using magic to find her?"

Helena's frown deepened. "Magic? Surely you don't

mean … the warlock?”

The Reeve couldn't hold her gaze but looked away. “I'm glad you're here, Helena, because I need someone to talk with about this, and there's no one on the Town Committee more experienced and trustworthy than you. I'd value your opinion and advice, because when this becomes known, it will cause widespread fear and panic.”

Helena's heart couldn't take any more distress as she said, “What is it? What has happened?”

The Reeve took a deep breath. “You know we have informants out in the towns and cities of the plains to bring us news of developments across the Empire. This morning a messenger arrived from Gorge City, reporting news he had learned in the Palace of the Earl of the Plains.”

Helena nodded. “What is Lord Vallance up to?”

The Reeve shook his head. “It's not about Lord Vallance. But it is being whispered around the Earl's Palace that the … um … Emperor … is moving.”

The Reeve held her eye, and the coldness of dread spread from her heart throughout Helena's insides. “The … E-Emperor?” she stuttered. “Is he coming this way?”

The Reeve gave a slow and deliberate nod. “Apparently, a couple of days ago, he made a definite change of course in his imperial progress. He turned to come in our direction … almost as though he'd been summoned.”

Helena struggled to swallow the air down into her lungs. Her thoughts turned immediately to Arthur's despairing words that the Dragon could come and finish them off. Had her husband inadvertently summoned the Emperor?

But all personal blame and guilt aside, the news that would terrify every soul in Albany was becoming real. This was their end: the doom of their town and everyone in it.

She spluttered to maintain her last shreds of logic and reason. “But … but we still have hope, and defences. The warlock. Yes, we must send for Philoe the warlock. He's helped us in the past and can do so again."

"I agree," replied the Reeve. "But he's ancient, and it's so long since anyone has seen him. Can we be sure that he's even still alive?"

"He has to be," Helena replied firmly. "We need him, and the town has always provided for him. Now is the time he must repay our trust in him, and save us, because we have nothing else."

"Thank you for confirming my thoughts in this matter, Judge Helena. And I was thinking that if our warlock manages to resolve our Emperor problem, then we should ask him to locate your Rozabella for you as well."

CHAPTER FIFTEEN

By the time the sun had lowered into the late afternoon, Roza had a list of questions she wanted to ask Philoe. She found him feeding the chickens and decided to disturb him there because otherwise she wouldn't be able to sleep.

"Excuse me, Mister Warlock Sir," she began, remembering to be polite. "I've been thinking about beauty, like you asked me to, but I'm a bit stuck over what I'm supposed to do with it."

Philoe straightened up and regarded her through the wooden fence of the chicken run. "Can this wait until tomorrow?"

"No, sir." She shook her head emphatically. "I won't be able to sleep tonight unless you sort this out for me."

"Give me a few minutes, and I'll meet you on the bench in the orchard."

Roza trotted off and made herself comfortable on one end of the bench while the sun cast slanting shadows through the trees. True to his word, Philoe joined her promptly, drying his hands on a cloth.

"Beauty," Roza said, before he'd even sat down. "Am I supposed to be thinking about it, or noticing it, or doing something more with it?"

Philoe sighed. "You really can't wait to get on with your next lessons, can you? I suppose I should be grateful for your enthusiasm."

Roza waited expectantly while he gathered his thoughts.

"Noticing beauty is an excellent start, Roza. Too many people simply miss it, walk past it, or take it for granted, wherever it occurs. Train yourself to notice it as much as you can. But yes, after that, there is more you need to do. You need to learn to appreciate it. To admire it, to revel in it. You need to let beauty touch you inside, to warm your heart. You need to drink beauty down deeply into your soul, because that is where it will kindle the spark and flame of magic inside you."

Roza stared at him, hardly understanding what he was on about. "Drink beauty down deeply into my soul. Right." She decided to move onto her next question before she got lost in the answers to the first one. "And I've been wondering that if magic flows from beauty, is there dark or evil magic, then, that flows from ugliness?"

Philoe drew in a sharp breath between his teeth. "A perceptive question, Miss Roza, and I can see you've been thinking long and hard about this all afternoon. The answer is complicated. Yes, magic is a tool, an instrument, a power, an energy, but it is not neutral. Since it flows from beauty, it tends towards the good rather than the bad. But if magic is misused by warlocks, is it the magic that turns evil, or should we pass judgment on the warlocks themselves who have twisted its beauty?"

"Hmm," Roza replied, not really understanding. "It's just that I've been thinking about things like the BodyCrusher Spell and the Bindweed ropes. They cause pain and incapacitate people, so I don't understand how those flow from beauty."

At once she caught the glare in Philoe's eye, his fury at being reminded of these things. Fearing she'd spoiled her chance of him answering her questions, she went on quickly, "Oh, I'm not getting at you at all." Well, not much, she added to herself. "I've forgiven you for everything you did to me, Warlock Philoe, but I want to learn as much as I can to be the best possible novice and trainee for you."

He grunted. "As I said, magic tends towards the good, but that doesn't stop warlocks from twisting it towards ugly things some of the time."

"But can you explain to me, please, if those of us who

use magic are supposed to occupy all our thoughts with beauty, how these painful things were created, or why they were invented?"

Philoe leaned forward, resting his elbows on his knees, and studied the grass between his boots. "A reasonable question, young lady. The BodyCrusher Spell and Bindweed ropes were developed for the exercise of justice and judgement. Sometimes a warlock became out of control and needed to be restrained. Fellow warlocks might be required to hold and contain him, render him unconscious, withdraw for a time his ability to use magic. The pain attached to them was intended as a deterrent to misbehaviour." He looked up at her. "But as you see, Miss Roza, it is too easy for warlocks to become a law unto themselves. Which is why our actions and attitudes need to be checked and corrected by others. As you did for me, my stubborn and forthright Rozabella." He offered her a grim smile.

She didn't know how to answer that, and found she was twisting her fingers together. "And what about the Forgetery Spell? Why is there something to mess about with someone's memories?"

Philoe sighed again. "That was originally intended as a kindness and a mercy. I realise that spell has ruined your knowledge of your former life, and I've apologised for that, and we'll do what we can to restore your memories. But sometimes as warlocks we encounter those who have suffered a terrible trauma, a crushing grief and sadness. People beg us for a way to forget what has happened to them, to put their past behind them and start again with a new life. So, we devised the Forgetery Spell to enable a clean slate for those who wish it. But again, it can be misused."

Roza was beginning to regret starting this topic of discussion, because the misuse of magic clearly troubled Philoe both deeply and personally. "Thank you for explaining this to me, Philoe," she said gently, "because I really appreciate it." She offered him what she hoped was a forgiving smile, and he seemed to accept it. Then she tilted her head. "Can I ask you something else, that might be a bit cheeky?"

He narrowed his eyes at her. "That depends on how cheeky."

"Well … if magic flows from beauty, then where does beauty come from?"

Philoe burst out laughing, and it was wonderful that the tension between them was broken. "A cheeky question indeed, and one worthy of a novice well beyond her first day of lessons."

Roza grinned. "Well, you asked me where magic comes from, and then said, beauty. So, you must expect me to ask you, where does beauty come from?"

"And there, Miss Roza, you have a question that divides the warlock community. I can offer you three answers that different warlocks will give you, and you must decide for yourself which you choose to believe."

"Very good," said Roza. "What are my three options?"

There was a twinkle in Philoe's eye as he said, "The first option I think you will like. Some warlocks insist that just as magic flows from beauty, then beauty flows from magic."

It was Roza's turn to erupt in laughter and then she rolled her eyes at him. "What? You mean that magic and beauty, and beauty and magic, are just like some never-ending circle that keeps going round and round and round?"

"Exactly," Philoe chuckled. "I thought you'd like that one. That the mysteries of magic and beauty are constantly replenishing and reinforcing each other to keep life and the Universe in motion. A variation upon it is that they might instead be a spiral, that magic and beauty are either growing or diminishing, in a widening or narrowing spiral, depending upon whether the warlock is feeling hopeful or depressed that morning. What do you think of that one?"

Roza gave him a sideways and dubious smile. "What are my other two options, please?"

"Option number two," Philoe began, "states that beauty is an external and objective truth in the Universe. Namely that beauty exists as an everlasting attribute of creation, brought into being by the Universe itself, or a Creator God, or gods, who themselves are beautiful. In this option, each and every single flower that grows in the depths of a forest, unseen by anyone, and then fading away, can still be intrinsically beautiful. The smallest and dimmest star in the night sky, unnoticed and unappreciated, still has its own beauty in the way it twinkles. Beauty is an inherent property of nature, out there, eternal, and infusing the whole Universe."

Roza sat there somewhat stunned by Philoe's eloquent little speech, and so said at last, "Okaaaay. And the last option?"

He drew a deep breath and said, "The third and final explanation for beauty is that it is an internal and subjective matter, entirely dependent on us living things to appreciate it. So, a sunset is only beautiful because we observe it and call it so. Otherwise, it is only the changing colours of light in the clouds and sky. Each flower and star, if unobserved by us, is simply a matter of biology or physics, and of no consequence to the beauty of the Universe. What gives power and magic and beauty to the Universe is that we living, conscious and sentient beings have appeared who can give meaning, wisdom and purpose to it all."

"Well, I'm glad I asked that question," Roza snorted. "Not complicated at all then, is it?"

Philoe smiled. "So, do you have a preference? The magic and beauty circle? The external and objective truth, or the internal and subjective appreciation? I'd be interested to hear what you think."

Roza blew out her cheeks, feeling completely put on the spot. There was so much she needed to learn and understand. But that was okay because she still had a lifetime to learn it. Or a few lifetimes if she could keep on rejuvenating herself. She thought grimly that it might take more than a few lifetimes to grasp this.

Philoe was waiting for her thoughts.

"Can I stick with a bit of all three?" she ventured.

He laughed. "Very wise. Hedge your bets. You can always come back to this later and see what you think then."

"And what about you, then, Mister wise, clever and all-knowing Warlock. Which of the three options do you choose?"

His eyebrows rose. "Since you ask, I'll tell you. I don't rule out the other two, but I find myself favouring option two, that beauty is an external and objective truth in the nature of the Universe. The first one confuses me, because how did either magic or beauty begin, to start their rotating circle? And the third one strikes me as the height of arrogance to claim that the source of all beauty is down to us. Given the vastness of the world – and in my travels I've seen only a little of it – and the intricacy of the moon, planets and stars, we seem very small living creatures to be at the centre of it all. The Universe is grander and more complex, more detailed and awe-inspiring, more diverse and beautiful than we will ever know or understand. So, I'm happy for beauty and magic to keep me humble and grateful that I can play a small part in the history of it all. And that is what I believe I have done, in finding you and discovering your gift."

She stared at him. "You feel you've achieved something important in identifying my gift?"

"Undoubtedly. It seems to me now that the Universe has kept me alive these last four hundred years precisely so

I could live long enough to meet you. Don't you think it an immeasurable tragedy if you'd lived out your normal life completely ignorant of the power you have to rejuvenate people? Wouldn't that seem a terrible loss and waste? When you could make such a difference to so many people's lives, to the Empire and to the world?"

Chills had washed their way across Roza's skin as Philoe said this. "Um, well, thank you, but I'm not sure I'm ready to make a massive difference to the lives of everyone in the world, if it's all the same with you."

He reached and patted her shoulder. "Don't worry about any of that, young Roza. It's my job to try and make you ready, and I'm very encouraged by your start with magic today. My guess is that your aptitude for magic more than matches the power and wonder of the unique gift within you. Please be reassured and confident that as time goes on, you will rise to the challenges you face. You're already keeping me on my toes, badgering me with questions, and for that I thank you. Well, it's getting dark and cold, so I'm going in."

Roza looked about. To her surprise, night was indeed falling around them, the gloom gathering between the trees and a breeze rustling the leaves. When Philoe stood up, she remained seated. "I think I'll stay out here for a while," she said. "You know, to enjoy the beauty of the evening and to watch the stars come out."

Philoe nodded and walked off into the cave. Once he was out of sight, she stood up and wandered back to the cliff edge and the boulder beside the waterfall. She sat on the top and breathed deeply of the sweet night air. The gentle gushing of the water made a soothing backdrop to the calm and quiet fall of twilight. An owl hooted in the trees behind her, and bats were swooping out for their night-time hunt. In the town below, lamps were kindled to usher tired workers home behind curtained windows to warm hearths and loving homes. The last rays of daylight above the mountains in the west painted fading colours across the ribbons of wispy clouds there. In the east, above the plain, the first and brightest stars were announcing the coming of their unnumbered host to fill the night.

Now she understood why Warlock Philoe lived here. It was a beautiful place. Magic would flow well here. If he, and she, needed to study and absorb and appreciate beauty in all its forms, then where better to do so than up here, away from the hubbub and distractions of everyday life in the town? Yes, she liked it here. Wherever she'd lived before, it could hardly have been better than this plateau. Maybe here, after all, she could find her peace, and purpose, and destiny.

It was only as the night cold seeped through her clothes that she too said goodnight to the stars and headed for her bed in the cave.

But as she tried to fall asleep, she couldn't escape an ominous dread that her peace and tranquillity were about to be shattered.

CHAPTER SIXTEEN

The next morning, Roza was walking along the clifftop near the path up from Albany when she spotted an unfamiliar man climbing towards them. She froze in alarm, wondering whether to hide, but decided she needed to make contact with the outside world soon. So, she waited where the path came over the edge of the plateau until the man was in earshot.

"Good morning," she called. "Can I help you?"

The man stopped, startled. He peered up at her, shielding his eyes. His face and clothes were sweaty from the climb, and he panted for breath. "I bring a message … from the Reeve … of Albany," he gasped. "I need to see … the warlock."

"Yes, he's here," Roza replied. "I'll take you to him."

She waited until he reached her and recovered his breath. The man fidgeted with the hem of his jacket, anxious either about meeting her, or the warlock, or because of something to do with his message.

"Who are you?" he asked.

She hesitated, but then said, "My name is Rozabella, and the warlock is training me in magic." An unexpected surge of pride rose within her as she described what she was doing here and saw the man's eyes widen in awe and respect.

He held out a hand. "I'm honoured to meet you, Rozabella," he said, and she shook his hand.

"Come," she said, and led him along the path towards the cave. It was a strange and welcome feeling, to have a place in the world, a role, a title, and one that a stranger recognised and admired. She liked it.

"Philoe," she called into the cave. "We have a visitor

with a message from the Reeve of Albany."

The warlock emerged into the morning sunshine, rolling up a scroll of parchment.

The messenger gaped at him. "Warlock Philoe," he gasped, "you look … well."

Roza glanced at the warlock and caught his eye.

"Yes, I am well," Philoe replied. "Better than I've been in a long time." He sneaked a wink at Roza, who suppressed her smile. "What can we do for you?"

The messenger wrung his hands and shifted on his feet. "I bring you an urgent and vitally important message, Master Warlock, from the Reeve of Albany. I'm asked to tell you we have reports that the … um … Emperor is coming."

Philoe turned to Roza and held her gaze, while the messenger looked between them. Was this because Kerenzi had called for him, or had the Emperor been coming anyway?

"Please tell me everything you know about this," Philoe asked the messenger.

"The Reeve receives regular news from the towns and cities of the plains," the messenger replied. "He considers it wise to keep abreast of the Emperor's movements as His Majesty makes his progress to collect his taxes. A messenger from Gorge City reports that a few days ago he changed direction to come towards us. We fear that he will arrive here in only a day or two." The man grasped hold of Philoe's arm. "Warlock, please, we beg you, you must help us."

Philoe patted the messenger's hand and loosened his grip. "I will come at once. I will do what I can, and Rozabella, as your next lesson, you could come too and watch what happens. We discussed visiting Albany, so if you wish, we can use this visit in that way also."

Roza nodded. She wasn't sure she was ready to discover what her former life had been, but as Philoe said, it might be a good opportunity to find out all she could while they were down there.

Philoe re-entered the cave to collect a walking staff, and Roza became conscious that she had no personal possessions or belongings other than the clothes in which she stood. It was hardly necessary for her to prepare for a trip away or make herself ready to meet any family.

The messenger was keen to start back towards the town at once, and edged away along the path, until Philoe and Roza followed along behind him. She found herself wondering what it would be like in the town, of which she had no memory. She'd become used to the natural beauty of the plateau: the grass and trees, the waterfall and stream, the hillsides by day and the stars by night, the silence except for the animals, birds and steady rush of water. Would it be dirty, noisy and crowded? How would she cope with everyone looking at them, the famous warlock striding into Albany, with herself as the uncertain teenage girl alongside? She knew none of the people there but would wonder constantly whether any of them recognised her.

They started off along the dusty path down the cliff, as she had done with Kerenzi days ago. Where was the spirit lord now, and was it really his call that had magically summoned the Emperor? The Emperor – was it safe even to think the word 'Dragon'? He was apparently still a day or two away, but her limbs trembled at the prospect that he was approaching, with only Philoe to stand in his way.

"What are you going to do about the Emperor?" Roza whispered as they walked along.

Philoe heaved a breath. "I've had time to consider and prepare my options since his last visit this way. In recent years, I've concentrated my studies and efforts on trying to avoid him coming here in the first place. It's so much easier to distract or divert him while he's still at some distance, rather than to negotiate, plead or threaten him face to face."

"You've met him face to face?" Roza was shocked. "And tried to threaten him? What is he like?"

Philoe's face was grim. "Yes, I've met him on various occasions, I forget how many. And yes, we've matched our magical wits and powers a few times, with better or worse results. I think he respects me by now and is wary of risking hurt or shame to himself. But I pray it doesn't come to that. He is truly terrible to encounter. Huge, ancient, arrogant, wily, vain, terrifying – whatever nightmares wake you screaming, add those to his list."

Roza swallowed hard. It was all she could do to keep walking downwards instead of turning, running and hiding in the farthest depths of the cave. "But … um … do you have a plan?"

To her immense relief, Philoe nodded. "Yes, we need to be within the boundaries of the town, and then I will cast a powerful protective spell. It has a good range, and I have high hopes that it will be effective. In any case, I consider it the best option we have." He gave her what he clearly hoped was a reassuring smile. "Now, if you will forgive me, I need some silence to think. I want to run through the spell in my mind and rehearse its components to be sure I get it right."

"Of course." Then she added, "I trust you as a great warlock, Philoe, and all the people of Albany have faith in you."

He pulled a face, but she hoped he felt encouraged by her confidence.

The only sounds were the tramp of their feet on the path, and the messenger didn't dare to disturb their concentration. Roza kept looking around, intrigued by how the cliff, the valley and the town looked different with every few minutes of their descent. The dry rock and dust of the upper path changed into shrubs and bushes along the way, and then into trees and grass. The way underfoot became softer and more level, from stones to beaten earth. The air became warmer and stuffy compared with the cool, clear breezes of the plateau.

Their path emerged through a stretch of forest, and they turned right onto a farm track. The first buildings appeared beside their route: barns, sheds, outhouses and cottages. Ahead Roza could see what she'd studied from the edge of the plateau, the town's walls and fences. On the east, towards the gap in the mountains and the entrance to their valley, there was a stone wall, but here in the south there was no more than a wooden stockade to mark the boundary of the town itself.

Roza drew in a shaky breath, and kept her gaze on the ground, as the messenger ushered her and the warlock in through the town gate, guards lining the way on both sides.

"I need somewhere high," Philoe said at once. "A rooftop or tower. The nearest you have, please."

The messenger consulted the captain of the guards, who indicated a lookout tower a short way along the stockade. Philoe and Roza started in that direction, and the messenger said, "I must let the Reeve know you've arrived," and sped off.

They reached the tower and began climbing the wooden steps, the captain clearing the way before them. At the top was an open platform, where guards could survey the vicinity in all directions.

"Clear the tower, please," Philoe ordered. "Just Roza and me up here."

The captain dismissed the guards, who fell over themselves to escape down the steps, afraid of being anywhere near when the magic started. The captain was last to leave the platform, and they heard him tramp back down to the street. A crowd of townsfolk had gathered to line the surrounding area, watching them from a safe and respectful distance.

Roza felt honoured to be here. Instinctively she reached

for Philoe's hand and squeezed it.

"Thank you," he breathed. "You encourage me more than you know, Rozabella. I'm comforted that you're here."

There was a cool breeze across the lookout platform, and from their raised position, Philoe pointed out to her the view across the town and its eastern wall, through the narrow gap between the mountains and out towards the distant plain.

It was facing this direction that the warlock positioned himself and said to Roza, "Stand back."

She retreated to the platform's rear corner and Philoe's spellcasting began.

There was much gesticulating and crying out, the chanting of words in a language Roza didn't know. An unexpected tiredness crept over her, and she fought against it. What was going on? What spell was Philoe casting?

The warlock's spell continued with a stretching of the arms and back and legs, followed by a slumping of the shoulders, and much yawning. The weariness and listlessness within Roza grew and she struggled to stay awake and alert. She wanted to watch, learn and follow what Philoe was doing, not fall asleep where she stood. She shook, pinched, and kicked herself to stay in the present moment.

At last, a crashing wave of tiredness seemed to break over her and then pass. She stirred, as though waking from a deep and restful sleep, and found Philoe leaning heavily against the platform's wooden rail. She hurried over to him, took his arm, and helped him to stand back upright.

"Are you all right?"

"Yes, thank you, Roza," he murmured. "A great spell like that always drains and wearies me, but if I can sit down for a few minutes then I'll soon recover."

She assisted him across the lookout platform and

helped him to sit on the top steps leading down to the street. She squeezed herself in next to him and supported him with an arm across his back.

"What was that spell? What did you cast?"

He glanced sideways at her with a small smile. "Tell me what you experienced, Roza. It helps me to know how it felt to you."

"I felt very tired," she said. "A weariness and a listlessness came over me such that I thought I might fall asleep. I pinched and kicked myself to stay awake, until it all ended with something like a wave of tiredness passing over me and away."

"Excellent." Philoe beamed. "It sounds as though it all worked correctly, then."

"What was it? Does it have a name?"

"It does indeed. It's called the Ennuissance Spell and is designed to make the whole town of Albany seem as boring as possible. The weariness and listlessness you described has the effect of making the target not be bothered with us. Coming here and dealing with us is simply too much effort, whereas anything else will be easier and more straightforward."

Roza couldn't stop a grin. "You mean you've just bored the Emperor so much that he won't be bothered with us?"

Philoe smiled back. "Exactly. Never underestimate the power of boredom and of not being bothered, my girl." They both laughed, and it felt a welcome release for her tension and fear. He tapped her knee, and they stood up. He indicated for her to lead their way back down to the street.

When they emerged from the base of the lookout tower, the guard captain looked enquiringly at them. "Was that it? Is it done?"

"Yes, my good captain," Philoe replied, "I believe that my spell has worked effectively. Could we trouble you for something simple to eat and drink?"

The captain snapped his fingers at a couple of the guards, and they rushed forward with water bottles. Another walked up with a small bag of biscuits. "We could arrange for some meat and wine if you prefer," the captain offered.

Philoe held up a hand. "These will be sufficient, thank you."

Roza took a swig from a water bottle and tried not to pull a face. The town's water held no comparison with the sweet, clear liquid that poured down Torrence's fall. The biscuits were dry, but they were sweet.

"Roza!" A voice called out from the side of the street. "Roza, is that you?"

A chill sank into her stomach and clenched all her insides. For days she'd been wondering about being recognised by someone in the town, and the working of the spell had driven it out of her mind. But now here it was, and she wasn't ready for it.

She scanned the townsfolk, trying to identify who had spoken. She didn't know any of them. But an ugly boy about her age was walking forward, skinny, with red-brown hair and scruffy clothes.

He was peering at her face. "Roza, it is you," he exclaimed. "My brother Rufus ran from his post at the warlock gate to find me and tell me he'd seen you. You've been missing for over a week, and we've been searching for you, and here you are at last. Rufus said he'd find you first." His lop-sided face grinned broadly at her.

Roza surveyed him and swallowed before speaking. "Um, I'm sorry, but I don't know who you are."

The boy's delight collapsed. "Roza, it's me, Jorxy. We went to the same classes together in the schoolroom."

She shook her head. "Listen, I'm sorry, Jorxy, but I don't remember you. You see, I've lost all my memories–"

"What?" Jorxy looked affronted now. "You don't remember me?" He glanced sideways at Philoe the warlock standing beside her. "Have you become so high and mighty you've forgotten your poor little friends from the schoolroom? Not good enough for you any more, are we?"

"No, listen to me, Jorxy, that's not it at all." Her anger was rising to counter his, and she struggled to maintain her self-control. "Something happened to me – like you said, I went missing. We think I must have hit my head, and it affected my memory, so I forgot my name, where I live, any family, my friends–"

"You think you must have hit your head?" Jorxy scoffed. He jabbed a finger at the warlock. "Is that what he told you to say? It's more likely he cast a spell on you, kidnapped you, and now he's bewitched you. How else can you lose all your memories and forget everything?"

Roza longed to deny it, but unfortunately it had been the warlock's spell that had done this, however much Philoe regretted it. The hesitation of them both to answer the accusation rippled through the surrounding crowd, and Roza wished this confrontation weren't happening in public. She longed to explain everything, but they weren't giving her the chance. "No, listen, Jorxy, I hit my head, and the warlock helped me–"

But the boy had turned to Philoe, almost poking him in the chest. "Is this something you've done, warlock? What have you done to her?"

"If you will listen to me," Philoe thundered, "then I will explain this to you. But it is a long story–"

Jorxy cut him off. "We don't need to listen to you, warlock. We can see what's happened, right before our eyes. Our Roza goes missing and then turns up with her memories wiped. What did you do, kidnap her? Make sure she can't remember who she is?"

Roza turned and walked away. She couldn't answer these questions, not without making it all sound much worse. Philoe was right beside her, and she said, "Can we go home?"

"I think that would be wise," Philoe agreed, as the two of them hurried along the street, away from the lookout tower and back to the gate in the town stockade. The crowd was surging forward behind them, their presence a menacing tide, with the boy Jorxy at their head.

Before they reached the gate, the guard captain caught up with them and turned them around. "Just one minute, if you please." He planted himself before them, blocking their escape from the town. "Do I understand this correctly? This young lady has gone missing, and now turns up here, and this warlock has wiped her memory? Are you a captive, miss? Is he forcing you to do anything against your will? If you wish it, we will rescue you from him."

"No, captain, no," Roza said at once. "Thank you, but I'm all right. The warlock rescued me from the forest after I forgot everything, and he's looked after me. He offered to train me as his novice, and I've agreed to that freely. It's true that I don't remember anything, but we're working to put that right. I'll return to Albany soon and piece together who I am, my family and friends. But for now, I need you to let us both exit through this town gate so I can return to the warlock's cave up in the hills."

The captain's eyes flicked between Roza and Philoe, whose decision not to say anything was probably wise for fear of making the situation worse. The whole truth was too long to explain, and the crowd clearly had no patience for that.

"Very well, miss, if you say so." The captain stood aside.

Roza glanced back as they hurried through the stockade gate and wished she hadn't. Jorxy's eyes were blazing after her, his anger and betrayal leeching into the other bystanders. If this was what Albany was like, she never wanted to come here again.

"I thought your spell was supposed to make the town boring," Roza muttered as they started off along the farm track. "If that's what 'boring' is like, I don't think I want to see 'interesting'."

Philoe gave a grim laugh. "Only boring to the Emperor. Too small and petty to be bothered about. But I'm very sorry that you had to experience that. We'll need to think and plan carefully about how to introduce you back into the town of Albany properly next time."

"But the news of my reappearance will spread. The Reeve's messenger, that boy Jorxy, the guard captain, and anyone else who was there and listening knows that my name is Rozabella and that I'm with you. I'm no longer lost, because they know I'm alive and up there at your cave on the plateau. If any family or friends want to find me, they can, and I'll only venture back down there when I'm ready."

They walked in silence, and Roza was glad Philoe knew where to turn off the farm track and up their path to the plateau, because she was too preoccupied to notice.

Had that ugly boy, Jorxy, really been her friend? It sounded like it. Couldn't she manage anyone better than him? If she'd chosen any family or friend as the first to recognise her, he would have been last on her list. He wasn't just ugly, but also scruffy, poor, suspicious, demanding and short-tempered.

Then a thought occurred. Had he been that boy she'd seen searching on the mountain spur, and then in the fields below the waterfall? So, he had been looking for her, for signs of her disappearance, and she felt glad now she hadn't called or waved.

The midday sun was warm, and the path climbed from the grass and trees up towards their scrubby rock and dust above, and they were sweating.

A movement high to her left caught Roza's eye and she glanced up at a shimmer near the sun.

Without warning, Philoe was lifted into the air beside her, and then his body slammed against the rock wall to their right.

Roza froze in shock.

As Philoe fell towards the ground he started casting a spell, but then a jet of fire blasted into his chest.

Roza threw up her arms to protect her face from the searing heat. The blaze of it blinded her, and she was thrown backwards by a deafening roar of thunder.

She could barely see, but the fire was followed by a bolt of lightning slamming into the warlock's body, hurling him back against the cliff wall. Then a spearhead of ice impaled his body to the rock, before he fell onto the rocky path.

Roza scrambled up and dived towards Philoe's body, but before she could reach him, he was lifted again.

"No! No! Stop!" she screamed.

Her eyes were seared as wave after wave of fire and lightning and ice rammed into the warlock, battering him against the cliff. As soon as he fell back towards the ground again, she ran forward and caught him.

"Stop, no, stop!" she wailed. And she must have got herself in the way, for the magical attack ceased.

She jerked her head around in time to see Kerenzi the spirit lord glide down and land on the path.

CHAPTER SEVENTEEN

S top, Kerenzi, stop," Roza yelled. "What have you done?"

The spirit lord stood on the edge of the path, his eyes still blazing with the violence he'd unleashed, but with a satisfied smirk on his face. "I've been waiting for that villain to venture further than a mile from his cave. Now I have my revenge, that's all."

"Go, Kerenzi, get lost," she shouted. "Leave us alone."

He folded his arms. "No."

Roza turned and knelt where Philoe's burned and battered body lay in a crumpled heap against the foot of the cliff. She cradled his head on her lap and touched his face, searching for any signs of life.

But his eyes did not open, and his limbs did not twitch.

Philoe the warlock drew in one last breath and gasped, "Hold … my hand … Roza … as I go."

Roza grabbed his hands and clasped them in both of hers more tightly than she'd ever held onto anything.

His body convulsed, and his lips breathed, "Call me…"

And then he was gone.

The seconds passed since Philoe's last breath and Roza stared at him, numb. She squeezed his hands and pressed on his chest, but no further breath came.

"Come, Rozabella," Kerenzi said. "He's finished."

"Shut up!" she screamed at him. "Don't you dare say a word. Go!"

But the spirit lord didn't fly away, although he took a few steps further up the path.

Roza tried to ignore him and focus on the lifeless body in her arms. She'd known this man for – what? – one whole week? For half of that time, she'd feared and hated him. Then she'd tried to forgive and understand, to trust and respect him. He'd offered her a future, a hope and a place in the world … and now that was all gone.

She held his hand and gazed at the face that now looked pale and old. Not as ancient as when she'd first met him, but without the life or energy of the last few days.

Then the tears came – as much for herself as for him – releasing her shock and grief, fear and doubt, hate and hope, and she didn't know how long she knelt there.

When the tears stopped, she wiped her face and looked around. Kerenzi was still there, looking out over the valley. She was too drained and numb to yell at him.

What should she do? She still held Philoe's body, and she couldn't leave it here. It ought to be buried, and probably up on the plateau. The resolve formed inside her that she would do it, because no one else would. She released the warlock's hands and head and laid them gently on the ground.

"Kerenzi," she called, standing up. "I'm going to bury Philoe up on the plateau. You will help me carry his body back up there." She refused to look him in the eye as she said this.

"No," the spirit lord replied, walking closer. "I'm not touching him."

Her anger re-ignited at once. She leapt forward and jabbed the spirit lord in the chest. "That was not a question. It was an order. After what you've done, you will do exactly what I tell you." She felt her eyes blazing just as much as his had done.

Kerenzi stepped back, shocked. "Don't you dare touch me or order me what to do."

"Why not?" Roza demanded. "You owe me, Kerenzi. Your life, your freedom. If it weren't for me, you wouldn't have either."

The spirit lord tilted his head, considering her. She glared back at him, determined that he would flinch first.

At last, he said, "You're upset, so I forgive your insolence. And you have a point that I owe you something. I will increase your strength so you can carry him. Because I'm still not touching that murderer."

"Fine," Roza snapped. "However you like. Just do it."

Kerenzi reached and held her shoulder, and the warmth of magical energy flowed into her. Just as it had when she and Philoe had held hands across the cave's kitchen table. No, that was too painful to recall.

Roza knelt and positioned one arm under Philoe's shoulders, the other under his broken knees, and found that she could lift and stand with him. His head lolled against her shoulder, his burned hands resting in his lap.

And she began to walk. It was a long, slow climb. The high sun was hot, and the dust clung to her sweaty face and feet. Her arms and legs grew heavy and aching from the carrying and climbing, but Roza didn't mind. She could have continued up this path for ever, because it was something to do. It distracted her from thinking or feeling. She made sure to lead the way in front of Kerenzi, so she didn't have to look at him. She wished he'd go away, but that seemed too much to hope for.

At last, the path reached its crest and levelled onto the grass of the plateau. Roza had already decided where she would bury him: among the trees and in front of the bench where the two of them had sat at night and he'd invited her to stay. So, she laid Philoe's body in the shade there.

Now she needed to dig. She entered the cave and found Standley in front of the bookcases. The grief surged back at needing to say this to someone, and she decided on plain and simple as the best option.

"Standley, I'm sorry to tell you that Philoe the warlock has been killed. I've carried his body back up here to the plateau, and I plan to bury him among the trees." She reached and touched the coat stand's pole in what she hoped was a reassuring gesture. "Do we have a spade anywhere that I could use to dig the grave?"

The coat stand seemed to stare at her in shock, and then tighten up his knot eyes and bow his head. She allowed him some moments of sorrow before he moved towards a storeroom at the cave's rear. It was where they'd found her bed, and a spade was among the tools leaning up in a corner. Roza took this, and Standley followed her back outside.

Kerenzi was standing near the warlock's body when they reached it. "You shouldn't bother with burying him, you know. You should burn him and scatter his ashes to the wind. There are so many of you mortals, and you die so quickly, that you'll soon fill up the whole world with your graves."

Roza marched up to him. "I don't care in the slightest what you think. And if you're not going to help, then get out of our way."

The spirit lord shrugged and wandered off towards the bridge over the stream to watch the waterfall.

Roza and Standley began by marking out where they wanted the grave to be. It turned out that the coat stand's clawed feet were excellent at gouging into the soil and working in straight lines. Together they lifted aside the turf, and then Standley broke up the earth while Roza shovelled it aside. They worked through the afternoon as the sun lowered towards the mountains across the valley. The irony that Philoe had once likened her to a spade was not lost on Roza as she dug a hole in the ground – a last resting place for him – with her face set in grim determination.

As the daylight neared sunset Roza decided the grave was deep enough. With Standley's help, she lifted and lowered the warlock's broken body into the earth, crossing his arms across his chest for his everlasting sleep. Before they covered him over, the two of them stood at the foot of the grave as the last rays of sunlight made their silence beautiful.

Since Standley couldn't speak, it was up to Roza to say something. She cleared her throat.

"Philoe the warlock, I'm sorry I only knew you for a few days, and that even those began so awkwardly. But as you changed in age and appearance, so I changed as well, from anger and fear, through compassion and forgiveness, to friendship and hope. Your life was long, and I'm sure you achieved much that I don't have the knowledge to tell. But your strivings for longevity are now over. Sleep well, my mentor, my friend."

Her voice broke at this last word, and she turned away. Standley moved next to her, his hooks gently touching her shoulder, and they stood like that until Roza's tears subsided. Then she picked up the spade and together they filled in the hole. When the earth was a smooth mound, they re-laid the turf on top of it, under the glittering stars and a crescent moon setting over the mountains.

Standley went back into the cave, but Roza sat on the bench for a while to rest from her exertions. She was thinking about how she might mark the grave when Kerenzi walked up and stood over her.

"Go away," she said. "I want to think."

He folded his arms. "Aren't you going to finish this? Aren't you going to call him?"

She squinted up at him. "What do you mean?"

The spirit lord let out an exasperated breath. "You were holding his hand as he died, weren't you? He asked you to. And then he said, 'call me'. So, go on then."

"I don't understand. What difference does holding his hand make? And how am I supposed to call him?"

Kerenzi adopted the tone of explaining something obvious to a stupid child. "When someone holds the hand of a dying person, they slow the spirit's departure. Trust me, I know about spirits, and the warlock's hasn't gone yet. He's waiting for if you will call him. So, are you going to?"

"Well, I'm not going to do it with you standing there," she retorted. "Clear off into the cave or something."

Kerenzi blinked a few times and then slouched off towards the cave. Roza made sure he'd disappeared before she turned back to face the grave.

Her breath formed a mist in the evening air. "Philoe the warlock," she said to the darkness in front of her, "I don't know if this is another trick of the spirit lord's to humiliate me, or whether you really can hear me. He says I might have delayed your spirit's passing, and if that's true, then I call you now to come, if you can."

The night was quiet except for the rustle of the leaves and the hoot of a distant owl. Mist was settling under the trees as the heat of the day cooled.

Roza sat up and stared. Goosebumps spread along her arms and hairs prickled up her neck. The mist wasn't just settling, it was gathering. It was rising from the ground, from the grave, to form a faint, luminous cloud. It coalesced, taking shape, filling out with further vapours flowing up from the smooth mound of turf. As Roza watched, it became a man, glowing, transparent, but with the unmistakeable appearance of Philoe the warlock.

When it was complete, it drifted across and bent in the middle to sit on the bench next to her. The glow from him lit up the grave and the copse of trees, a small circle of light in the surrounding darkness.

"Hello, Rozabella." His lips didn't move, and the voice sounded inside her head. In any other circumstance, she'd have been petrified by this. She'd grown up with ghost stories, of course, but here on this magical plateau, anything seemed possible. She'd been prepared for his spirit coming, even called for it, and the presence of her friend was comforting rather than frightening.

"Hello, Philoe," she thought back. She copied him by not using her voice, and his smile told her he'd heard her.

"Thank you for holding and calling me, Roza. I hoped you would."

"Standley and I buried you here. We hope you approve."

Philoe's spirit nodded. "Perfect. I'm sorry the way things have worked out, but I accept that I deserve it."

She bristled. "No, you don't. Not like that, anyway. Not taken by surprise with sudden violence. In a court of law perhaps, after consideration of the evidence. But not with him as your judge and executioner."

Philoe held up a hand. "Thank you for standing up for me, but I'm afraid you know only a fraction of the crimes I've committed during my long life. I am guilty, Roza, and have lived way past what is due to me. I can accept that this is my time to go, and I ask you to accept it too."

"But we had so short a time to know each other. And you have so much that you need to teach me. What is going to happen to me now – a novice without a warlock to train her?"

"This is one of the things I need to tell you. There are some parchments on the desk in my bedchamber, which I wrote a day or two ago. You can show them to the Reeve of Albany or whoever you like, and I assure you they are perfectly legal. They outline my wishes in the event of my death, which I thought it prudent to record, given Kerenzi's threats."

Roza didn't know what to say to that. How might the warlock have amended his will during these last few days of knowing her?

"First of all, I leave to you, Miss Rozabella, the ownership of the cave, this orchard, the fields, the animals, Standley, and everything else I possess. This whole plateau is now your property, to live here or to do with as you wish."

Roza's jaw dropped. She didn't think she'd ever owned more than a few clothes in her life. Her family background might have been rich or poor, but certainly nothing compared to this. At seventeen years old, she might now be one of the richest landowners in the whole valley.

"But … but…," she stammered, "I don't deserve to inherit all this from you. You only knew me for a few days."

Philoe smiled, and his voice sounded clear and close in her head. "For one thing, I have no one else to leave it to. I don't want it to go to the town of Albany, who will divide it up and sell it off, and spoil the beauty of this place."

Roza nodded and understood that.

"And secondly, I feel you do deserve it because I want to make things up to you. I captured you and stole you away from your life. I was cruel and threatened you, and even now have made you a stranger in your hometown. I'm sorry, Roza, and hope you'll accept these gifts from me as my final apology."

She swallowed. "Apology accepted. But I don't know how I'll get on with looking after fruit trees, or crops, or animals, or anything."

"I didn't know much either when I started, but I learned, and so will you. And Standley will help you. You are a smart, determined, resourceful young woman, and I'm sure you will succeed in all these things when you put your mind to them. I was afraid you might not have a home to go back to, or a loving family to welcome you in. I want to give you somewhere to belong, where you can feel safe and at peace, and I hope my cave and this plateau can be that for you."

"Yes, I'm starting to love it here," she said, and her gaze drifted off to the trees and stars.

"I have also, under the authority of the Master of the Warlocks, promoted you from novice to apprentice, and therefore appointed you as my successor as warlock."

Roza jerked back to stare at him with a jolt. "*What?*"

"You were my only novice, and the most promising I have ever known. So, it is only fitting that you now become my apprentice and take over my role after my death."

"But I was your novice for about *three days* and know next to nothing about magic. How am I supposed to learn to be a warlock?"

"I can help you there."

"What, after you're dead? Are you going to stay around in spirit form for the next thirty years until I've learned all I need to?"

Philoe's spirit chuckled and then leaned forward. "I'll let you into a secret, Roza. Part of the magic of warlocks is that we can pass on our wisdom and experience to our successors. My mentor did that for me, and also before him, and so on back through history and all the generations. We consider it vital that no learning is lost. That is one reason why I tried so hard to stay alive, so I could bequeath my magic to a worthy apprentice before I died."

Roza scoffed. "A worthy apprentice? What on earth makes you think I'm one of those? I'm seventeen, and naïve, and inexperienced, and have had a total of about two lessons in magic."

Philoe held up a finger. "Ah, but the main thing about an apprentice, is not what you know already, but your potential, that you have an aptitude and a willingness to learn. I've been searching for such a person for decades, for centuries, and you, Rozabella my girl, have these in abundance."

"How can you reckon I have any aptitude or potential? I've never even tried any magic."

"Oh, but you have." Philoe beamed. "Have you forgotten your unique and remarkable gift? I grant that the power for my youthful transformation came from me, not from you, but you still channelled it and let it flow through you. I consider that an excellent recommendation of your worthiness."

"But how can you pass on what you've learned? Is it all written down in those books in there?"

"Yes, it is, and I encourage you to read and study them. But I can do better than that. If you're willing, I can leave you a portion of my spirit."

She frowned. "A portion of your spirit? What does that mean?"

"Before I finally pass on from this mortal life, I can breathe some of my spirit into you. It will combine with your spirit and live within you for ever. That's what my forebears did for those who came after them, such that within me live all the warlocks who have ever lived here. Our spirits, our souls, our essence and our magic lives on for ever in those who succeed us. We can guide and teach you in all you need to learn, and give you an excellent start in developing your own source of magical power."

"But I don't have any magical power of my own. You said so yourself. It all had to come from you."

Philoe chuckled. "You may not yet, but you will. Most humans have magic within them, but too often they neither recognise it nor develop it. It's such a shame."

"Is this what you were saying about magic coming from beauty? That if we open our minds and hearts to it, then the mystery of magic is revealed to us?"

The warlock nodded. "I'm glad you remember that much, Miss Roza. The fact that you grasp these things already is a promising sign. Search down deep inside yourself and see if you can locate the spark of magic starting to kindle. My spirit will dwell and burn there as a small flame for when you need it."

"All right, so you can leave me a portion of your spirit, but what about my training? There is still so much I need to learn."

The spirit Philoe sighed. "I regret very much that we

didn't get the time together for me to accompany you on your long, rigorous, warlock training. I would have enjoyed sharing that adventure with you, but I can still be with you in my spirit. You are right that training yourself is not ideal, but in time you will manage it. Read the books. Study and learn them. Practise what you read. And keep on practising."

"But … but what about music? I told you I'm rubbish at that and will never understand it, so you said you'd give me extra lessons. Will I miss out on those too?" A small part of Roza was relieved about this.

"Yes, I regret that you will need to teach yourself everything as best you can."

Roza looked around the darkened plateau. "It still feels as though you're leaving me an awful lot. This plateau, your title and position, your spirit and magic – and I don't feel I've given you anything."

"On the contrary, my Roza, you have given me everything. You saved me. Although my capture of the spirit lord resulted in my death, you came along just in time to make things right. You held up a mirror for me to see the monster I'd become and helped me to change my ways. I found an apprentice for my magic and an heir for my estate. But most of all, you made me feel young again, and offered me what I had lived without for far too long: friendship."

If Philoe's spirit could have had tears in his eyes, Roza knew she'd be seeing them now. She reached out to grasp his hand, but there was nothing but mist and vapour. Her fingers passed through cold air to rest on the wood of the bench. There would be no more holding of hands, no warmth of embrace. The finality of death and goodbye and departure swept over her, and she wanted to weep.

"Thank you, my Roza," he said in her head, "for giving me a most precious gift at the end of my life. My last few days with you have been my best for three centuries. We talked and argued, learned and laughed, living together in the way that human beings should, in company and friendship. You reminded me and gave me what I had lacked and missed for so long, and I can leave this life content at having had a friend with me at the last."

The old warlock's spirit moved closer along the bench, and Roza heard him say, "It is nearly time for me to go. May I leave you some of my spirit so you will always remember me?"

Roza shuddered a breath and then nodded.

"Then I will say goodbye to you in this form and for now. Good night, my dearest Rozabella, and sleep well, my friend, and I will be with you in the morning."

Philoe's spirit moved closer still, as though to kiss her. Then he breathed out, and Roza breathed in, and it was the longest, deepest, fullest breath she'd ever taken. She closed her eyes, and it seemed to fill her up, with more contentment than she'd ever known.

When she could breathe in no more, she opened her eyes, and all that remained were a few wisps of mist drifting gently upwards towards the twinkling stars.

CHAPTER EIGHTEEN

When Roza went back into the cave, Kerenzi had disappeared. Perhaps he'd mustered enough sensitivity to know she'd want to be alone after the events of the day. If so, she was grateful. She said goodnight to Standley and lay down on her bed. She didn't want to explore what had been Philoe's bedchamber. But was this cave now her home?

As Roza woke the next morning, a crushing sense of loneliness overwhelmed her. She'd never felt more desolate. She could only remember the last ten days or so, and her only company in that time had been the warlock and the spirit lord. With both of those she'd had one argument after another. Now the bitter feud between the two of them had led to Kerenzi executing Philoe, and she was supposed to be the next warlock.

She buried her head under the pillow. Maybe she would be better off forgetting this whole experience. Forget about magic and her gift of Rejuvenate, walk down the path into town, find that angry boy Jorxy and pick up the pieces of her former life. That had to be easier than trying to be the warlock, right?

But then that feeling of magical power coursing through her body nudged at her resolve. More than anything, she desperately wanted to feel that again, didn't she?

A slight tapping sound disturbed her thoughts. She poked an eye out from under her pillow. A gentle daylight was filtering into the cave, and Standley the coat stand was peering around the entrance to her bedchamber.

Oh yeah, of course, she thought wryly, she'd had more company than a warlock and a spirit lord these last ten days. Her best and only friend in the whole world was now an enchanted piece of furniture, who seemed to understand her, but whose conversation was limited to yes and no.

Slowly, she sat up and swung her legs out of bed. "Good morning, Standley," she sighed.

The coat stand gave the rock wall a couple more taps and jerked his top towards the cave entrance.

"What is it?" Roza asked him. "Has something happened? Is someone here?"

Standley nodded his hooks and scuttled away again. Roza jumped up, dressed quickly, and followed him into the main cave chamber.

Kerenzi the spirit lord was sitting at the table. Part of her was still furious with him for what he'd done yesterday, but the other part was relieved to have the company. Here at least was the one person who knew what had happened with her kidnap and captivity by the warlock.

She ignored him for a few minutes while she gathered some food for breakfast, and the spirit lord had the good sense not to intrude on her sulking. He watched her, of course, and when she finally sat down opposite him to eat, she broke the awkward silence.

"What do you want, Kerenzi? Why are you here? I thought this place might hold too many unhappy memories for you." She didn't want to sound too unfriendly, but she was suspicious.

"I thought I'd see if you wanted any company."

Well, yes, of course, she wanted and needed some company, but was it any of his business? Would she prefer to be on her own, to have a chance to think, or did she need to talk with someone about it all? He was the only one who knew her situation and might understand. But then it occurred to her what was really going on with him.

"What's the matter, Kerenzi? Weren't you welcomed back into the forest with open arms? Wasn't there jubilation and rejoicing among your fellow spirits when their lord and master returned to them safely?"

She wasn't surprised when he glared at her. He looked to be trying to decide whether to admit the truth to her. "No," he said at last. "There were no celebrations. As I expected, I returned to the forest to find a full-scale civil war going on between different spirit factions over who would succeed me. So, no, they weren't pleased to see me. And when they saw my maimed wing, none of the factions wanted to welcome a crippled former spirit lord into their ranks. Consequently, I decided to leave them to it."

"And chose to come and annoy me instead."

"Something like that." He forced out a smile at her.

He was still annoyingly gorgeous, she reflected. Why couldn't this arrogant spirit lord be the ugly one, and that angry mortal boy down in the town be the gorgeous one? Then her choices and decisions might be a little easier. Or would they? All these boys and men might be more trouble than they were worth.

Then she remembered her own loneliness and an ounce of pity nudged at Roza's heart. "You mean that you've been banished from your forest in much the same way as I've been cut off from my hometown. I suppose we could share some of our lonely exile together from time to time, but whether that means I want your company right now, I'm not so sure."

Kerenzi shrugged and they sat in silence while she ate some breakfast. Then he leaned forwards. "I saw you called the warlock's spirit last night. You were talking so I thought I'd leave you to it. What did he say?"

Her first reaction was to say 'it's none of your business' but realised he'd find out soon enough and it was easier just to tell him. "He's left me all of this place and wants me to be his successor as warlock."

Kerenzi nodded. "I thought he might. Congratulations, then. Do you want the job?"

"Since I've no idea what on earth being a warlock entails, or how to do any of it, I can't answer that question yet."

The spirit lord narrowed his eyes at her, as though examining her. "He's left you a portion of his spirit, hasn't he?"

Roza swallowed, thinking that ought to have remained a secret between her and Philoe, but supposed a spirit lord might know about such things anyway. "Yes, he did."

"I thought so. I can sense him still here, and the beginnings of magic within you."

Her fury at him for what he'd done to Philoe boiled up inside her again, and it burst out before she could stop it. "Why did you have to come back, Kerenzi? Philoe had apologised and let you go. Couldn't you have gone on your way, enjoyed your life and freedom, and left it at that? If you hadn't killed our warlock, he'd still be here to protect the town and train me in the ways of magic."

"And if Philoe hadn't captured and injured me," the spirit lord snapped back, "I wouldn't have needed to avenge myself by killing him."

"And if Philoe hadn't captured us, then we might never have discovered my gift of Rejuvenate, which can help so many people. But no, you had to get your revenge, didn't you?"

Kerenzi glared at her again. "It wasn't just revenge, it was justice. He committed crimes by capturing, imprisoning, and assaulting us, and he deserved what he got."

"With you as judge and executioner? Yes, he made numerous mistakes, but people are allowed to learn from them and change. He regretted what he'd done and tried to make amends. Otherwise, it all ends in a cycle of violence, revenge, and bitterness, doesn't it? Sometimes it's better to exercise some mercy and forgiveness and let these things go."

"It's easier for you than for me to forgive him when I'll fly with a maimed wing for the rest of my immortal life. For you mortals, the consequences of your crimes are so short-lived it's no wonder you don't bother about them so much."

"Whereas you immortals," Roza retorted, "have the whole of eternity to nurse your grudges, cradle your injured wing and be consumed by bitterness. I know which I prefer."

"Ah, but now justice is satisfied. I've had my revenge, Philoe has paid for his crimes, and I can let it go, with no grudge or bitterness. Yes, I have my injured wing, but I can nurse my wound knowing that the perpetrator paid for it."

"But the question is: will *I* ever forgive *you* for killing my friend?"

When Kerenzi was silent, Roza looked up at him. The spirit lord looked taken aback but clearly wasn't about to apologise for what he'd done. He went on the offensive instead.

"How could you ever consider that cruel, lying, disgusting man as your friend?"

"No, of course he wasn't my friend to begin with, but I told you: he changed. And not just in a younger physical appearance. He put away his lying and cruelty and became considerate, trustworthy, and generous. I'm going to miss him."

Kerenzi was staring at her. "Listen to yourself. Haven't you accepted by now that he bewitched you? He was always trying to trick and persuade you into staying, and he almost succeeded. I saved you from him, Roza. I rescued you from his clutches. You say you saved my life and gave me back my freedom; well, I did the same for you."

"But I didn't want rescuing!" Roza bellowed back. "I could have been happy here, in this beautiful place, with a role as his novice and learning about magic. You had no right to take that away from me. You've robbed me of my future, my teacher and mentor, and stolen away my training in the ways of magic. My rescue or freedom wasn't your decision to make, it was mine."

Kerenzi was wagging a finger at her. "No, no. Your capture here was my fault. The warlock wasn't after you in that forest clearing, he was after me. You just happened to get in the way, and any young mortal would have done. He needed an immortal the most, any spirit of the forest, and he struck lucky in capturing me. Your being here in the first place was because of me, and I couldn't leave you stranded here either."

Something in the spirit lord's tone surprised her. "You feel responsible for me? You care about what happens to me?"

Kerenzi looked abashed, as though he'd said too much and been found out. But he seemed too proud to back down now. "Yes, I do. As I told you before, I noticed something different about you, that unique and powerful gift you have. You have a spirit with enormous magical potential. Why do you think I appeared to you in that forest clearing in the first place, Roza? You intrigued me, and yes, I like you. I watched you then, and I like you more with all I've seen of you since."

Roza couldn't believe what she was hearing. "Hang on a minute, you *watched* me? You, an immortal spirit lord, took a fancy to some random mortal girl, and thought you'd have some fun, did you? You could flatter her with your supernatural charms, toy with her feelings, and then too bad, you went and got captured. Well, thank you for liking me, Kerenzi, but have you considered that I might actually *not* like you?"

Part of Roza ached to be saying this. The spirit lord sitting opposite her far surpassed any mortal boy she would ever meet, in looks and power, but with it went an arrogance she found repulsive.

"Be careful, Roza," Kerenzi warned. "I offer you a friendship that could be greatly to your advantage. Do not spurn it lightly."

"You were jealous, weren't you? Of my friendship with Philoe. As far as you're concerned, my plan to earn his trust and arrange our escape worked far too well. So now you had to come back, 'to rescue me from his clutches', and claim me for your own. Well, I hate to burst your bubble, Kerenzi, but I have feelings too. I happen to get a say in this matter, whatever you think your looks and power might achieve for you."

The spirit lord adopted a condescending tone. "I can see you're upset, Roza. This is an emotional, grieving time for you, and you need the chance to consider your life and your future. But I can be patient. I have more time to wait than you do."

"Yes, I'll take some time to think about my future. But there's one thing that losing my memories has taught me: to enjoy the present and live for the future, because my past isn't even there."

Kerenzi frowned. "Haven't your memories started coming back to you? I thought they might have done by now."

"No, not a thing. Philoe said it could take a very long time for them to reconnect through natural healing."

"I don't mean that. It's just that with Philoe's death, all the spells he cast will start to unravel. Including the Forgetery spell on you. You should start remembering things."

Roza stared at him. "You mean my past, my family, my friends? They'll all start coming back to me? How long will that take? And what about his other spells? Like Standley – will he stop being enchanted?"

Kerenzi chuckled. "No, Standley's enchantment is far older even than Philoe's four centuries. He is an ancient coat stand, made with the same wood as my own forest.

I've heard of him for my whole life and have great respect for him. He's been handed down through a long line of warlocks."

She smiled at Standley, who seemed to smile back and incline his hooks. "But what about Philoe's other spells? Can you tell me what else around here he enchanted?"

The spirit lord gave her a sideways look. "It isn't the spells around here you should worry about. What about yesterday? If I'm not mistaken, he cast an Ennuissance spell over the town of Albany. What will happen when that one starts to fail?"

A weight of dread slithered down Roza's throat and thumped into the pit of her stomach. "The … um … the Emperor?" she whispered. "He might be bothered to come here after all?"

Kerenzi gave a slow nod. "And who do they have to protect them this time?"

"No one," Roza croaked.

"Wrong," Kerenzi chimed. "They have you. The town of Albany will look to their new warlock to save them. Good luck with that." He stood up, turned, and started walking towards the cave entrance.

"No, wait, stop," she called. "You must help me. I haven't the faintest idea how to save a town from a Dragon."

"Tut, tut," Kerenzi mocked. "You shouldn't say that word, you know."

Roza's anger flared. "This is all your fault. Not only did you call out to the … Emperor before you left here, but you also slaughtered the one who was protecting the town. It is your responsibility to step in and help us."

"I don't care about the town or people of Albany. You mortals come and go so quickly I can hardly keep up with your passing."

"All right, then. You promised never to harm me. This is going to harm me. I insist that you repay me for saving your life and arranging your freedom, by helping me when I ask for it. Not to mention that you've robbed me of my magical training. You owe me, Kerenzi, and now I'm calling in your debt."

The spirit lord considered her for some moments. "Very well. I agree that your intervention rescued me from being killed in this cave. I also stand by my promise not to harm you. If you call, I will answer. I'll be listening. But understand that I insist on remaining invisible. I will be there, but I refuse to allow all those worthless Albany townsfolk to gawp at me. And after this, my debt to you is repaid, and we are even."

"Agreed," Roza said, and held out her hand.

Kerenzi took it and they shook.

"Now, how do you suggest I deal with the Emperor?" Roza demanded.

"That, I'm afraid," Kerenzi said with a smirk, "is your problem, not mine."

And he vanished before her eyes.

She had no time, though, to wallow in dread, for at that moment a cry came from outside the cave. Had the spirit lord sensed that someone was coming and hidden himself? Had he gone, or was he still here but invisible? She had no way of knowing.

The cry from outside came again, so Roza shook herself and hurried out the cave entrance. The town messenger from Albany was running along the path towards her, more out of breath and sweaty than she'd seen him before.

"Help, help," he was gasping. "The warlock, we need him. Where is Philoe?"

Tightness constricted Roza's throat, and she found she couldn't answer the man's question. "Why, what is it? What's happening?" she managed.

"The town needs Philoe the warlock," the messenger insisted, coming to a stop in front of her. "Where is he?"

Roza swallowed down her grief and forced out the

words. "Philoe is dead. I buried him among the trees last night." She indicated the low mound of grass beyond the bench.

The messenger didn't even glance that way, for his face had fallen into horror. "The warlock, dead? But how?"

She didn't know how to explain this. "Um … he was killed yesterday afternoon while walking back up the path to this plateau. It was a magical attack … by one of his enemies."

The messenger stared at her, his eyes fixed into a glazed dread. "Then … we have no warlock. We are lost. The town is doomed, and we're all going to die."

The clenching in Roza's stomach tightened into an icy vice. "Why?" she whispered. "What did you need him for?"

The messenger's voice was a dry croak. "The Dragon has come."

CHAPTER NINETEEN

Roza's first thought was to rebuke the man for having said 'Dragon', for fear of summoning the beast, and then realised how stupid and pointless that was. It was too late. Philoe's Ennuissance spell had broken, and the Dragon had remembered Albany.

In that instant, as though to reinforce the man's message, a deafening roar erupted from the valley below. If all the world's thunders had broken right over her head, Roza didn't think it could have been louder. The ground shook beneath her and she staggered. Rocks cracked and tumbled down the mountainsides from above. Trees in the orchard cracked and swayed, crashing into each other as some of them toppled over. The messenger fell to the ground, hiding his face, his hands over his ears. The roar's echoes reverberated around the mountains for some minutes before at last they faded away into silence.

"The Emperor announces his arrival," the messenger sobbed into the earth.

Roza stared about. After centuries of delay, distraction, and reprieve, today was Albany's day of reckoning. Their Emperor had come to collect his taxes. And there was no one to protect or save them.

Except for her.

The realisation hammered into Roza like a thunderbolt and her knees gave way. She collapsed to the grass and rolled herself into a tight ball. Maybe if she hid like this, or somewhere at the back of the cave, buried under broken furniture, then the Dragon would never find her. She might be safe, and escape, and survive.

But what would be left? The Dragon would lay waste to the valley. The town would burn to ashes, the farms and forests too. The plateau would be destroyed, the groves of trees, the fields and animals too, as Dragon-fire licked up every last blade of grass into smoke. She would emerge from the cave's hideout into a desolate wasteland, empty of food or life, and starve to a lonely death among the ruin.

No. She refused to die like that. If this was going to be her end, and everyone else's, then she wouldn't face it alone, or as a coward. She could find whether she had any family and die alongside them at least. She would not surrender to despair, not while there was anything left to try.

She uncurled herself from her ball on the grass and sat up. She wiped her face, heaved some breaths, and cleared her throat to get her voice working. The messenger was still shaking and sobbing on the grass.

"Excuse me," she said, and after some moments the man managed to look over at her. "Um, before he died, Philoe the warlock appointed me as his apprentice, and so now I succeed him in the role. So, if you'd like me to, I'm willing to come down into the valley and see if there's anything I can do."

The messenger sat up and stared at her. "You? The new warlock? But you're so young … and a girl. What can you hope to do against the Dragon?"

That was enough to set Roza's hackles rising. She jumped to her feet. "I think you will find," she snapped, "that girls are equally as capable as boys. And that some of us younger people have qualities you older people seem to have forgotten, like courage, resourcefulness and hope."

The man stood up. "What did you say your name was?"

She was determined to put some authority into her voice. "My name is Rozabella, and I am the Warlock of Albany. If you give me one minute, I will come with you down into town."

Roza turned and marched back into the cave. It wasn't

as though she needed to fetch anything but wanted to try to control her trembling. A surge of tears had risen into her throat, and she gripped the edge of the table to force her arm and leg muscles to be still. She closed her eyes and thought of Philoe. Come on, then, my mentor, my friend. If your spirit is still inside me, then you landed me in this mess, and you'd better help me to survive it.

Something touched her arm. Standley the coat stand had sidled across to her. She rested a hand on his polished wooden hooks, and said, "You're in charge here, Standley, while I'm gone. Please try to look after everything as best you can. And if things don't go well down in town, then I'm very pleased to have known you."

The coat stand edged closer, and his hooks curled at her shoulders and hips into the nearest thing to an embrace. She squeezed him in return and then leaned back. His knots for eyes seemed to blink at her, and then he let go.

"Thank you, Standley," she breathed, and then left the cave.

The messenger was waiting for her on the path, and she followed him across the plateau. She supposed she ought to try to think of a plan, but her mind was in too much fear and turmoil to function.

When they reached where the path tipped over the edge of the cliff, the messenger skidded to a halt and gasped. Roza stopped beside him and forced her gaze downwards.

The town of Albany nestled on the floor of the valley as it had always done, with one glaring change. She couldn't help but turn her eyes eastwards, where the eastern walls of the town faced the gap in the mountains and the plain. Only today there was no gap.

A new mountain lay curled before the gates of Albany's eastern walls, a deep russet red in colour, with scales that shone like metal in the morning sun. Rows of spikes like a forest of bone ran along the crest of the ridge that was the

Dragon's back. Wings the size of a canopy to shade the whole town lay folded along its sides, above a tail that stretched the length of the wall. Roza could not bring herself to look at its head. Even from this distance the beast emanated such terror that no one could dare to approach it.

She jerked her head to the left and grabbed the messenger's arm. "Come on," she said. "Don't look at it. We need to go down to the town."

He stumbled after her, and she realised that she was now leading him. She needed to think. She had the duration of this walk down the path in which to come up with a plan. And it needed to be a good one. The best that any mere girl her age had ever devised. She snorted at the messenger's incredulity that a young girl could ever be a warlock. So, she was young, and female – what did that matter? She'd been chosen to be a warlock's apprentice, and she had a gift...

Her gift. That had to be it. It was the only thing about her that was different or special. What had Philoe told her? The ability to make people younger was so rare and remarkable that nations would go to war to possess it. The whole world would be clamouring for her to give them extra years, and longer life, and renewed vigour, a return to their youth. Was this the key? That she could offer herself to the Emperor to be his slave, to use her gift in his service for the rest of her life? Was hers an ability that was valuable enough that he would spare their town in return for it? Maybe he would, but did she have the courage to make such an offer? To sacrifice her life to be a Dragon's slave so that others could escape and survive?

Roza trudged down the cliffside path, and no matter how she turned the situation over in her mind, she could find no other conclusion. This had to be the deal that the Emperor might accept, whatever the cost to her. She was walking towards not the town's doom, but her own.

She kept her gaze down towards the dusty path beneath her boots so as not to notice the beauty of the cliff, the mountains, the forest or the valley around her. If she was right, then this would be the last time she would pass this way or see these views. The Dragon would whisk her away to some unknown land where she would spend her days in some lightless dungeon until she died. But how long would that be? Would the Emperor insist that she use her gift on herself, to make herself young again, and so go on serving him as his slave for ever? It was a destiny too terrible and horrible to contemplate.

The path beneath her turned from rock to grass to beaten earth, as the town's messenger tramped along behind her. At least the man had the decency to remain silent during her long, last walk as a free girl. The path came down to the farm track, and Roza looked up enough to turn right towards the town.

The town. Soon she would need to see people and talk to them. They would all be watching her. And then she needed to face … him. These were the last choices and decisions she would ever need to make for herself, until her will and freedom were taken away and she served the wishes of another. She had only a few more conversations to get through and she could manage this. She drew some deep breaths and composed herself.

How had she won over Philoe the warlock when he'd started off as a wretched, ancient bully? Through politeness, determination, and self-control. She still had these, at least for the moment, so she plastered onto her face a calm, confident expression and looked towards the town gate.

A crowd of people thronged there, and there looked to be a commotion. No doubt they were all waiting for Philoe the warlock to come down from his cave to save them. She could imagine the messenger's announcement: Sorry, everyone, our trusted warlock is dead. All we've got in his place is this presumptuous girl. What can she do? You might as well go back to your homes and prepare to die. Or something like that.

As she approached, the commotion seemed to pause at the sight of her and the messenger having descended from the warlock's plateau. Shouts arose from the people ahead, a craning of necks, the sounds of relief, a rebirth of hope. No, she thought, don't deceive yourselves, it's only me. But still, she supposed that if her plan succeeded, and the Dragon accepted her slavery in return for sparing the town, then they might be safe after all. Her sacrifice might achieve something useful, and she tried to console herself with this thought. But everyone in Albany was a stranger to her, so she struggled to care for them or make this reinforce her resolve.

She was close enough to see their faces, that they were frowning. Perhaps she ought to say something, to explain her presence before they lynched her. She raised her arms to gain their attention.

"People of Albany," she called, and a hush fell. "There has been a change of warlock. Philoe died yesterday afternoon, but I was his apprentice and have now accepted the role. Please do not be afraid. I will meet with the Dragon our Emperor and have a plan for our town to be saved."

But her last words were drowned out by a second roar from the Dragon. It wasn't as loud as the first, but Roza was nearer to it now, and like everyone else, it made her jump and cower.

The commotion erupted anew. People were hurrying back and forth within the town, perhaps trying to find loved ones or gather their possessions. As Roza watched, a handful of townsfolk broke through the cordon of guards and fled past her along the farm track. Each was carrying a bundle or pack, and she guessed they hoped to escape the valley altogether over the mountains, if that were possible.

Part of her couldn't blame them. She might have gone with them if she could.

Then above all the noise came a cry of "Roza! Rozabella!"

She turned to locate the source of the call, and saw Jorxy, that ugly red-haired boy from yesterday, leading a man and a woman towards her. The man in the middle was being led by the hand, and stumbling, as though he couldn't see, and the woman was clutching her chest. They were middle-aged … about the age her parents might be.

And something clicked. It was the first clear memory that had reconnected since the Forgetery spell.

They stopped in front of her, the woman and the boy staring. The man wasn't quite looking at her, but was saying, "Roza, my Roza, are you there?"

"Um, you're my p-parents," she stuttered, aware at once how strange and stupid this sounded. But before further words came, the three of them fell into an embrace of tears and kisses and squeezes and laughter and relief. Her parents were touching her face and hair and shoulders, and Jorxy was standing there, a grin all over his face.

"I told them I saw you," Jorxy said. "I found them and said you were alive and with the warlock now. So, with the Reeve sending for the warlock, we thought we'd wait here and catch you."

"But what's this about you being the warlock now?" her mother was saying. "About meeting with the Emperor and saving the town? What are you on about?"

It was the cruellest irony, that she should meet and recognise her parents again now, only to leave them at once and become the Dragon's slave. But she couldn't allow them to divert or distract her from the plan. After all, it was now their lives she would be saving, and that was her first comforting thought.

"Listen, Mum, Dad, there's so much I need to explain. Philoe the warlock discovered I have a gift, an ability, something unique and wonderful. I'm going to use it to save our town from the Dragon. Please trust me about this because I know what I must do."

Her heart ached not to tell them more about her gift, or what her plan involved, or that they'd never see her again. How could she tell them, because they'd never let her go if they knew?

Overhead, a jet of dragon-fire exploded above the town, and everyone ducked as cinders and ashes fell around them.

Did Roza have time for this family reunion? The Town Reeve and the Emperor would be waiting for old warlock Philoe to descend from the plateau, so she probably had some minutes before the Dragon would fulfil his threat to lay waste to the town.

Her mother and father were holding each other, speechless. She turned to the boy and took his hand. "Jorxy, I'm sorry about yesterday. Thank you for going and finding my parents. I'm very grateful to see them again before I do this." She squeezed his hand and let go.

Jorxy grinned. "No problem," he said. "I can't wait to tell everyone I'm friends with the new high and mighty Rozabella the warlock."

And something about this boy's grin also clicked in her memory. Somehow, he didn't look ugly when he smiled, compared with when he was angry. "And now I think I remember you, Jorxy. Yes, from the schoolroom. You were my ... my best friend." Tears prickled at the back of her eyes as she said this. "And you were angry with the old warlock yesterday because you thought he'd wronged and hurt me, because you care about me like that."

The boy's eyes were shining. "Taken you long enough to remember, hasn't it?"

"And we used to meet, and hang out, at the ... at the town's rubbish ditch?"

Jorxy winked. "Best place in town."

She laughed, but underneath it stabbed at her heart that she now had to leave her best friend as well. *You're saving his life too,* she told herself. But she wished there was something more she could do for all three of them.

And more memories clicked. Being here with her Mum, Dad and Jorxy reminded her of the niggling, unsatisfactory feeling she'd had up on the mountain spur about her family and home. Her parents weren't well. That's right, her Dad was blind, and her Mum always tried to hide her chest pains. So, she'd had to look after them, do lots of things for them. Tending the animals, going into town, making up the fires, chopping firewood in the forest...

Now her past started to make sense. That's what she'd been doing when Kerenzi first visited her, and the warlock surprised them. But the unsatisfactory niggle was that she'd felt trapped. She loved her parents, and wanted to care for them, but still longed for the chance to be free, to make all her own choices and chart her own course in the world.

With a jolt she remembered that she was now leaving them after all. If the Dragon took her away, who would look after her parents?

And an idea occurred. If this really was the last time she would see her parents, she could try and do something for them. Help them to live by themselves again. Like they had when they were younger. *Younger.*

She was in the position to give them something. A memento, a keepsake, a legacy to remember her by. And the only thing she could give them was her gift.

While all this flashed through Roza's mind, they were gazing at her, holding onto her and smiling. She had planned to keep her unique ability secret for as long as possible, but if she was about to reveal it to the Dragon, what did it matter if her parents and Jorxy knew? In saving her town, she could save her parents too. And something told her that to test her ability now, to wield magic by herself, might be a good idea rather than trying to do it for the first time ever in front of the Dragon Emperor.

She drew in and let out a deep breath. "Jorxy, since you're my best friend, I want you to see and know this. Come over here for a moment, with my parents, because I'm going to do something for them." She led the three of them away from the commotion and the guards to the side of the farm track.

"What is it, dear?" her mum said, concern all over her face. "Is there something we can help you with?"

"No," Roza replied, "it's something I can do to help you both. I'm going to touch your eyes now, Dad, so please don't flinch when I do."

"What? Why?"

"I told you I have a unique and wonderful gift, and this is it, so please just let me." She reached and placed a gentle finger at the corners of her father's milky eyeballs.

Now, how did she do this?

Roza closed her eyes and thought back to how she'd made Philoe's hands younger when they sat across the cave's kitchen table. It had started with the warlock sending her his magical energy, a tingling warmth through their joined hands. But now she wouldn't receive the magic from outside, but had to find it within herself, from the portion of his spirit that Philoe had left her.

Where was it? She searched for some long seconds, deeper and deeper inside her, and then there it was, down in her belly, or gut. It was no more than a spark, and she gazed and marvelled at it in wonder for a moment. This had certainly never been there before. Thank you, Philoe. But now what must she do? Ignite it into a flame?

She imagined herself breathing on the spark, and it burst into a single, steady flame. She willed the fire to grow, and then fanned it into life, energising, empowering, strengthening her. It warmed her insides, and then she channelled it, down her arms and into the tips of her forefingers, and across into her father's eyes.

Younger, younger, she thought. Make his eyes like they used to be. Like when I was a little girl. When he was a younger man. Make his eyes younger and restore his sight.

Her Dad gasped and Roza opened her eyes. She was looking into the warm brown of her father's gaze that she hadn't known since early childhood. And he was staring at her, tears streaming down his cheeks.

"My Roza," he murmured. "But you've grown. And my Roza is a gorgeous young woman, and I've got to see you at last. But how?"

Roza was leaking tears too. "This is my gift, Dad. Do you like it?"

Arthur's jaw dropped open in wonder and gratitude and speechless love. That's right, his name is Arthur. It was coming back.

"And Mum, let me fix your heart."

Helena's eyes widened as Roza laid a hand on her mother's breastbone. The magic came easier this time, because it was already burning, and she knew where to find it. She channelled it across, and it seemed to know where to go, to repair the muscles and ease the blockages. To make a younger heart.

When Roza lifted her hand, her mother sighed and stretched her shoulders back. "The tightness," she breathed, "and the aches have gone. Will I be free from the stabbing pains too?" Roza nodded. "But what have you done, Rozabella? And how did you do it?"

"Er ... it's called magic, Mum. I'm the warlock now, remember?" She flashed them a wide smile, and the look on their faces was her reward, whatever came next. She leaned closer and whispered, "I've given you younger eyes and a younger heart. They should last you for many years now."

Jorxy was standing there, jaw agape. "You ... you've just done magic?"

"Yep." She gave him a playful poke in the chest. "I'm Rozabella the Warlock now, and don't you forget it."

The look of awe and respect in Jorxy's eyes as he gazed at her was heart-breaking because she had to leave him too.

The Dragon roared again, and they all shook.

"All right, I'm coming!" Roza yelled, even though the Emperor couldn't hear her.

She took her parents' hands and stood between them, reminding herself of being a little girl going out to play, with them keeping her safe. But now she was grown up, and the world was not safe, and there would be no one to protect her where she was going.

"Come on," she said. "Albany needs me. Will you come with me? I need to meet this Dragon."

CHAPTER TWENTY

As they hurried towards the gate in the stockade, Roza caught a whiff of smoke. She looked up to see flames spreading across a thatched roof. Falling embers from the Dragon's fire had kindled the thatch. She needed to face and confront this beast before anywhere else was set alight.

Some of the town guards at the gate were fighting the fire, while others restrained the panicking crowds to allow Roza, her parents and Jorxy to enter the town. It soon became clear that Helena and Arthur were well-known, because there were cries of amazement that her father could now see.

Roza left it to her mother to explain what the town's new young warlock had done and turned right through the jostle of people towards the eastern walls. She needed to meet this Dragon sooner rather than later before her resolve weakened. The longer she spent with her parents, or Jorxy, or anyone else who knew her, the harder it would be to leave them all behind.

Jorxy kept up with her determined stride, and the guard captain from the stockade gate marched right behind her with an escort of town guards. Were these to keep her safe or to make sure she didn't run away?

"I may have lost my memories," she said to the captain, "but I can find my way to the eastern gate well enough."

He shook his head. "Not my decision to make. The Reeve insists that the warlock is given every protection and assistance, so let me know if you need anything."

"Nothing I can think of, thank you."

"I apologise for doubting you yesterday, Miss Warlock. I can see you're a young woman who knows her mind and will go a long way."

Roza forced a smile in acknowledgement but didn't reply. She wondered how far away she might end up going as the Dragon Emperor's slave.

They reached the open courtyard that lay behind the town's east gate, and she was conducted at once to an old man with thinning grey hair who held a gold-tipped staff of office.

"Mister Reeve," said the guard captain, saluting him, "the warlock."

The Reeve looked around, clearly expecting to see Philoe. "Where?" he snapped. "What are you talking about, man?"

The captain indicated Roza, who wanted to disappear between the cobbles. The Reeve's eyes finally landed on her, and he frowned. "Who the hell are you?"

It was time to assert herself and make a good first impression. The Reeve's attitude grated on her, but she was determined to practise her polite, determined, and confident persona. She held out her hand and he took it automatically.

"Mister Reeve, I am pleased to meet you. My name is Rozabella, the daughter of Helena and Arthur. Philoe the warlock chose me as his apprentice before he died yesterday afternoon. His responsibilities therefore fall to me, and I am ready to meet the Emperor to try to save our town."

The Reeve's eyes had gone wide. "Philoe the warlock is dead? And now we have this girl in the role as our last hope of survival?"

Roza's indignation increased with his sneer at her youth and gender. "Mister Reeve," she pressed on, "as he died, Philoe the warlock bequeathed to me a portion of his magical spirit. He chose me because of my particular gifts and abilities. I have a plan of what to offer to the Emperor, and the resolve and the power to follow it through. Or perhaps you have some better ideas of your own of how to save our town from destruction? If you have, please say so, and I'll go back up to my plateau and leave you to it."

"No, don't do that," he said at once. She could tell that, despite himself, the Reeve was becoming impressed with her. "What did you say your name was, Miss Warlock?"

"Rozabella."

The Reeve was clicking his fingers. "You're that girl who's been missing for the last week. Judge Helena asked for my help to find you. Someone told me you'd been spotted."

"I've been in Philoe the warlock's cave during that time and learned much to our advantage. So, will you allow me to speak with the Emperor on behalf of the whole town?"

"What is your plan?" he demanded.

Roza hesitated. "I'd prefer to reveal that to the Emperor alone. But you can rest assured that I will extract from the Dragon a promise that no one in Albany is to be harmed, and that all our outstanding debts and taxes are to be written off."

The Reeve's eyes narrowed. "What on earth can you offer to make him accept such a deal?"

Roza lowered her voice. "As I said, Philoe discovered in me a unique and remarkable gift. If you wish proof of my powers, then speak with my parents and they will show you what I can do. They are on their way here from the warlock gate."

The Reeve considered her and then nodded. "Very well. We have no other options, so I suppose we might as well let you try. You may speak with the Emperor for us. And I will talk with Helena and Arthur as soon as they get here."

"One more thing," Roza said. "When I speak to the Emperor, no one must interrupt, contradict, or otherwise stop what I plan to do. It will be a very delicate negotiation, and you must trust that I know what I'm doing."

The Reeve narrowed his eyes at her again, and she was relieved he had little option but to agree to her terms. "We will allow you to see if you can save us. If you succeed, you will be rewarded with anything you wish. And if not, well, we'll all be destroyed anyway. So, good luck to you, Rozabella the warlock."

As he bowed his head and moved away, Roza suppressed a grim smile. How gracious of him to *allow* her to sacrifice herself for the safety of the town by becoming the Dragon's lifelong slave. They might appreciate in due course the cost to her once the deal with the Emperor was concluded. And as for the reward, that would have been nice, but she wouldn't be around here to receive it.

She watched the Reeve head to where her parents had now entered the open courtyard. There would be exclamations of wonder at the healing of her father's eyes – and sure enough they came a few moments later – but Roza needed to turn her thoughts from her parents to the Emperor.

As if to remind everyone, a second spout of flame seared the sky above, and Roza felt the heat of it on the back of her head.

Jorxy was still with her. He'd hung back as she spoke with the Reeve, but now stepped close and whispered, "Speak with the Dragon? Are you mad?"

She searched his eyes. The longer she was with him, the more she remembered. They'd spent a lot of time together at the rubbish ditch, sitting and talking. They knew, and understood, and trusted each other. Which made it all the harder to leave him. So, she couldn't tell him anything of her plan. Could she muster enough confidence to fool him?

"Jorxy, don't worry about me." She touched his arm. "I've learned a lot over the last few days about magic and warlock stuff, and I have a plan for this. Trust me."

He was staring into her eyes. "I do trust you. But you're

trembling. You're petrified. What are you going to do?"

No, she couldn't fool him at all. Of course she couldn't. "I'm going to go and speak with this Dragon, that's what I'm going to do. Because it's me or no one else. And the fate of our whole town and valley depends on it. So, wish me luck? Please?"

Jorxy swallowed. And then his lop-sided grin was back. "Go get him, Roza. That Dragon won't know what's hit him."

She managed a shaky laugh and gave him a quick embrace. Then she had to turn away. She couldn't let him see any more of her shaking and fear. Could she draw some strength from the boy's confidence? A few more steps towards the gate.

Roza filled her lungs with several deep breaths but had to cough as more smoke caught her throat. Did she have all she needed for this? She had her gift of Rejuvenate and was grateful now for the opportunity to confirm and practise this with her parents. She had the portion of Philoe's spirit and knew how to access the spark of magic he'd given her. The only other piece of the puzzle was the presence and support of Kerenzi the spirit lord. Was he here? She wouldn't be surprised if he'd accompanied her, invisible, all the way down from the warlock's cave, just to watch and enjoy the show. But she needed to be sure.

"Kerenzi, are you here?" she breathed.

In response, an invisible hand squeezed her left shoulder.

"Good," she said. "Just be ready when I ask for you."

She stepped forward and her escort of town guards moved with her. Receiving an armed entourage wherever she went wasn't bad for an otherwise unknown young woman of seventeen years, she thought with a wry smile.

But the town gates lay open before her, and her smile failed. Through the opening in the town wall, she saw a hillside of deep russet scales, topped with spikes of bone, where the view to the plain should have been. The dread and terror of the beast assailed her as a physical blow, and it was all she could manage to move each foot forward after the other.

She dropped her gaze to the cobbles. It wouldn't serve any purpose to petrify herself before she even stood in front of the Emperor. It would take more will and determination than she thought she possessed to walk up to him. But she had to do this. There was no other way, either for her or for the town. Walk yourself forward, Rozabella the warlock, and prove to this town and the world what a young woman can accomplish.

She reached the line of the town wall and crossed the threshold where the gates would close. The guards escorted her this far but then stopped. She didn't need to look up at what had stopped them. She knew. A stench of raw meat and a shadow over all the ground told her the Dragon was there in all his terrible splendour and no mortal could behold him without fear.

She walked on and glanced to her left and right. A huge crowd of the townsfolk had also exited through the gates and now cowered against the walls on each side. Their fear could only be as great as hers, and yet they had come, in morbid fascination to watch their fate unfold before their own eyes. If this was going to be their doom, then they were determined to witness it first-hand. Their safety was in numbers, to be no more than one in the vast crowd, trusting that the Dragon could not single them out for torture and death any sooner than he executed sentence on them all.

The lines of townsfolk stretched in a wide semi-circle all the way to the rising hills to the north and south. Here the mountain ranges that enclosed their valley met in a narrow cleft to the east where the highway from Albany ran out to Gorge City in the plain and to the rest of the Empire. But today there was no narrow cleft and the highway was blocked.

Still Roza didn't look up. She knew that if she did, she might turn and flee and hide and disgrace herself as they all expected. A buzz of murmurs and whispers ran through the throngs behind her, no doubt asking who she was and what she was doing. The answer would be passed along: Philoe is dead and she's the new warlock. What, her? they would say. Yes, me, Roza insisted. She would show them. That a female young person could have as much courage and resilience as anyone older or male. If not more.

But her arms and legs were shaking, and her stomach churned so much she was in danger of vomiting in front of them all.

She walked on, placing her boots carefully, one by one, on the paved slabs of the highway. By now she had to be conspicuous, approaching far closer than anyone else in the crowd of townsfolk. So, she stopped. The time had come to look.

As she'd seen from the edge of the plateau far above, the Dragon's scales gleamed like metal in the midday sun, but now she was so close that they towered above her like a cliff. She lifted her head and saw the lines of bone spikes that ran in serried ranks along the ridge of the Emperor's back, white against the blue of the sky. To her left and right lay the folded leather of great wings, tipped with clawed fingers, whose unfurled span she couldn't imagine. Underneath and beyond were vast legs and a tail, containing acres of muscle, lined and jointed with spines, ending in talons the size of a man.

Then at last Roza turned her gaze to behold the Dragon's head. He wasn't even looking at her. His head rested on the ground, half-lidded eyes flicking lazily along the crowds of fearful townsfolk as though choosing which to eat first. Menacing wisps of smoke rose from each cavernous nostril, and the closed mouth hid all but a few jagged and razor-sharp fangs. From time to time a blood-red tongue flicked out between the rows of teeth to taste the fear in the air.

The blood pounded through Roza's head, but she'd locked her muscles to prevent their natural inclination to turn and run. She was here. She'd made it this far. A lone figure in the middle of the vast open space before the presence of the Emperor.

The Dragon must have noticed her. He was mocking her, belittling her, reckoning her not even worthy of his attention. Through her terror and dread, her determination rose that this beast would look at her before she spoke.

She stepped forward again. After all, it couldn't get any worse than being this close to a Dragon, could it?

Yes, it could.

At last, the Dragon's wandering slit-like pupils deigned to come to rest on the tiny, single figure approaching him. And Roza wilted.

The force of the Dragon's gaze drained all but the last remnants of her will. How had she presumed to come and meet this beast? What utter folly had prompted her to attempt to speak, and reason, and deal with her Emperor? He was so far above her, and she a mere nothing, that comparing her to an ant before a mountain flattered her. How dare she?

A rumble through the ground made Roza's boots tremble and she braced herself for an earthquake. But the sound emanated from the Dragon before her, and with horror she realised that his eyes and mouth had opened to laugh at her.

Despite her dread, Roza bristled. If anyone was entitled to think little of her, it might be a Dragon or an Emperor, but a fire rose inside her to overcome her humiliation and shame.

The Dragon's jaws opened wide, rows of sharp teeth glistening in the sun, and she thought her end had come. He would lunge and bite her in half and strew her remains across the highway. Or burn her to a cinder by simply breathing out. Most of her hoped for this, because then her ordeal would be over. But no, the mighty throat uttered a deafening laugh, followed by a wide yawn.

He settled his head back to the ground and then spoke in a boom that filled the valley.

"I remember the olden days when villages used to offer me maidens to eat. It was a quaint custom, and I used to be fond of their soft flesh, but now I crave tougher meat. And besides this one would hardly make a mouthful."

Roza gulped down her indignation and fear, for she knew she needed to respond. So, he considered her no more than a peace offering as a young maiden to eat, did he? She would show him. Her throat was dry, but she marshalled her voice, remembering: polite, determined, brave.

"Your Majesty, you may eat me if you wish, but it would be your loss."

She'd aimed to call out the words, and was amazed when they seemed to ring out, filling the space between the mountains and the wall. The throngs of townsfolk behind her stilled, keen to catch every word of this exchange between their warlock and the Dragon.

The Emperor glanced away again, clearly refusing to be intrigued. He sighed in boredom and still wouldn't speak to her directly.

"I thought they'd have sent that Philoe the warlock out to meet me by now. Or maybe the old codger is too slow on his pins to make it down from the hills yet."

"Your Majesty, Philoe the warlock is dead. He was killed yesterday afternoon."

The Dragon flicked his wide eyes towards her. "The old warlock allowed himself to be killed?" The Emperor's voice cracked with amusement. "How careless of him. Too slow and dim-witted even to watch his own back. Still, I shall miss the exchanges with him. He always came up with some diverting proposals and riddles."

Roza decided it was time for some flattery. "He spoke of you with the utmost respect, Sire. As the town of Albany mourns for him, we are deeply touched that you share our grief and will miss him too."

The Dragon sniffed. "The town of Albany has come to a sorry state when it can find no better than a girl to give me this important news." There was a sneer on the word 'girl' that she couldn't miss, and it stirred her hackles. Patience, Rozabella, self-control, politeness.

"Your Majesty is too kind, for this messenger girl is no more than a warlock's apprentice and is honoured to speak with her Emperor."

"A warlock's apprentice?" the Dragon rumbled. "I see that old Philoe's brain became addled to choose such as this to train."

"Nevertheless," Roza pressed on, "I am the one he chose as his apprentice, Sire, and he had his reasons." Her confidence was growing the longer this conversation lasted. She was managing to do this, to speak with her Emperor, the Dragon, and she hadn't been eaten or incinerated yet. "He even thought of me highly enough to appoint me as his successor and bequeath to me a portion of his spirit."

For the first time the Dragon focused his attention on her. At last, she'd communicated to him that she was no trifling messenger or lackey, but someone to be reckoned with, the one through whom the town of Albany would present its requests.

"You are the new warlock?" The Emperor's tone was half doubtful, half amused. "I suppose you'd better tell me your name, girl, although I'm likely to forget it."

"I am Rozabella, Sire, the daughter of Arthur and Helena, upstanding citizens of this town, and I am at your service." She'd been going to curtsy, but at the last minute decided she'd prefer to give him a deep bow instead.

"At my service, are you?" the Dragon thundered, as though she'd reminded him at last of why he was here. "I trust then that you are well informed about what the town of Albany owes to the Empire. There is the small matter of centuries of outstanding taxes and duties which I have had to come here in person to collect. Do you have the authority to deal with me about all that is due?"

"We are truly sorry that you have had to trouble yourself with this matter in person, Sire. But the honour of your presence enables us to suggest a solution that will resolve our outstanding debts to you once and for all. Yes, the Reeve of Albany has appointed me to speak with you on behalf of the people here. Will Your Majesty be kind enough to listen to the proposal from your humble subjects to set things right between us?"

Here I go, Roza thought. It's now or never, and this is it: the moment when I offer myself to this tyrant as his abject slave until death releases me. There's no turning back.

CHAPTER TWENTY-ONE

The Dragon lifted his head into the air so that it overshadowed Roza from the midday sun and flexed the rippling muscles in his neck. When it came down to the ground again it was closer to her and facing her squarely. He breathed out, and the heat from his nostrils blasted into her, scorching her face and singeing her hair. If he'd been trying to intimidate her, it worked, but Roza stood her ground.

"Now then," the Emperor began, "do you understand the vast sums of your indebtedness to the Empire, and how you have no grounds for mercy or appeal?"

Roza held out her hands. "I do not know the exact figures, Sire, but only that the total exceeds the value of all the land, buildings and people in the valley. As such, there is no way that we can pay in gold, silver, jewellery and gems all that is due and so we ask you to consider accepting instead something else that is even more valuable."

The Dragon's slit eyes narrowed as though trying to imagine something more valuable than treasure to add to his hoard. "How dare you insult me by suggesting you have anything I could possibly want more than treasure? Are you trying to trick me?"

"I apologise if I have in any way offended you, Sire, but please hear me out. I know that Your Majesty is wise and cunning, and able to detect any lie, so I would not presume to try to deceive my Emperor. I swear on my life that all I say to you is true, and you can test and examine me on any point you wish."

"I'm waiting to hear what you think you have that is more valuable than my treasure."

Roza heaved a breath. She remembered discussing with Philoe the worth of her unique and remarkable gift, and how she would never be safe if its existence became widely known. They'd agreed to keep it in absolute secrecy for as long as possible, and yet Roza had already used it to help her parents. Now she was about to announce it to the entire population of Albany, and to the ruler of their whole Empire. In a few minutes, it could hardly be less secret.

"It begins with the reason why Philoe the warlock chose me as his apprentice. He was not addled when he did so because he discovered in me a unique and remarkable gift. He informed me that the ability I possess is so rare that it has never appeared before in the whole history of the world. It is so remarkable that Empires have gone to war over the mere rumour of it, and Emperors and Lords would give everything they own to control or have access to it."

The Dragon looked unimpressed. "You stretch my patience. Get on and say it."

Roza swallowed hard. Once uttered, her secret could never be stoppered again. She lifted her voice, slow and clear. "My gift is called Rejuvenate, the ability to make people physically younger." Now she'd done it.

There was silence across the space between the walls and the mountains, followed by an outbreak of chatter among the townsfolk. It rose in volume, as though they'd forgotten for a moment the terror of the Dragon before them.

"Silence!" the Dragon roared, spewing a jet of flame into the sky over the town, showering down in sparks and ash. The people of Albany hushed, although Roza thought she heard the conversations continue in whispers.

"Explain yourself," the Emperor ordered. "What do you mean?"

Roza drew in a breath. Her leg muscles had rooted her to the spot for too long, so now she made the conscious effort to move. As she spoke, she paced back and forth in front of the Dragon's head, his eyes following her progress.

"When I met Philoe the warlock some days ago," she began, "he was continuing his study of longevity. He'd already succeeded in prolonging his life to the four hundred years or so of his existing mortal lifespan." She decided not to mention that he'd captured her, or anything about the potion. "He soon discovered that something in me had effected a remarkable change in him. When I first met him, he was ancient and decrepit, and yet when he died yesterday, he was no more than middle aged. I had made him physically younger again."

"Do you have any proof or witnesses for this?"

Roza had expected this, although she wished she could have kept it all under wraps for longer. "First of all, can you detect within me the portion of Philoe the warlock's spirit? He would not have bequeathed to me his memories, his magic and his very soul unless he trusted me and considered me worthy. This ability of mine is the only thing that qualifies me to be a warlock."

The Dragon narrowed his eyes again and leaned closer, scrutinising her. It was as though his gaze sliced through her, worming his way into the deepest recesses of her body and soul.

He leaned back. "Yes, I do sense Philoe within you, and you certainly possess a spark of magic. His spirit feels more vigorous, contented and youthful than I remember, so I will grant you that. You said, 'first of all', so what else?"

Roza hesitated. "There was a witness to the time I spent in and around the cave of Philoe the warlock, namely Kerenzi, lord of the spirits of the forest. Your Majesty may not have noticed him yet, but he is here beside me and invisible."

At once the Dragon's eyes roved around her immediate

vicinity before coming to rest behind her left shoulder.

"Ah, Kerenzi, my old friend," the Dragon rumbled. "What brings you out here today?"

Roza heard the spirit lord's voice come softly so that the Emperor could hear, but not all the crowds along the town wall.

"My lord the Emperor, I am here because Rozabella the warlock asked me to come. I can confirm that everything she has told you is true. She is an impressive and spirited young woman, and I can vouch for her honesty and integrity. I am in her debt but have every reason to believe that her dealings with us will be both forthright and trustworthy."

If she hadn't been face-to-face with a Dragon, Roza would have spluttered and gaped at the compliments Kerenzi had given her. As it was, she lifted her chin and held the Dragon's gaze calmly as he spoke.

"Well, well, having spirit lord Kerenzi to vouch for you, and he says he is in your debt. I detect the scent of an interesting story between the two of you, and only regret that we have these pressing matters to attend to first. Very well, Rozabella, warlock of Albany, you have a gift. Explain to me how this might be more valuable to me than treasure."

And that was the moment when the better idea hit her.

All morning she'd been intending to offer her gift in service to the Emperor as his slave. That he would amass vast wealth and power through exploiting her gift, selling it to those who wanted it.

But could this better plan work instead? She needed to think fast and keep the Emperor talking while she worked it out.

"Your Majesty, in order to discuss the value of my gift to you, I beg your indulgence to answer a few of my questions. It will help us to establish how this could profit you best. So, please excuse my ignorance, but are Dragons immortal?"

The Emperor threw back his head and laughed. "Are we immortal? That's hardly something you lesser mortals need to worry yourselves about. We outlive you by many of your lifetimes, and after all of you have died, I will still be here."

"My point is, Sire," Roza pressed on, "that if you're not immortal then you have a lifecycle. You hatch from an egg and grow from hatchling to adolescent to adult. You mate and produce eggs. You progress to maturity, and to ancient. If Dragons are not killed by the sword or magic or accident, then eventually you reach old age and die of natural causes. You remain undefeated and your spirit passes on peacefully in your sleep. Forgive me if I'm only guessing, but is that correct?"

The Emperor paused, seeming to consider Roza's words. "You are correct, but the lifespans of Dragons are reckoned in thousands of human years."

Roza nodded. "I understand that, Your Majesty. Our Empire has been blessed with your gracious rule for centuries, if not thousands of years already, and I can see that you have matured to huge and ancient size. I wonder, therefore, if the years behind you outnumber those ahead. Are you nearer the end of your life than its beginning? We pray, of course, that we will benefit from your wise and generous rule for many hundreds and thousands of years still to come. But in the case of human old age, we experience increasing aches, pains, frailty and infirmity, until our eventual death by natural causes. We would hate for any of these to afflict you, Sire."

The Emperor's eyes were fixed on Roza, boring into her. "You dare to suggest that I will weaken, that my powers will fail, to become a decrepit, impotent, pitiable Dragon? My splendour and might have been undimmed for centuries and will remain so for centuries to come."

"We pray indeed that this will be so, Sire. Nevertheless,

the march of time runs in one direction only – forwards – from birth to maturity to death, the inexorable course of our mortal lifespans, and can never be stopped or reversed. Except, of course, through the use of my unique gift of Rejuvenate.”

The Emperor licked his lips, and Roza hoped he was pondering her words, acquiring a taste for longer life. “You said you had a proposal to make. I suggest you present it.”

“I would like to offer, Your Majesty, to use my gift for your personal benefit. I propose to see if we can make you younger again, to increase the span of years that you still have ahead of you. You can enjoy again the vigour and energy of adulthood and expect to rule our Empire for hundreds or thousands of years longer than otherwise. You will forestall the onset of frailty and old age, and cheat death out of creeping up on you. In short, Sire, you will become the longest-lived Dragon of all time. As well as being the greatest Dragon of this age, you will become the greatest Dragon there has ever been.”

Roza hoped she was presenting her offer in glowing and irresistible terms. It remained to be seen whether her gift worked on Dragons as well as on humans, but it was certainly worth a try.

“And what do you ask in return for using your ability to benefit me in this way? I assume your offer is not a free gift.” If she hadn’t known better, Roza thought he might be teasing her.

“As you might expect, Your Majesty, in return for my gift, the town of Albany asks for all outstanding taxes owing to you to be cancelled. This will wipe the slate clean, and we can start again with a new and mutually beneficial relationship with you, Sire. We also ask for your promise that neither person nor property in this valley will be harmed by you from today for the next hundred years into the future.”

During the pause in which the Emperor considered Roza's terms, Kerenzi the invisible spirit lord spoke. She jumped because she'd forgotten he stood behind her shoulder.

"Forgive me for intervening, Sire, but these short-lived mortals have little concept of a meaningful passage of time when compared with those of us who count in centuries. As a girl in the prime of her youth, Rozabella the warlock has reckoned only with the years that the residents of the town of Albany might be expected to live. I speak for the immortal residents of this valley and would ask that in return for the warlock's gift you should promise to leave this valley in peace not for a hundred, but for a thousand years."

Not a hundred but a thousand years of safety and peace? Roza thought this might be too high a promise to extract from the Emperor, but in a negotiation, it was always worth asking, and to start high. Maybe she'd set the value of her gift too low. Was the prospect of rejuvenation sufficiently irresistible for this Dragon to accept whatever they asked?

A rumble issued from the Dragon's chest, and he said, "Hmm, you ask a high price. To write off all the past tribute from Albany for the last four centuries, and not to trouble you again for another thousand years?"

"Ah, but in return, Your Majesty," Roza interjected, "suppose I gain for you another thousand years of life. You would have lost nothing from us. And you would receive a thousand years of tribute from all the many other towns and cities in your Empire. Those years would be yours to direct how you please, with only this small pocket of land left untaxed, and in return you gain the priceless gift of a restored youth and strength and energy. If I were an old woman, I know which I would choose. I would return to my youth, which I could never otherwise regain, and trade it for any amount of treasure, which death robs from us all anyway."

Roza was tempted to keep talking, trying to persuade the Emperor to agree to her offer, but she clamped her mouth shut. The Dragon was clever enough to understand the terms asked, and also what the benefits of rejuvenation might be. She needed to be patient.

She looked around and saw again the lines of townsfolk along the wall, who also seemed to be holding their breath for whether the Dragon would accept. Yes, this was their fate that was about to be decided too.

The Emperor cleared his throat and Roza looked back at him. "Are you sure you can perform this miracle?"

"I will be honest with you, Sire, and say that no, I am not completely sure. I have never tried to use this gift with a Dragon. However, I know that it certainly works with humans, and it might even work more powerfully with you because of your inherent magic. We can only try it and see."

"And how would you do it? What would be involved?"

"I need to touch you, Sire. I have only a small amount of magic of my own, but that would be channelled through my touch into your body. This is why I asked Kerenzi the spirit lord to be here now, to contribute his considerable magic to effect your transformation. We would ask that you supply your own magic to the effort too, because it is a mighty task that we attempt. We pool the magic of the three of us, combine it with our common desire for you to be younger, and it all becomes reality through the exercise of my gift. That is the theory, anyway."

"Very well," the Dragon declared. "Rozabella the warlock, I agree to your proposal."

There were some cheers from the townsfolk behind them, but these were soon silenced when the Emperor flicked his eyes in their direction.

Roza breathed out a long breath and rested her hands on her hips. "Thank you, Your Majesty. Please make your promises."

The Dragon lifted his head from the ground and his proclamation echoed around the mountainsides. "I hereby swear by my life and Empire that if – and only if – Rozabella the warlock can make me significantly younger today, then I cancel all outstanding payments due to me from the town and people of Albany. I also swear that at the successful conclusion of our rejuvenation effort, and for the next one thousand years, I will neither enter, nor trouble, nor harm, nor expect any payment from the residents of the valley of Albany, except with your permission. I express also a desire that we might negotiate further mutually beneficial agreements in the future."

"Agreed," said Rozabella, and there were more cheers from the townsfolk. This time the Dragon did not quell them, for there seemed a mood of celebration in the air. If Albany could be freed from dread and debt, to live in prosperity and security for a thousand years, and if the Emperor could be freed from the fear of old age and death, then this was a wonderful day for them all. It was a day of peace and joy and hope.

The only thing remaining was for Roza to deliver it.

CHAPTER TWENTY-TWO

Roza swallowed hard. She never imagined herself in the position of negotiating a successful deal with a Dragon and Emperor, let alone trying to use magic to rejuvenate him. And now here she was, and everything depended on the successful use of her gift. The sooner she got this over with, the better.

She stepped forward, reaching out with her hands. "If possible, Your Majesty, I should touch you somewhere softer, or otherwise the natural defences of your armoured scales might deflect the magic. Perhaps in the folds under your neck?"

The Emperor gave her a sidelong look, and Roza thought he almost winked. "As long as you promise not to tickle me," he rumbled. What was she to make of that? Could she possibly be on friendly and joking terms with a Dragon and her Emperor?

He stretched out his neck along the ground and rolled sideways, revealing the paler coloured scales underneath. Roza forced her footsteps forward because her trembling had started again. She was now so close that the Dragon's body towered over her, even his neck thicker than her height. If he decided to roll back over again, he would crush her to death. She also felt dangerously trapped and enclosed, with vast wings above and clawed feet to the side. This was no place for a girl in her right mind to be.

But she had one ally. "Kerenzi, are you with me?" she breathed.

"I am," came his voice in her ear. "So far, so good. It's time for you to change the history of this valley and Empire. I believe in you, Roza, so go ahead." His two hands took a firm hold of her shoulders.

Everything now depended on her, and on this. She reached out her hands and placed them on the Dragon's neck. The scales were hard, but not metal, and she adjusted her fingers into the cracks between them where she could feel the warmth of the Dragon's flesh beneath.

"Your Majesty, when you feel the magic from me and the spirit lord begin," she called towards the Dragon's head, "please send all your magical energy into me, concentrating on wanting to become younger. I will channel it through my gift and back into your body."

"I understand," came the rumbled response.

She closed her eyes. This was it.

Roza reached deep down inside for her spark of magic, and there it was again. She fanned it into flame and felt its heat begin to build. Kerenzi's hands tightened on her shoulders, and the flow of magic from behind her joined it, filling her up fast. She needed to start channelling this out or it would overwhelm her.

She focused on her hands, on where her palms and fingers touched the Dragon's flesh and started sending the power out again. It was working, sending Kerenzi's energy and hers into the Dragon's body.

At once she became aware of how minuscule and insignificant she was, and how vast and massive was the Dragon's huge bulk. She wasn't trying to rejuvenate only this small portion of his neck, as she'd done with Philoe's hands, or with her parents' eyes and heart. This time the object was his whole body, and it felt like dipping her fingers in the waters of a small bay in the corner of an entire ocean.

She sensed the Dragon's willingness to receive from her, and their desires were united – Rozabella the warlock, Kerenzi the spirit lord, and the Dragon Emperor – to make this massive creature younger. But it seemed too great a task, too hard and vast for her to accomplish through her small, mortal frame.

Then the Dragon's magic began to flow. Just as Philoe had done as they held hands across the cave's kitchen table, the Emperor was sending his magic to help her. But this was a vast flood, huge and overwhelming, and Roza feared to be washed away in its tide.

Kerenzi's hands squeezed her shoulders, and his voice sounded in her head. "Hold on, Rozabella, because you can do this." Were they so united in their magic they could communicate without speech, as Philoe's spirit had done? "Don't try to turn, or hold, or control it, but let it flow through you freely. Don't narrow or restrict the flood but open yourself up. Abandon yourself to the magic. Be a wide and clear vessel for the magic's course, and it will work."

She tried to relax her tense muscles and let the magic wash in, and through, and out, but her arms and hands were tingling and fizzing and crackling with such raw power that she lost all feeling in them. The warmth and contentment of the magic in every corner of her body was building to an ecstasy of joy and energy and purpose that overwhelmed all sense of self. She was no longer a person, but the tide itself, the magic, the flow, the power, that came and went in an endless rhythm of creation.

She was no longer a girl. She was a warlock. Her spirit had grown, as though she stood towering over the whole valley. The people of the town bustled around beneath her feet like ants, and she was as high above them as the clouds above the soil. And she cared for them, in their little concerns, as though she were their mother, and they were all her children. She would protect them, and provide for them, and save them all from death. With one finger's touch, she could restore youth and strength and vigour, and banish old age, disease, infirmity and death.

For she was more than just their warlock. She was their saviour and deliverer, their liberator, the one who would set them free from fear. She was their queen and empress.

Their goddess. Here at last was her life's work, her destiny and purpose.

And then something shifted. What was that? Cupped in her mighty hands lay this curled Dragon. Had it worked? Was the Dragon beginning to rejuvenate? She reached out with her senses, and yes, there was the Dragon's body, the whole vast form of him, as though she were the mountains and cradled the Emperor in her arms. And it was working.

The beast was no longer ancient. The years were slipping away, reversing, as the flow of time ebbed backwards, like water running uphill. She was doing this, leeching away his old age and fear of death, and sending them into the earth and the sky.

Had she doubted she could do this? With her own budding magic, with the wealth of Kerenzi and the Emperor, this task was no longer formidable, but manageable, and she set to work. One by one she attended to his vital and inner organs, his outward appearance, his bones, his blood, his flesh – younger, younger, younger.

She felt his body changing beneath her fingers, moving, shrinking. Because of course, Dragons kept growing larger and larger throughout their lives, until they became both ancient and huge. As he became younger, the Emperor was also becoming steadily smaller.

Then she wondered, when were they supposed to stop? How young did the Emperor want to be? They hadn't set a specific age or stage of life. They'd been so uncertain of doing it at all that the Dragon had only said 'significantly younger'. Well, he was certainly that already. How much younger did he want: old, mature, adult?

As soon as she thought this, Kerenzi's voice answered her: "Keep going." Had he read her mind? "Keep going, Rozabella, further, more."

She kept going … and the Dragon continued to shrink before her. The feelings came through her hands and fingers again, as the scales moved, and shrank, and softened, and warmed.

"No, wait, stop," the Dragon roared, and he seemed to be trying to pull away.

Not only was the flow of magic from the Emperor abruptly cut off, but his desire ceased too. A body-wrenching shock slammed into Roza as their magical union shattered. With a final blast, Kerenzi's and her magic crashed into the Dragon's scales and rebounded, catapulting them backwards high into the air.

Roza had never flown, and she flailed her arms and legs in a helpless and hopeless attempt to save herself. She braced herself for the inevitable and fatal impact with the ground ... before she realised that Kerenzi's hands were holding her. In fact, his invisible arms now enveloped and lifted her as his wings flew for them both. Their descent slowed into a safe and graceful landing back on the wide slabs of the highway. Roza's legs gave way in shock, and she would have crumpled to the ground if the spirit lord hadn't still been holding her up.

No sooner had her feet hit the ground than a jet of flame roared towards her. Before it struck them, Kerenzi reacted, deflecting the flames skywards. Had that been Dragon-fire?

The shock of the attack stunned Roza back into reality. She shook herself free of Kerenzi's arms and leapt forward.

"You promised," she screamed. "Stop!"

The Dragon's head before her inhaled his next breath as smoke billowed from his nostrils.

"You swore by your life and Empire that you wouldn't harm any of us in this valley," she yelled. She would have shouted more but the words died in her throat. The vision before her was struggling to register in her brain.

The Dragon stood before her, the Emperor, but he no longer lay on the ground, filling the cleft between the mountains. The spikes on his back had previously reached up towards the mountainsides, but now they stood only two or three times her height. His vast bulk had overflowed past the rising hillsides on each side, but now if he stretched out smoking nostril to bony tail tip, he might only just reach from side to side. His wings were unfurled, and instead of a vast canopy overshadowing the whole valley, their shade didn't even reach as far as the town walls.

Rozabella gulped. What had she done? She was no expert on Dragon ages or sizes, but here was no huge or ancient Dragon. In fact, the Emperor looked no longer old or mature, or even an adult. If she had to place him, she'd have said larger than a child or young Dragon, so perhaps adolescent or young adult.

"Your Majesty," she called, "what have we done to you? I had no idea this would work so well. I didn't know when to stop. I never dreamed your rejuvenation could go so far."

The Dragon's eyes blazed into hers and she quailed before the fury in them. "You did this on purpose," he spat. "You had 'no idea', did you, you 'never dreamed'? You have deceived and tricked me, Rozabella the warlock."

"No, I have not," she protested. "I offered this in good faith. My gift is untested, and I told you I'd never tried this with a Dragon. It was your own greed for extra years of life that sent too much magical power my way, and I could only reflect it back to you. I refuse to take any blame for how this worked out."

The Emperor's eye shifted to behind her, and Roza realised he was now addressing the still-concealed Kerenzi. "If the girl protests her innocence, then you, spirit lord, certainly knew what you were doing. I felt you pressing for further and more, refusing to stop even when you knew I no longer desired it. You wanted me smaller and weaker, didn't you?"

The viciousness and mockery in Kerenzi's voice shocked her. "Yes indeed, Your Humbler Majesty, I wanted it. For too long you have ruled over this Empire with dread and violence, and today I saw a chance to end it. You are a cruel and vain tyrant, oppressing and mistreating your subjects, who live out their lives in abject fear of you. But no longer. You are vulnerable now, O Smaller Emperor, and your fire-breath less hot, such that even I can deflect it. Your scales have become soft and tender, such that even our archers might penetrate them. Yes, I admit it, in this warlock's gift I saw the chance to diminish you, and for the sake of the Empire, I acted. But you will remember that the promise of your word remains, and you will keep it for a thousand years, if you manage to survive that long."

"Wait, Your Majesty." Roza stepped forwards, arms outstretched. "I know I am young and naïve and inexperienced, but I do not wish us to part as enemies today. Accept my apology for making you younger than you desired. Today's agreement between us must stand, and Albany will be free of debt and fear for longer than we can imagine, but I hope that our future relations can be peaceful, not antagonistic."

"Your wishes and hopes are admirable, warlock, and may be wiser than your years, but they carry no weight with me. I must honour my word and promises, but you have all made for yourselves an enemy today."

The Emperor turned his head away, lifted his wings and leapt into the air. With a mighty downdraft of wind, he beat his way up into the sky above the valley, making a vast, rising circuit above the town. His roar echoed up to the peaks, but it no longer split rocks or felled trees. Roza's last sight of him was a jet of fire above the cleft and the highway, and then the Emperor turned north and disappeared behind the mountains.

CHAPTER TWENTY-THREE

The Dragon's roars had not faded into silence before they were replaced by the erupting townsfolk. They cheered and shouted and whistled and clapped, surging forward to where Roza stood.

"Enjoy your glory," came Kerenzi's voice in her ear. "I'll see you soon, Rozabella the warlock." Behind her, she felt him rise invisibly skywards to escape the oncoming crush.

The first to reach her was Jorxy, who grabbed her into a rib-crushing squeeze. And then the rest of the people were on her. Everyone wanted to touch and embrace and congratulate the girl who had saved them. The crush risked becoming too great, so Jorxy and another boy hoisted her onto their shoulders and carried her towards the town gates. She had no opportunity to say even a word above all the shouting and crying. All she could do was to wave and smile and acknowledge them all.

But she didn't know any of them and felt exhausted. At last, when she reached where the Reeve and her parents stood, the town guards restored order, keeping the jostling masses away from her. The crowds of townsfolk gave them a little more space, and the boys lowered her onto her feet. The tightest hugs were from her mother and father, and the Reeve shook her hand, wiping the tears from his face. And they proceeded through the town gates.

"To the marketplace," the Reeve cried. "A feast in the Town Hall, an assembly in the square, and today will be a public holiday for ever!"

The people lined the streets, shouting until they were hoarse, waving their arms, blowing kisses, crying their eyes out in laughter and relief, and there was only one name on everyone's lips: Rozabella.

It began to sink in that she'd done it. She hadn't really appreciated all that was at stake, but it was over and past now. She walked with her parents on one side and Jorxy on the other, holding their hands in the procession to the Town Hall, but it all felt unreal and a dream. This was not like her, to be the hero of the town, the saviour, the one who had defeated the Dragon. Long before the feast and speeches, the honours and awards began, Roza found herself yearning for the quiet beauty of the plateau and cave.

But she played her part. She smiled and waved and thanked everyone. When they called on her to say a few words, she explained that it hadn't been only her. Philoe the old warlock deserved the recognition for identifying her gift and starting her on the path of magic. Kerenzi the spirit lord, and the Dragon Emperor himself had provided the magical power for the transformation.

But the people seemed reluctant to share her credit with anyone. After all, they hadn't seen anyone but her outside the town gates, facing the Dragon. She had negotiated the deal that the Emperor had accepted and worked the miracle that had vanquished him. In the end, Roza stopped arguing about it, because no one wanted to believe it hadn't been all her doing.

She made sure that Arthur, Helena and Jorxy always sat with her in the places of honour, because she didn't know anyone else, and they were the best company for conversation. Although her parents might have been used to public occasions and banquets, Jorxy was clearly having the time of his life, stuffing as much free food, not to mention silverware, as he could fit into his jacket pockets. They had the best rooms in the town's Mermaid Inn, and Roza's exhaustion caused her to sleep long and late.

By the time she awoke the next morning, there was already a queue of people at the doors of the inn asking for her to rejuvenate them, or someone they loved.

This was a predictable development, and at first Roza was only too pleased to help, but it was a foretaste of what was to come. During the day, increasing numbers of townsfolk brought to her those who were sick or elderly, for her to heal them. What she had done for her parents, as well as for the Dragon, was now the main topic of conversation, and everyone knew someone who needed her touch. Time and again she had to explain that she had only very little magic of her own and couldn't heal all diseases or re-grow limbs with a touch. But anything that was an age-related condition, such as her parents' eyes and heart, she found she could rejuvenate. When it worked better than people could possibly imagine, the tales of Rozabella's miracles began to spread beyond the valley.

By that evening, she called a halt and announced that she would accompany her parents back to their Meadow Cottage in the forest the next morning. It was a relief to be back in the peace and solitude under the trees, and to see her parents settled into their home. Jorxy's sister, Joidi, had loved living in the cottage and looking after their animals and was clearly sad to relinquish that role and return to town.

Arthur was busy looking at everything, pointing out to them the most ordinary sights with wonder and delight. He talked about being able to 'pick up the threads' of his old life, and they groaned at the weaving reference. Helena was walking everywhere with a brisk pace, bustling over the household chores, and wondering whether the town still needed her services as a judge.

The only person Roza would allow to visit them at Meadow Cottage was Jorxy, but she didn't let him stay with her there. Although she enjoyed his company, she also needed lots of solitude to think about all that had happened, to recover her memories, and consider her future.

In the end, she told neither her parents nor Jorxy the truth about everything that had happened to her, but kept to the story of having hit her head in the forest clearing, and that Philoe the warlock had rescued and helped her. She reasoned there was no benefit in adding to their fear about the world of magic, and they would fuss forever about whether she was fully recovered. She would let old Philoe rest in peace, forgiving him for his crimes against her, because she'd now succeeded him, and her gateway into a life of magic was wide open. Only Kerenzi the spirit lord knew the truth about their kidnap, mistreatment, captivity, and the dreaded longevity potion.

When the townsfolk started seeking her out at her parents' cottage, however, Roza decided it was time to retreat to her own plateau and cave. She explained that she needed to study and grow in her own magic to be able to help them all better in the future. So, one evening she bade farewell to her parents and sneaked off at night back up the path to the plateau. The town guards at the warlock gate were supposed to prevent unauthorised people from venturing out of town that way and trespassing along the farm track onto the path up to the plateau.

Everything was as Roza remembered it. Standley had looked after the animals as best he could, and the next morning she marvelled to watch how a coat stand could milk a cow, carrying a bucket to underneath their cows called Dairy, and using his middle hooks. He was also adept at collecting eggs from their chickens, Boil, Scramble, Poach and Fry. He could pick them up with his wooden feet, toss them upwards to catch them in his hooks and lay them in a basket he carried. Roza wondered whether he might actually be able to juggle with the eggs but decided not to test that or let him try.

After their chores, she sat on the bench in the orchard while he stood beside Philoe's grave, and she told her coat stand of all that had happened with the Dragon. Standley was an excellent listener, in that he nodded in all the right places, and didn't interrupt at all.

When she finished, she stood up and gazed at this amazing piece of furniture she seemed to have inherited. "Thank you, Standley, for all you've done for me so far, and for looking after this place."

The knots at the top of the stand seemed to crinkle into a smile again, and he inclined his top hooks towards her.

Roza smiled back. "I don't know how long you've lived here, serving successive warlocks, and I don't suppose you'll ever be able to tell me. But it struck me that Philoe wasn't all that kind or considerate towards you. Did he treat you well?"

Standley was discreet enough not to say anything, but she thought his hooks shook slightly to left and right.

Roza reached and rested a hand on one of his polished wooden hooks. "I'm going to try to make things better for you from now on, Standley. I'd like us to be friends, if that would be all right with you?"

At this, Standley's knots definitely smiled, and he scuttled forward and gave her the nearest to a warm and gentle embrace that hard-edged wood could manage.

When they stepped back, the coat stand scuttled off into the cave and Roza was intrigued enough to follow him. She found him rummaging and searching through all the piled-up junk in one of the storerooms at the rear of the cave. At last, he seemed to find what he was looking for, because he hooked out a small jar and offered it to her.

Roza took it and examined the faded label. Gymbo's Furniture Polish. She looked up at Standley. "Is this for you?" He nodded. "Would you like some?" Another vigorous nod of the hooks.

She unstopped the lid and at once a wonderful woody aroma filled the cave. Standley seemed to breathe it in too. She peered at the thick, dark brown liquid inside. "How much do I use?"

He held two hooks very close together to indicate a very small amount.

Roza found a cloth, dipped it into the jar and scooped out a small blob. She raised her eyebrows at him. He nodded.

Laying down the jar, she began to apply Gymbo's Furniture Polish to all of Standley's wood, from hooks to pole to feet. He seemed to relax and sigh with relief as she worked the fragrant ointment into his knots and joints, and the grain in his wood seemed to shine. He even closed his eye knots when she came to polish his top.

"I guess that old Philoe didn't bother to do this for you very much," she mused. He shook his hooks. "And you can't exactly do this for yourself. There are some things that require a human touch."

When she finished, Standley flexed and stretched like an old man who'd long suffered with stiff and aching joints and was finally free of the pain. She giggled to herself to see him enjoying his renewed bending, twisting and scuttling so much. Almost as though he'd been rejuvenated, she thought to herself with a wry smile.

That afternoon, Kerenzi the spirit lord appeared. Roza wondered whether he'd been watching and waiting for her return. He was leaning nonchalantly against the cave wall near the entrance when he popped into view from invisibility. It was disconcerting, and she wondered how long he'd stood there, hidden from her view, or even following her around.

"You're not allowed to snoop around here invisibly, you know," she scolded him. "I insist on some privacy, so you will appear at the top of the path and walk across the grass like everyone else."

He raised his eyebrows. "As you wish, Miss Warlock." He sauntered closer, looking around at everything again. She'd been cleaning and tidying, deciding to rearrange the cave into how she liked it. Standley had helped her to move the furniture, and the first priority had been to clear out Philoe's sleeping chamber.

Kerenzi sat down on a kitchen table stool, and it seemed that the spirit lord wouldn't leave until they'd had a proper conversation. So Roza seated herself opposite him.

"Did you intend from the outset," she began, "to humiliate the Emperor the other day by making him as young as possible?"

"Yes and no." Kerenzi tilted his head. "Like you, I was surprised at how well your gift worked. I knew that between us, the Emperor and I have some impressive magical energy, but it all depended on how strong your Rejuvenate gift is. Very strong, as it turns out. Before we started, I didn't think we'd make him younger by more than a century or two."

"So why did you persevere when it became clear we could make him as young as we wished? Why make an enemy of him, when we could have stopped with him as a mature adult Dragon, and we could all have gone away happy and as friends?"

"Ah, Rozabella," he sighed. "At times I love how naïve and trusting you are. At other times it's a huge frustration how short-sighted and parochial you mortals are. The deal you negotiated with the Emperor was impressive in its scope, writing off centuries of payments due from Albany and securing the safety of everyone in the town. I hope you didn't mind my increasing his banishment from this valley from a hundred to a thousand years?"

"No, I didn't mind at all. I didn't want to ask him for too much in case he refused."

"Asking for too much? For him and for me, a hundred years is nothing. A thousand years isn't much more. It's the predictable short-lived mortal thinking: a century means you'll all be dead by then and so it won't concern you. Rozabella, have you forgotten your gift? Now that you've started rejuvenating all the elderly in the town, what do you think will happen to Albany's average life expectancy?"

"Um, it will go up?"

"Er, yes, I should think so. In fact, if you stay here and use your magic and gift to keep making people younger, then everyone alive today could live for at least another hundred years. And if you also use your gift on yourself to extend your own life, then you could make all the residents of Albany practically immortal."

Roza sat there stunned. "I hadn't thought of that. If I keep making myself younger, and everyone else who comes to me younger, then there's no reason for any of us to die of old age, is there? Only from other diseases, accidents, or violence."

Kerenzi was nodding. "And suppose that no one is dying, and people keep having babies. What will happen to the population of the town?"

"That will keep rising too. So before long the town will become crowded or run out of food to eat or something."

"Exactly. They will need more houses, farms, schools, and so on. Which means you need to think about wider than the future of just this one valley. How long will it take for the news of what happened here to spread across the towns and cities of the plain and across the Empire? Or how long until the rumour spreads that the town of Albany has someone who can heal the sick, can stop the old from dying, and is a source of eternal youth and practical immortality?"

Roza's cheeks turned cold as the blood drained from them. This is what Philoe had talked about: Empires going to war to possess an Elixir of Life or a Fountain of Eternal Youth. And what everyone would want access to, to possess or control or exploit, was her.

"What can we do?" she whispered.

"We need to be able to defend ourselves," Kerenzi

answered. "To control access to the valley through the cleft and along the highway. We're blessed with a naturally defensible position, but we need to be on our guard at once. And so, the first thing to do was to get the Emperor out of the way."

"Why did we need to remove the Emperor? Wouldn't he have helped to keep law and order, to stop the peoples of the Empire from besieging the town of Albany? With him on our side, we'd have been able to hold our own against everybody."

"Don't be naïve, Rozabella. The Emperor would never have been on our side. He has only ever, and always, been on his own side. He wouldn't defend our interests, but always look to exploit the situation for his own ends, to profit from you and use you to extend his power."

"But what will happen to the Emperor now? Can an adolescent Dragon rule an Empire?"

Kerenzi shook his head. "Not a chance. An Empire this vast, with so many cities, towns and peoples, was kept together only through fear of their Emperor who had the power to destroy them. Now that he is weakened and vulnerable, everyone will seize their chance to become free. All will rise up against him and seek to claim power for themselves. War is coming, Roza. The Empire will fall apart. The Dragon will be overthrown or killed. When chaos and uncertainty come, we must remain strong and safe, and you will be key to that."

Roza stared at him and then turned to look out of the cave entrance at the grass and trees outside. How had she ended up in the middle of this? Was her gift as much of a curse as a blessing? Was it bad luck, rather than good luck, that the Universe had given her this ability? If her gift had not appeared, or if she hadn't used it, then Albany would have been enslaved or destroyed. Now Albany was saved, but what of the Empire?

Kerenzi stood up. "I guess you have much to think

about, so I'll leave you now. If you want to talk, call me and I'll come. I'll be listening." He gave her a roguish smile. "And I promise I won't sneak up on you invisibly. Well done so far, Rozabella the warlock, and good luck."

He turned and wandered back out of the cave, and Roza watched him go. Yes, she'd need the help of people like Kerenzi if she and their town were to survive the coming days and months. She would also need the advice of wise people like her parents and the Reeve. She ought to go and talk with them sooner rather than later about what Kerenzi had told her. Those who ran the town needed to be aware of what the spirit lord expected would happen, if they hadn't worked it out for themselves already.

But what about herself? Her gift of Rejuvenate seemed to be working with excellent results, and she was determined to make it more of a blessing than a curse. After all, if rejuvenation offered people health, strength, youth and longer life, then that had to be better than illness, weakness, old age and death, didn't it? Yes, it was a wonderful blessing, what her gift could do for people, and she wanted to share it with as many people as possible, starting with those who needed it the most. It only became a curse when selfish or greedy people sought to control, exploit or abuse her gift for their own benefit. How dare they? That was the one thing she wouldn't allow.

Could she manage all this on her own? She had Kerenzi as an ally, and she hoped the Reeve would be on her side. And her parents and Jorxy. But that was the limit of her list of friends, as far as she could remember.

Then her coat stand caught her eye. And Standley, of course. She smiled and stood up from the kitchen table.

"Well, Standley," she said. "It looks like we've got a lot to do."

Roza heaved a breath. What did she need to do most? The first area she needed to understand better and grow in was magic.

She looked around. Behind Standley, shelves of Philoe's books stretched up towards the cave ceiling. Did these contain what she needed to know? The old warlock's spirit had said she could start with these.

Roza turned to the coat stand and said, "I need to understand all I can about magic. Which book should I start with, Standley?"

The coat stand edged across and hooked out a small book at one end of a lower shelf. Roza lifted it out. 'From a Spark to a Flame – First Principles of Magic for Beginners'. That sounded about right.

Rozabella the warlock poured herself a cup of water, sat down at the kitchen table, opened the book, and began to read.

Roza's story continues in Book Two of the Immortality series,
War for Immortality.

Roza's story continues in Book Two of the *Immortality* series, *War for Immortality*:

What if you could make people physically younger?

Roza's secret is out.
All she wants is to learn magic and cure people of old age,
but those seeking her rejuvenation power are
overwhelming her hometown of Albany.

When the Plains erupt into a "war for immortality"
against the weakened Emperor,
how can she keep herself safe and free?
And how can she stop the war being fought in her name,
when each side is as power-hungry as the other?

If you enjoyed this story,
you might also enjoy the *Destiny's Rebel* trilogy:

Can you escape who you're meant to be?

Kat never asked to be in line to be Queen.
Eleven days until she comes of age,
and she feels suffocated. Bullied by her guardians and
oppressed by expectation, Kat dreads the Coronation Day
that will end her dreams of freedom and adventure.
She refuses to surrender to her fate and runs away –
straight into a different kind of trap.

Will Kat get back to Anestra in time to save her Kingdom
from their enemies' schemes? Can she accept the fate from
which she flees? Can she, on this last quest, restore the lost
and broken Crown of Anestra with its sacred powers as a
relic of the Divine?

Kat's adventure weaves through treachery and intrigue to
discover the truth about herself, her friends and her place
in history.

ACKNOWLEDGEMENTS

This book has taken a long time to write – thirteen years since the first idea for it came to me in a dream. As might be expected, the story has grown, changed and developed a lot over those intervening years. Writing is mostly about thinking, rather than typing, so this is my chance to thank those of you who have helped my thinking along the way.

I'd like to thank my fellow members of the Society of Children's Book Writers and Illustrators, and of the Association of Christian Writers, who have supported and encouraged my writing journey. A special thank you to those who have read and commented on this manuscript at proof stage, and particularly to Rae, Fran, Sheila, Jamie, Philipp, Edmund, Daisy, Ellie, Savanna, and Heidi.

My chief delight has been to share the progress of this story with the young readers and writers in the secondary schools I visit. I'm sure they don't realise it, but as young people they succeed in casting their own version of a rejuvenate spell on me and so keep me younger than I am.

I'm grateful also for the creative expertise of others – artist James Hayball for the cover illustration and map, and cover designer Liz Carter.

A final thanks also to my loving, supportive, encouraging, and long-suffering family – to Ann, Mark, and Rachel – who keep me believing in both beauty and magic.

Philip S Davies, 2023.

ABOUT THE AUTHOR

Philip S Davies has been a full-time author since 2012, and the highlight of every week in term-time is to run Creative Writing Clubs in four local secondary schools and colleges.

His first books, the *Destiny's Rebel* trilogy, were bestsellers in Teenage and Young Adult Fiction at Blackwell's Bookshop in Oxford, and were Shortlisted as Finalists for the Crystal Kite Award from the international Society of Children's Book Writers and Illustrators in Los Angeles.

He spends too much of his time enjoying the beautiful view of an Oxfordshire valley outside his study window, while also wishing there could be mountains out there like those surrounding Albany.

You can find out more about Philip at:
www.philipsdavies.com.